THE AMARNA AGE:BOOK 3

EYE OF
HORUS

KYLIE QUILLINAN

ONE

I left Memphis as a slave and a prisoner. I was no longer the queen — that title was stolen by Ay who forged my signature on a marriage certificate and thereby made himself pharaoh. Once he had secured the throne, he no longer needed me, so he sent me to labour as a slave in the Nubian gold mines.

Now I was walking to Nubia, surrounded by guards who were not my own men. They had little interest in my well-being, let alone my comfort, and would likely give me no more than was necessary to sustain my life. Hannu — one of the men who had caught Renni and I when we tried to flee the palace — was the only one I knew by name, and only he might show me any kindness.

I could count on nobody other than myself. If my unborn babe and I were to survive this journey, it would be up to me. Thankfully the babe was still small and the hottest months of *akhet* had passed. Now the days eased into *peret*, which was the coolest time of year and the shortest days. Nights would be cold out here, but at least the days would be bearable.

We walked all through the afternoon and didn't stop even for a few moments. The soldiers ate and drank as they walked and nobody thought to offer me anything. My mouth was dry and my stomach growled but I was determined to ask for nothing from these men. Ay had taken from me everything he could, but the one thing I had left was my dignity. I could barely remain on my feet by the time we stopped for the night.

"Tie her to the wagon," the captain said to nobody in particular.

"Is that really necessary?" Hannu asked. "We are in the middle of nowhere. She will die if she tries to run off."

The captain shot him a look. "Don't make me repeat myself."

"Yes, captain."

Hannu retrieved a length of rope from the wagon. He pitched his voice low so that only I could hear. "I am sorry, but you heard him."

"I need some privacy first."

He shot a glance towards the captain.

"Please."

"Be quick."

He led me behind the wagon so that I was somewhat concealed from the rest of the squad and turned his back while I relieved myself. When I was finished, he held out the rope.

"Give me your hand," he said.

As he tied the rope around my wrist, he glanced down at my feet. He had offered me some bandages earlier when he noticed I was limping.

"Did the bandages help?" he asked.

I wanted to snarl at him. However nice he was being right now, he was still Ay's man, but I swallowed down my pride. If

Hannu was inclined to help me, I couldn't afford to alienate him.

"They did."

He made no further comment as he finished tying the rope around my wrist.

"What did you do to get sent away?" I asked.

Before Hannu could answer, a shout came from the other side of the wagon.

"Over here," Hannu called and led me back to where the rest of the squad was. "She needed to relieve herself."

"She is a prisoner. She could have gone where she was." The captain shot him a disgruntled look.

"Come on, man," Hannu said. "She's a lady. We can afford to give her a little privacy when she needs to do her business."

The captain huffed and turned away.

Hannu tied the other end of the rope to the wagon's wheel. "The wagon will give you some cover from the breezes overnight. Someone will bring you food later. I would not suggest trying to get away. Even if you could untie the knot, we are a full day's march from anywhere. There is nowhere to hide out here."

He returned to the soldiers. They were setting up camp for the night: making a fire, laying out their blankets, tending to the horses that pulled the wagon.

I spread out my cloak and sat where I could lean against the wheel. It seemed nobody had thought I might need a blanket and I thanked Isis for Istnofret's forethought in giving me the cloak. I tucked her little bag beneath my skirt where it would be out of sight if anyone came near. Then I waited.

As darkness fell, two of the men returned to camp, each bearing a pair of hares. I hadn't even realised they had disappeared. I should take more notice of the men guarding me, starting with how many there were. Study them. Learn their habits. Despite Hannu's words, there might be an opportunity to escape and I would need to know all I could about these men. The two guards handed over their hares, and others quickly got to work skinning and gutting them, and setting them to roast over the fire. My mouth watered. We would have a hot meal tonight and that was more than I had expected.

Under the cover of darkness, I began to investigate the little bag. There were several small packets, presumably food of some sort. Dried meat perhaps, maybe some dried figs if I was lucky. Something hard — a chunk of cheese? A tiny bottle with a stopper, which I would have to examine by daylight. It was too small to ease my thirst and I couldn't imagine what else Istnofret might have thought I would need. A narrow roll of cloth. Ha, I hadn't needed Hannu's bandages after all. Four finger rings. Why on earth had she thought I would want jewels?

A shadow loomed and Hannu crouched down to offer me a mug and a chunk of bread. I glanced towards the fire. Were the hares not ready? Hannu read the question in my eyes.

"Only bread and beer for prisoners," he said. "I am sorry."

Surely they wouldn't make me sit here smelling their meal and then not let me have any? I needed the strength that meat would give me if I was to walk so far every day.

"Take it. It is better than starving."

Hannu was still holding the miserable meal out to me.

I took it silently and he retreated back to the fire. To his portion of the roasted hares. I was thankful for the dark as I gnawed on the bread because it meant nobody would see my tears. The beer didn't quench my thirst but at least it washed the dry crumbs away.

Nobody else came near me for the rest of the evening. It

was like I was trapped in a shadow world as I sat alone in the dark, with the wagon wheel hard against my back and the rope around my wrist. The men paid no attention to me as they sat around the fire, gnawing on hare bones, drinking mug after mug, and laughing and talking amongst themselves. Eventually I wrapped the cloak around my shoulders and lay down, cushioning my head with my hands. I may as well sleep while I could. Tomorrow would be another long day.

I was almost asleep when I heard footsteps and opened my eyes in time to see a shadow pass by. Something dropped onto my cloak with a soft thud. I waited to make sure that nobody was watching before I took up the small package wrapped in linen. I pulled it in under the cover of my skirt while I unwrapped it. The chunk of hare it contained was cold and greasy by now, but it was the most delicious thing I had ever tasted. I ate every morsel and licked my fingers clean. Feeling more like I had eaten a meal, I fell asleep.

TWO

I woke with a start. Men shouted. There were thuds and thunks and groans. The fire dipped, then flared as somebody fell into it. Someone screamed. A shadow came flying towards me, firelight glinting on a dagger. I froze.

"Get up," somebody said.

He didn't wait but grabbed me by the shoulders and hauled me to my feet. I had been sleeping with the cord from Istnofret's bag wound around my fingers and I managed to keep hold of that, but there was no time to retrieve my cloak. With one stroke of his dagger, the man sliced through the rope that bound me to the wagon.

"Go." He shoved me towards another man before leaping back into the fight.

The second man grabbed me around the waist, threw me over his shoulder, and ran. I could do nothing other than hold on, even as my wig fell off. We reached the cover of some scrubby trees and he dropped me on my feet. My knees buckled, almost pitching me to the ground, and my head spun as I suddenly found myself upright again, but he grabbed my arm before I could fall.

He was short and muscular, and his face was concealed by a linen scarf, revealing nothing other than his dark eyes. He pointed behind me.

"Get up."

I turned and came face-to-face with a donkey, which drew back its lips and snorted at me.

"Hurry up."

He shoved me closer to the donkey, then someone grabbed me from behind and boosted me up. In very short order I found myself sitting astride the beast. It was only then that I noticed a second donkey bearing another man with a scarf wrapped around his face.

"Go," someone said and the other donkey took off.

My beast followed. They ran straight back to where the guards were still shouting and fighting and dying. I caught the glint of firelight on bronze spears and axes but there was no time to see anything else. I still didn't know who these men were.

"Haw," the man on the other donkey cried as we raced past the melee.

Someone called out, "They have her."

"That will keep them busy for a while," he yelled over his shoulder at me. "Now hold on."

We sped past trees and shrubs, no more than shadows in the darkness. I clung to the donkey's neck, waiting for an explanation that never came. The spell bottle, which still hung on a length of string around my neck, was cold. It had never failed to warn me of danger before so I could only trust that I was being rescued, rather than abducted.

"Who are you?" I asked. "Where are we going?"

The wind whipped the words away from my mouth and if the man heard, he made no reply. I didn't ask again. A long time passed, at least a couple of hours. The donkey slowed to a brisk trot. The night air was cool and I shivered, wishing I had my cloak.

The sky was still dark when I saw a dom palm tree up ahead, its distinctive spiky outline framed against the moonlit sky. As we reached the palm, the donkeys finally halted, their sides heaving. Nearby was a small fire.

"My lady?" a woman called and I recognised her voice instantly. "Do you have her?"

"Istnofret?"

I scrambled awkwardly off the donkey. My legs were stiff and I almost fell. Before my feet reached the ground, Istnofret was there and we wrapped our arms around each other. I couldn't speak for some time. My shoulder was damp with Istnofret's tears and I shed more than a few myself. At length I unwound myself from her.

"What are you doing here?" I asked.

"Are you harmed? Did they treat you badly?"

"I am well, but where are we? Why are you here?"

"We came to rescue you," she said, with a laugh. "You didn't think we would abandon you, did you?"

"Rescue me?" I had had no thought of rescue until the moment I found myself on a donkey racing away from my guards. I had believed it would be up to me alone to keep both myself and my unborn babe alive.

A man approached from behind Istnofret.

"Renni? What are you doing here?"

He and Istnofret shared a long look before he answered.

"Intef charged me with getting Istnofret and Behenu out of the palace."

"Behenu? Is she here as well?"

"I am here, my lady," came a sleepy voice from the other side of the fire. "Mau, too."

"You brought Sadeh's cat?" I laughed, hardly knowing what to make of all this nonsense. "But how did you get away? How did you find me? Who are the men with the donkeys?"

"We are Medjay," came a voice from behind me. "We serve the true Pharaoh."

I turned in time to see the man remove the linen scarf from his face. He was Nubian, that much was clear, with black skin and a slender build. He reminded me of Intef in the way he held himself, his back straight, his limbs ready to spring into action at a moment's notice. He was no common soldier. He was alert, prepared, efficient, just like Intef.

"There is no true Pharaoh at present," I said.

He bowed his head. "The lady speaks truth, but that does not mean the time will not come when Pharaoh again sits on his throne. Until then, we serve as we may."

"Thank you for coming," I said. "It was going to be a very long walk to Nubia."

He bowed his head again. "It would be better that we are far from this place before others come searching. Better that you are long gone also."

"We will be leaving as soon as Intef finds us," Renni said. "Thank you for your aid tonight."

The Nubian nodded at him, then turned without another word. He mounted his donkey and set off again. The second beast trotted after them. I turned back to Istnofret and Renni.

"What are you doing here?" I asked. "How did you get out of the palace? Who knows you are here?"

"Your questions will need to wait, my lady," Renni said. "We need to break camp and be ready to leave. Ay's men will search thoroughly for you and we need to be away before then. But here, let me remove that rope."

Using his dagger, he quickly sliced through the rope still tied around my wrist. Then he returned to the fire and started dumping sand over it.

"My lady, where is your wig?" Istnofret asked.

"Oh." I put my hand to my head, feeling its shaved baldness. "It fell off."

"You should take mine." She was already reaching for her wig, but I put out my hand to stop her.

"No," I said. "I will not wear a wig again until I return to Memphis."

She studied me for a moment and then took off her own wig. "Then neither shall I."

We looked at each other and she gave me an awkward smile.

"I should go help Renni, my lady," she said. "It will not take long."

"It is truly good to see you, Istnofret."

She smiled again, less awkward this time. "You too."

As Istnofret left, Behenu darted in and wrapped her arms around my waist. Unlike Istnofret and I, she had never worn a wig. It was her own hair which dangled in little braids to her shoulders.

"I thought I would never see you again," she said.

"I didn't expect to see you either. I thought I had left you safely at the palace."

She pulled away and gave me a dark look. "There is no safety there for me without you. Horemheb would have claimed me again. I would slit my own throat before I went back to him."

Her bald assertions shocked me and I had no reply.

"Where is Mau?" I asked instead.

"Asleep on my blanket. I tied a rope around her neck and the other end to a basket so she cannot wander off and get lost. She doesn't like it very much. She hissed at me at first but she is getting used to it."

"Sadeh would be very pleased that you are taking such good care of Mau for her."

"I know."

I didn't know what else to say. What does one say to those who have risked everything to rescue you? Thank you seemed too inadequate. Surely they knew I could give them nothing in return. Ay had taken everything from me.

The thunder of approaching donkeys made my heart pound. Had they found us already?

"It is all right, my lady," Renni said. "It is Intef."

Intef climbed down from his donkey and came straight to me. I didn't know what to say and couldn't bring myself even to look him in the eyes. This man had been in my bed. I had begun to think of him as something more than just the captain of my guards. But then he betrayed me to Ay. Or at least I thought he had. Now I was beginning to wonder if it had all been one of Intef's unknowable plans. After all, Renni had said Intef did nothing without a plan. But if his betrayal was an act, what else had been a pretence? The only thing I knew for certain was that he had killed Sadeh. I hardened my heart and gave him a steely glare.

"You could have trusted me," he said.

"You gave me no reason to."

"No reason? After ten years of service in which you never once doubted my loyalty? After saving you from three assassins? After supporting your plans to usurp the throne? After..." His voice broke. "After inviting me to your bed. My lady, I may be foolish, but I thought we had a connection. I thought… I thought you felt something for me."

His words felt honest and the armour with which I had shielded myself began to crack. I couldn't let him see that, though. If he wanted me to trust him again, he would have to earn it. So I gave him my haughtiest voice.

"You told me once that you were paid well to look after me. I suppose I am no longer in a position to ensure that you receive payment so…"

Maybe I was trying to give him a chance to leave. I wanted him to go. I could never trust him again. But, also, I wanted him to stay.

"I thought you would want to be rescued. Perhaps I was wrong. Regardless, we need to leave before they come looking for you."

He turned his back on me and walked away. Over to the smothered fire where Istnofret, Renni and Behenu waited, a pile of packs and baskets beside them.

"Any trouble getting away?" Renni asked him.

Intef shook his head but if he responded, I couldn't hear him.

"Come, my lady," Istnofret called. "We are ready to leave."

"Where are we going?" I asked.

She laughed. "Anywhere you want."

"What is the plan?" I turned to Renni since I couldn't look at Intef. "You must have some destination in mind."

"Intef thought you would want to go to your sisters," he said.

The world swam around me.

"My lady?" Istnofret moved to reach for me, but Intef was quicker, leaping back to grab my arms and hold me up until my legs steadied. As soon as I could stand by myself, I shook off his hands and took a few steps away from him.

"My sisters?" I still couldn't bring myself to look at him. "I thought you didn't know where they were."

"I don't, but I know someone who can give us a clue. We travel to him first."

"Let's go. We should have been away from here already." Renni began picking up various packs.

My feet had grown roots down into the sand.

"I cannot. It would endanger them. Ay will be looking for me and I could lead him straight to them."

"We will be careful," Intef said. "Nobody will follow us."

"You cannot be sure of that."

"We will take every possible precaution."

"No. I will not go to my sisters. They must be free to live their own lives."

"Where will we go then?" Istnofret asked. "We cannot go back to Memphis."

"Akhetaten?" The word was a whisper, but even as I said it, I knew my childhood home was too obvious. If there was anything of the city still standing, Ay would send men there. Intef and Renni both shook their heads. "Where then?"

"You spoke of sending Sadeh to Babylon once," Istnofret said, slowly. "Perhaps we could go there."

Babylon. The world's centre for learning. I had suggested Sadeh might want to go there to learn something. If we went to Babylon, it would feel like her *ka* was following us.

"No," I said. "Behdet."

"Behdet?" Renni shot me a quizzical look.

"There is an artefact there. It could help me regain the throne, restore my father's dynasty."

"You mean the Eye of Horus," Intef said.

Of course, he had overheard my conversation with Hemetre when she came to my pleasure garden to tell me about the Eye.

"The Eye of Horus?" Istnofret sounded sceptical. "What is that? It sounds gruesome."

"I don't know exactly," I said. "It is a very old artefact which is reputed to give much power to its holder. It could help me take back the throne."

"And it can be found in Behdet?" she asked.

"I asked Hemetre once where one would go to seek the Eye. She didn't know but said that she would start in Behdet."

"Horus is greatly revered in Behdet," Renni said.

Istnofret raised her eyebrows at him. "How do you know such a thing?"

"My grandfather worshipped Horus," he said. "Many years ago. I remember an old family story about him travelling to Behdet to worship at an ancient temple there."

"Have you ever heard of the Eye of Horus?" My hopes were crushed as quickly as they had risen when he shook his head.

"If my grandfather ever knew of such a thing, I never heard him tell of it."

"No matter," I said, briskly. "I will go to Behdet and see what I can find out."

"We must leave." Intef was looking up at the lightening sky. "We have lingered here for far too long."

THREE

We departed on donkeys, five of which had been waiting quietly, tied to some nearby bushes. Mau's basket was fastened to Behenu's donkey by way of a rope across the beast's back. Mau hissed as she was deposited into her basket, clearly uneasy at her mode of transport.

Our party was quiet as the donkeys walked and the sun rose. I marvelled at my luck at having been rescued. Surrounded by guards as I had been, I hadn't expected any possibility of rescue. It was Istnofret who finally broke our silence.

"Why did Ay make you walk?" she asked. "It would take months to walk all the way to Nubia. I doubt you would have arrived before the babe was born, but you could have sailed there in a few weeks."

"Had I sailed, I would have arrived whole and strong. I don't think he wanted me to survive the journey. Even if I managed to walk all that way, I would not be in any condition to work. He was ensuring I would not last long."

"He may as well have killed you at the palace," she muttered. "It would have been a lot less effort for him."

"Good for me that he didn't, though. How did you get away?"

"I left in a load of laundry." She laughed a little. "Intef set it up."

I shot her a puzzled look. "Laundry?"

"We waited until the bed linens were being washed and when they were taken down to the river, I was right in the middle."

"And nobody noticed?"

"Oh, they knew, but there are still people in the palace who are loyal to you. When I came crawling out of the middle of the laundry, everybody was looking in a different direction. I ran off and hid in the place where we had arranged to meet."

I had often believed myself to be surrounded by intrigue, but I had never been smuggled out of the palace in a load of laundry.

"And Behenu?"

"She went out in a cart that was fetching wine from Pharaoh's vineyard. It was full of empty crates and she hid inside one. They were not far from the palace when they had to stop to fix one of the cart's wheels. That gave Behenu a chance to jump out and come to meet me."

"The wheel just happened to break?"

"Of course not. Intef arranged that, too. Renni slipped out later that night. He came to find us and we went to the Medjay to ask for their help. I don't know how Intef got out. He needed to do something so he was leaving after us."

"I am surprised Renni went to the Medjay."

"Renni wanted to come for you ourselves, but Intef said we

needed more men. He said we would only have one chance to rescue you and the Medjay owed him some favours."

I was overwhelmed at learning how much effort had gone into rescuing me, but before I could reply, I realised that Intef and Renni were making plans and I really should understand what they intended. If we were to be separated, I wouldn't have the first idea how to survive out here alone.

I knew vaguely where Behdet was. My father had taught his daughters to understand maps and I could still picture the one he made us memorise. It had pins where each town stood, and we had to tell him which mark was which. Behdet was way down to the south, past Akhetaten. Past Thebes even. There was a long journey ahead of us and Behdet might turn out to be only the first stop.

There were two possible routes, it seemed, and Intef and Renni disagreed on which was best. Intef wanted to go back to the Great River, which stretched through the entire length of Egypt. If we made our way along its banks, sooner or later we would reach a place where boats pulled in to purchase supplies. We could buy passage and sail to Behdet from there. The other possibility, which Renni favoured, was to cross the desert and make our way to the Red Sea. From there we could board a ship and sail down the coast, then cross the desert again to Behdet.

"There is more chance of encountering a boat on the Great River," Intef said. "We might wait days for a ship travelling down the coast."

"But there is less danger of discovery," Renni said. "Ay will likely send messengers along the Great River once he learns she has escaped. He won't expect her to go to the Red Sea."

"It makes the journey unnecessarily long," Intef said. "And

long means risky. We need the shortest and quickest route to Behdet."

"How do you propose to ensure we are not discovered if we travel on the Great River?" I asked.

Intef knew my question was for him, even though I stared straight ahead, between my donkey's ears.

"We will pose as peasants," he said. "On a pilgrimage to Behdet. Two men and their wives."

"What about me?" Behenu asked.

"A cousin," he said, promptly. "And her cat companion."

"How long will the journey take?" I asked.

"Two weeks. Maybe a little more. Depends if we have good weather and strong winds."

"And if we go via the Red Sea?" I asked.

"A few days to travel overland," Renni said. "Maybe a couple of weeks on the ship, and another few days back overland."

"Twice as long," I said.

"But safer," he said.

Both plans seemed sensible, but someone needed to make a decision and it was clear Intef and Renni were not going to reach agreement.

"I don't have the luxury of choosing the safest path. We must reach Behdet as quickly as possible. We will travel by the Great River."

"South aways first then," Intef said. "We cannot risk approaching the river too close to where you escaped. There is a checkpoint not far from here where your guards were expected to stop for supplies in the morning. It won't be long before someone realises they are not coming."

"We should find somewhere to spend the day," Renni said. "Travel under cover of night."

"Closest village is a half day's travel from here but they will look there," Intef said. "They would be stupid not to."

"Inland then," Renni said. "The Medjay camp."

"Too obvious," Intef said. "If they realise it was the Medjay who helped her escape, they will check the closest camps. And besides, time we spend travelling away from the Great River now is time we need to make up tonight."

"Then we head south from here," Renni said. "And veer east towards the river once the sun sets."

"Too exposed. There is no cover for leagues around. If they spot us, they will easily keep us in sight until they catch up."

They stared at each other and both seemed to reach the same conclusion at the same time.

"Back to where they camped last night," Renni said.

"It is the first place the guards from the checkpoint will search. By the time we get there, they should be long gone," Intef said with a nod. "We find some shrubbery, stay out of sight, and move on after dark."

"What about the donkeys?" Istnofret gave hers a tentative scratch on the neck. "Will not five donkeys with travelling blankets be rather conspicuous? We can hardly ask them to hide behind the shrubbery with us."

"We will remove the blankets and send them on their way," Renni said. "There is enough traffic along the road that they will likely be captured before night fall."

"I hope they find a good home," Istnofret said. "They look like they have been well cared for."

"They came from the Medjay," Renni said. "They treat their animals well, especially those that must carry them."

"We will be exposed until we get there," Intef said. "So we move as fast as the donkeys can. Be quiet; sound travels far out here, and stay alert."

Istnofret and I nodded. I glanced at Behenu who sleepily leaned against her donkey's neck.

"Behenu, are you paying attention?" I asked.

"Yes, my lady," she murmured. "Quiet and alert."

Intef led the way, pushing his beast into a fast trot that was just short of a run. Istnofret, Behenu and I followed, with Renni bringing up the rear. I clutched my donkey's mane as we jolted along, not trusting its halter to help me stay on the beast and certain that if anyone was going to fall off, it would be me.

The orange and red streaks of sunrise had long faded by the time we approached the place where the soldiers had camped last night. We stopped behind some scrubby bushes and climbed down.

My backside ached and I could barely stand, having never ridden a beast before. My thigh muscles were cramped from holding on for so long. Istnofret seemed just as uncomfortable, but Behenu sprang down from her mount and busied herself with untying Mau's basket. I had forgotten about the cat, for she had been entirely silent after her initial hisses. How strange it must be for a cat who knew nothing other than my chambers to suddenly find herself tied to a donkey and travelling through the dead of night. Intef and Renni seemed as stiff as me, and began stretching their legs.

"We will release the donkeys as soon as Renni confirms the camp is clear," Intef said, very quietly.

"And then what?" I asked.

"Then we wait."

Renni crouched down low and approached the camp. The wagon was still there, but the horses were gone. I could see no sign of men, not even bodies on the ground. Surely some had died, or had at least been injured in the fight. While we waited,

I tried to imitate the way Intef and Renni had stretched, and found that it did indeed help me to feel less uncomfortable.

Renni returned swiftly. "I think they have already checked here. There are far too many sets of footprints for the number of men the Medjay sent."

We got on with removing the various bags that were strapped to the donkeys. Behenu made herself useful offering the donkeys some water in a bowl. Once the supplies had been unloaded, we removed their blankets and slapped their rumps. They wandered off willingly enough. Then we sat down to wait.

I was so tired I could barely keep my eyes open. I needed to stay awake, though. None of us had much sleep last night and I could hardly expect to rest if nobody else was. It was time to admit that I was no longer the Queen of Egypt. I was just another member in our travelling party. These four that had come searching for me did so out of loyalty. How long would they remain loyal if I pretended I was still queen and treated them like the servants they no longer were? I wasn't sure I even understood why they had come for me. What had I ever done to inspire such loyalty in them?

"You should lie down and sleep, my lady," Istnofret said. "Here, I brought a spare cloak, in case they took yours away. You could put it beneath your head so you can rest more comfortably."

"You should not call me that any more. I am no longer your queen."

She gave me a puzzled look.

"But of course you are."

"No, I don't know what I am now, but I am certainly not a queen anymore."

"What should we call you then?" Renni asked.

I looked around at them. Were these my friends? I supposed they were the closest thing I had to friends, even if I didn't understand why they cared for me so much that they gave up everything to rescue me. They could never go back to the palace now.

"Ankhesenamun will do as well as anything." My no-nonsense reply was rather ruined by the yawn that followed.

"Sleep for a while," Intef said. He glanced at the others, including them in his words. "All of you should sleep."

"You have had no more sleep than anyone else," Istnofret said.

"I will wake you in two hours," he said. "Then I will sleep."

"I will take a turn at keeping watch, too," I said.

I expected he would argue, but he merely shrugged. "Get some rest first. You cannot keep watch if you are falling asleep."

Satisfied, I took the cloak from Istnofret and lay down. A rock dug in between my ribs, but before I could move it I was already asleep. I woke to a hand shaking my shoulder.

"My lady," Renni said. "It is your turn to keep watch."

I sat up, groggy from my deep sleep.

"Should I stay up with you for a while?" he asked.

"No, no, sleep while you can. I will feel better once I stretch my legs."

"You cannot walk around. We must remain out of sight behind the bushes. Stay seated. They probably won't come back here to check again, but we cannot take the risk."

"Of course." How daft of me. I could have exposed us all without even a thought. "Is there anything else I should know?"

He studied me, probably wondering whether he could

really trust me to keep watch while he slept. Eventually, he shook his head.

"Just be quiet. If you see or hear anything, wake me. I will lie right here so that you can poke me with your foot if you need me to wake up."

He looked around one last time, then lay down. Like Intef, he lay on his back with one hand on the dagger stuck through the waist of his *shendyt*. He seemed to fall asleep immediately. I edged away a little so I wouldn't accidentally jostle him.

With nothing else to do, I looked around. The shrubs gave decent enough cover from the direction of the camp and anyone wandering around over there probably wouldn't see us unless we moved. I couldn't even see the camp, except in small patches between the branches of the shrubs. The road lay on the far side. On either side of us stretched scrubby plainlands, a vast expanse of flat land.

My eyes were already starting to droop. I had had several hours of solid sleep but even that felt like too little. To keep myself alert, I held my eyes open wide and looked around, watching for changes in our surroundings. I scanned the sky for smoke, quite pleased with myself that I thought to do such a thing. Hopefully if someone came by, it would be on my watch and I would spot them. I would prove my worth to my companions.

But as the hour dragged on, boredom set in. The sky was clear of smoke. Not even a bird or a cloud interrupted its expanse. I could see nobody creeping up on us and although I listened intently, I could hear nothing other than my companions breathing. After some time, I realised Intef breathed differently to the others.

"You don't have to stay awake to keep an eye on me," I said, quietly.

He opened his eyes and gave me a rueful look. "You have never kept watch before, and you were sound asleep when Renni woke you."

"Did you stay awake during Istnofret's watch too?"

"No."

I glowered at him and he grinned a little.

"Renni did."

"I may as well go back to sleep if you are going to stay up," I said. "There is no point us both being awake."

"Oh no, it is your watch," he said. "I am not done sleeping yet."

He closed his eyes and didn't speak again, even when I cursed him.

FOUR

The day passed with no sign of anyone searching for us. Intef was correct when he said they wouldn't return to this place once they had already searched it. We kept Mau in her basket for most of the day, although Behenu let her out briefly with a rope tied around her neck. It would have pained me greatly to lose Sadeh's cat out here and I was pleased that Behenu was taking such good care of her. Mau was my last link to the first woman assigned to serve me when I became queen. But, I reminded myself, I was queen no longer, and in a way, I was glad that Sadeh wasn't here to see this.

We passed chunks of hard-baked bread and handfuls of dried dates between us. There was a stoppered bottle filled with beer and I drank deeply, still dehydrated from yesterday. I replaced the wrappings on my blistered feet with the roll of linen that Istnofret had included in my little bag. I didn't know what to do with the dirty bandages until Renni dug a hole in the sand. I dropped the bandages in and covered them up. With my belly full and my thirst quenched, I felt more content than I might have expected as we waited for nightfall.

Even once the sun had sunk beneath the horizon, Intef didn't let us get up. It was only after the sky was fully dark that he sent Renni to scout around once more to be certain that nobody lay in wait. When he finally allowed us to stand, my legs were stiff. I stretched, trying to remember the movements I had seen Intef and Renni make when they got off the donkeys. Behenu jumped up, as lithe as ever, but Istnofret seemed as sore as I was.

"I am not meant for sitting in the dirt all day," she said to me, rubbing her behind.

"You should have stayed in Memphis," I said. "You would have been more comfortable there."

"I am your lady. It is my duty to follow wherever you go."

"Istnofret, I can offer you nothing for your service. If you wish to return to Memphis, or to go somewhere else, I release you. I don't know where I am going and you don't have to follow me there."

She shook her head. "I am your lady."

"This journey will be arduous, Istnofret. Likely dangerous. You should go back now. Maybe they haven't noticed your absence yet."

"I don't know how to make you understand," she said, echoing my own unsaid thought. "There is nothing in Memphis for me, without you and Sadeh and Charis. Why would I stay there?"

"Your family is there."

"I would be just another mouth to feed, and my parents would likely marry me off as quickly as they could. I prefer to choose my own fate, and I choose to follow you, wherever you are going."

"What about—" I glanced towards Renni, unsure as to whether there were any promises between them.

She followed my gaze and smiled a little. "That is another reason I cannot go back to Memphis. He will go wherever Intef goes and Intef will follow you. So I have no choice in the matter."

"Do you intend to marry him?"

She looked at Renni for a moment longer before she turned back to me. "Maybe. Maybe not. I would like a companion, but I am not so sure I want a husband."

Her casual words brought a pang to my heart. I would have married Thrax, or so I had thought until I learned the truth of his identity. Once I had discovered he was a slave, I knew there was no future for us. The Queen of Egypt could no more marry a slave than she could... My thought suddenly halted and I wasn't sure where it had been about to go. I could no more marry a slave than I could befriend a servant, perhaps? And yet here I was, travelling with three servants and a slave, all of whom had chosen to leave behind their lives and come with me to the gods only knew where. What did that say about them? About me?

Ay had sentenced me to slavery before he sent me away. Did that mean I was a slave now, even having escaped from his guards? Was I still a slave if nobody other than those with me knew of my sentence? If had gone to Ay when he first summoned me, instead of sending Sadeh, would he still have sent me to Nubia? Was Sadeh's life worth the price I might have paid had I gone to him myself?

While I had been lost in my tangled thoughts, the others were preparing to leave, packing away the remaining food and returning Mau to her basket. Istnofret rolled up the spare cloak she had given me earlier and tucked it under her arm. I suddenly realised I had nothing but the clothes I wore and my little bag. I was entirely dependant on my companions.

"Pass that to me," I said to her. "I will carry it."

She handed it over in silence, barely seeming even to notice. Were her thoughts as morose as my own?

Intef relayed some final instructions before we set off.

"If we encounter anyone, stay silent unless they ask you a direct question or it would seem strange if you didn't speak. Leave the talking to me if you can. If you must explain anything to anyone, Renni and I are cousins. My lady and Istnofret are our wives. Behenu is Istnofret's cousin, born to her sister who married a Syrian. We are travelling to Behdet to ask a boon of Horus. It is a private family matter and we don't wish to share the details with strangers. When we are done, we intend to return to our homes in Memphis."

I wondered whether anyone who saw Behenu would believe she was only half Syrian.

"Memphis?" Istnofret asked. "Will that not give us away?"

"We must stick as close to the truth as possible," he said. "It makes the story easier to remember and it sounds more convincing. The less we have to lie, the less we give folk reason to question."

I looked out into the dark plainlands as Intef spoke. I didn't want him to be right about anything but his words did seem sensible. Every time I looked at him, I saw him stepping up behind Sadeh and slitting her throat. I was grateful he had arranged for my rescue, but I could not forgive him for killing her.

So we set off. Istnofret walked with Renni on one side and Behenu on the other. Intef stuck close beside me, although I kept edging away. I wished I had thought to walk with Behenu, but I would rather walk alone than with him. For more than ten years, he had walked ahead of me everywhere I went. I was more familiar with the back of his head than I was with my own face. It was strange to have him walk beside me, to see the path ahead for myself without it being obscured by his form.

We saw nobody as we walked through the night although we often heard rustling in the grass and once the cry of an owl. Time seemed to stand still and I lost any sense of how long we had been walking.

We paused briefly to rest when the moon was high in the sky. I yawned and hoped we might stop long enough for a short sleep, but although Renni sat down, Intef continued to prowl around us. We ate and drank, and Behenu let Mau out for a while. But all too soon, Intef was motioning at us to get up and it was time to walk again. My blistered feet hurt, despite the bandages, but I didn't want to be the one to slow us down so I did my best to ignore the pain.

I smelled the Great River before I saw it. Its marshy scent was instantly familiar. I perked up a little at the knowledge that our walk was almost at an end. We would wait here for a boat to take us to Behdet.

But as the river came into sight, its waters sparkling in the moonlight, Intef veered off to walk alongside it and my heart sank. I desperately wanted to ask whether he intended for us to walk all night, but I held my tongue. I would not ask Intef for anything.

Dawn broke before a group of houses came into view. At least, I assumed they were houses. They were ramshackle things, built of worn mud bricks. A boy played in the dirt in front of one of them. When he noticed us approaching, he stood and put his thumb in his mouth. He was wretchedly skinny and looked like he had not bathed for months.

"Wait here," Intef said, quietly. "I will see whether they are welcoming of strangers."

He walked on ahead and stopped when he was still some distance from the boy.

"Hello there," he called. "Is your father at home?"

The boy took his thumb out of his mouth and howled. A woman came running out of the house. She stopped short when she saw us, then rushed over to the boy to grab his arm and shove him behind her.

"Who are you?" she demanded.

"I didn't touch him," Intef said. "I came no closer to him than I am right now."

"He does not like strangers," the woman said. "Who are you?"

"Travellers," Intef said. "We are on our way to Behdet. Would there be somewhere we can rest for a few hours? We can pay."

She eyed him suspiciously, then turned her glare on the rest of us. After inspecting us for what seemed like a long time, she shrugged at Intef.

"What will you pay?"

He took the bag from his shoulder and rummaged through it, then removed something small which he offered to her in the palm of his hand. The woman's eyes lit up although she quickly tried to hide her interest.

"Is that all?" she asked.

Intef closed his fingers around the item and went to put it back into his bag.

"We merely seek somewhere to rest for a few hours. We are not asking for food or anything else from you. We don't want to trouble you, though. Perhaps the next house…"

"I did not say no." She turned and walked back into her home, dragging the boy with her. "Come inside and hurry up before anyone sees you. I don't want anyone asking questions."

Inside, the windows were still shuttered and the chamber was hot and stuffy, despite the early hour. We stood in what seemed to be a living area of sorts, with a threadbare rug on the floor and a single chair in the corner. The chair was rickety and looked as if it would collapse should anyone actually sit in it. I tried not to stare, but I had never been inside a house like this before.

The woman held out her hand to Intef and he passed her the trinket. She inspected it briefly and, seemingly satisfied, tucked it away within her gown.

"You can rest in here."

She took her son by the arm and went into the other chamber, which looked to be a sleeping area, although there were no bed frames nor cushions nor soft linens, just a couple of woven mats on the dirt floor. Was this how the common folk lived? I had known I lived in luxury but I had not realised their accommodations were so poor.

The chamber in which we stood seemed clean enough, for all that it was bare. I spread my cloak out on the floor and lay down.

"I am not ready to sleep yet," Istnofret said, quietly. "I can keep first watch."

Intef and Renni lay down, and within moments they both seemed to be fast asleep. Behenu fussed with Mau's basket, whispering to the cat and feeding her a sliver of something. I lay still and tried to pretend I was asleep. It hadn't even occurred to me that somebody should keep watch. I had assumed we were safe behind the closed door.

FIVE

With the door closed and no window to let in a breeze, the chamber quickly became stifling. Beads of sweat already trickled down my neck. I opened my eyes just a tiny bit and saw that Behenu had finally laid down. Istnofret sat with her back against the wall. She glanced in my direction and I quickly shut my eyes. I must have finally fallen asleep because I woke to someone shaking my shoulder.

"My lady, it is time to go."

My skin was sticky and I felt like I had melted into the floor while I slept.

"Is it my turn to keep watch?" I asked through a yawn as I peeled myself off my cloak. The darkness was relieved only by the lamp from the other chamber.

"The sun has set," Istnofret said. "We are preparing to leave."

"Why did nobody wake me? I didn't take my turn to keep watch."

"You were sound asleep and we thought it better to let you rest while you could."

She busied herself with shaking out my cloak and folding it neatly. I snatched it from her. How soon would they tire of me if I demanded special treatment?

"I can fold that myself. And somebody should have woken me."

She retrieved her own cloak from the floor and said nothing.

"Stand back against the wall," Intef said. "Renni is going to scout around and I want you out of sight while the door is open."

I tucked my cloak under my arm and we both stood with our backs against the wall. Behenu joined us with Mau bundled away in her basket. Intef waited beside the door, dagger in his hand. Renni sauntered out, looking as if he merely headed off for a wander, and the door closed behind him before I could see anything more than darkness.

Renni seemed to be gone for a long time and I was beginning to worry when a series of quick knocks sounded on the door. Intef, his dagger held at the ready, motioned to us to move.

"Quickly, let's go. Behenu, go thank our host."

Behenu darted over to the doorway and gave the woman a polite thank you for her hospitality, then we left.

There were only half a dozen huts in this small village. Lamps shone from behind closed doors and the aroma of cooking fires and fresh bread lingered in the air. Intef set a fast pace until we were well away from the village. Although he and Renni looked as casual as ever, nobody would sneak up on us without them noticing.

"Will she tell anyone?" Istnofret asked.

"The trinket I gave her should be enough to buy her silence," Intef said. "But you can never be sure how someone will react when questioned. The boy bothers me more than his mother. I don't think he has enough wits about him to know to hold his silence even if she ordered it."

The moon was high before Intef allowed us to stop for a short rest. Istnofret passed around bread and beer, while Behenu tied the rope around Mau's neck before releasing her from her basket.

We walked for another hour or two before we saw flickering lamp light in the distance. Intef stopped us at a small stand of dom palm trees, on one side of which lay the crumbled remains of a mud brick wall. On the other was something that might once have been a well but was now almost entirely disintegrated.

"We wait here," he said. "Up ahead is a small village where boats often pull in to shore. Renni will go watch for a boat. The rest of us will stay here, out of sight."

Renni and Istnofret had their heads together, speaking too softly for me to hear. He squeezed her hand, then headed off into the darkness.

"How long until a boat comes along?" Istnofret asked.

Intef had set down his bags and was collecting some stones. "No more than a day or two, I would think. We are reasonably out of sight of the village here. I think we could risk a small fire behind the wall, at least while the sky is still dark."

He sent Behenu in search of sticks and dead leaves while he set down a ring of stones in the dirt. I noted where he had placed his bags and laid out my cloak on the opposite side of the fire pit.

I sat on my cloak and wrapped my arms around my legs. The night air was cool and despite our long walk, I felt chilled. A fire would be a welcome relief. My blistered feet throbbed, but I was too tired to bother unwrapping the bandages. Hopefully tomorrow we would be on a boat and I would not have to walk much for a few days. My feet would heal soon enough.

Istnofret passed around food.

"This is the last of the bread, and that is a good thing because it is nearly too stale to eat. We are almost out of beer, too. We will need more supplies tomorrow."

The last seemed to be directed at Intef.

"We should be able to get some things in the village," he said.

I stared into the flames as Intef coaxed the fire to a blaze, memories of Sadeh running through my mind. The look of delight on her face when Thrax first presented her with Mau. Her intense concentration as she focused on making up my face just right. The moment on the journey to Memphis when we had laughed about the toothless man her father had intended to marry her off to. She had served me for ten years and it was hard to believe she was really gone. I must have made a noise because Istnofret suddenly crouched down beside me.

"My lady, are you well?" she asked.

"I told you not to call me that."

"Habit. I doubt I will ever remember."

I sighed and stared into the flames.

"Sadeh feels close tonight, does she not?" Istnofret said.

"I was just thinking about her."

"She knew it was a dangerous thing to do. She did it willingly."

"I feel like…" I stopped, unsure whether I wanted to share my thoughts. I had been thinking about Sadeh in happier times. Istnofret was obviously thinking about her death. I wasn't sure I wanted to admit that for a few moments I wasn't thinking about the way she died — or about who killed her. "It is my fault. I should have gone myself."

"She did it so that you could get out," Istnofret said, fiercely. "If you had gone, it likely would have been you who died."

"They wouldn't have killed me."

"She knew she would die if anyone realised."

"So why did she do it?"

"Because she loved you."

Tears filled my eyes. The realisation that my ladies were actually my friends was still new to me. I didn't know how I was supposed to feel about Sadeh now, but it hurt that she was gone. From the other side of the fire, Intef spoke and although I tried not to, I couldn't stop myself from hearing him.

"Sadeh was not the only one," he said. "There are other people who care about you."

"You." I glared at him across the fire. My sorrow disappeared, replaced by rage that bubbled up so fast, I could hardly spit out my words. "You killed her."

"It was her or you." His words were simple and his tone matter of fact. "If I had refused, they would have killed her anyway, and then they would have come for you."

"You don't know that," I snarled.

"I know you are angry with me," he said. "But Sadeh made her choice knowing it likely meant her death. I made my choice knowing it likely meant you would live. Ay wanted someone dead and he didn't really care who. If I did it myself, I could ensure it was quick. She didn't suffer."

His words were like a slap on my face. How could I judge him for giving Sadeh a quick death when it was no more than I had done for Thrax? We both had blood on our hands. In truth, it was myself I was angry with, not Intef. I felt like I had traded Sadeh's life for my own, and I was furious about it.

SIX

Intef roused us shortly after dawn.

"There is a boat," he said. "Time to go."

His face was haggard. Had he had kept watch all night by himself? I hadn't been woken to take a turn and Istnofret looked rested enough that I guessed she hadn't either. Why had he kept watch all by himself?

My stomach growled, but it seemed there was no time for food. We swiftly gathered our belongings and set off. As we came in sight of the jetty, my heart lifted, for the boat that waited there was of a decent size and looked well made. Despite the many boxes and baskets being loaded on board, there was plenty of room for passengers. We would be travelling in comfort.

But when we reached Renni, he motioned towards another, smaller boat. It was barely as wide as a man was tall and its hull showed clear signs of repeated patching. It looked like it would fall apart as soon as the current took hold of it.

"Why can we not travel on the other one?" I asked, barely even trying to conceal my disappointment.

"This boat is less conspicuous," Intef said. "We are trying not to draw attention to ourselves."

The captain was a wiry little man named Ramose. Renni introduced us, calling me Samun and Istnofret only Ist. Behenu was left unnamed, described as Ist's cousin. Ramose bowed briefly to each of us and then left to tend to his boat. He clearly had little interest in his passengers.

There was not much room to sit on the crowded deck. Behenu wedged Mau's basket between some crates, then perched on a box that looked sturdier than the boat itself. Istnofret and I found spots where we could sit with our backs against crates. There was not enough room to even stretch out my legs. It would be a very different journey from the last time I had travelled by boat, when we left our desert city to sail to Memphis. Then I had sailed on my own vessel, with servants and guards to attend to me. I had a soft pile of cushions to sit on and a shade cloth strung above my head. Trays of food and jugs of melon juice were presented to me at regular intervals. There would be none of those comforts this time.

I sat with my legs pulled up to my chest and waited for the boat to set sail. Intef and Renni would be serving as crew it seemed, for as Ramose made his final preparations, they joined the other men at the oars and began rowing us out into the middle of the river.

Istnofret, Behenu and I sat in silence. The boat creaked and wobbled, and I waited for it to tip over, but once it caught the wind, it seemed to steady itself. This late into *akhet* the flood waters were still high and we needed a strong wind to travel south against the current.

The rowers drew in their oars and took up other chores around the boat, with Intef and Renni still helping. With five of us, the six crew, the captain, and Mau, it felt like far too many occupants for a vessel of this size.

"Will this boat be taking us all the way to Behdet?" I asked Istnofret. I kept my voice low, not wanting to offend the captain who, after all, had obviously not planned for so many passengers.

"Renni said the captain is only going as far as Hebenu and then will turn back to Heliopolis."

"So we will find another boat at Hebenu?"

"I am sure they have a plan."

"It would be nice if they deigned to share it," I muttered.

"Do you intend to stay mad at Intef for the entire journey?"

"I don't understand why you are not mad at him. Do you not care that he killed Sadeh?"

"He is distraught over it. But he bought you time to get away and he gave her a quick death. Have you even thanked him for that?"

"Thanked him?" I shot her a look, trying to gauge whether she was joking. I would think later about her comment that Intef was distraught. He was well practised at keeping his emotions from his face and if he was indeed distraught, I had failed to see it. "Thanked him for killing the woman who served me for more than ten years? Who was the dearest of my ladies to me?"

"I know she was always your favourite." Istnofret's tone was stiff and I realised with a sudden surge of regret that I had offended her. "But she chose to go. She knew they would realise that she was not you sooner or later, and she knew they would kill her when they did."

"So why did she go? Why didn't she be sensible and stay in my chambers?"

"And how would you have gotten out of the palace? One

of us needed to go in your place and she was the best option. I would have gone willingly, but I am too tall. They would have realised much sooner and you would have had no chance to get away."

"And then it would have been you who died," I muttered. Renni and I had made it only a few blocks from the palace before we were caught. I couldn't tell her how much it hurt that Sadeh had died for nothing.

"It had to be one of us. I know you wish it was me and I would have gladly taken Sadeh's place, but I am grateful to be the one who lived."

"I never said I wished it was you."

"You don't need to. I see it in your eyes every time you look at me."

I didn't know how to reply. I could not even say for certain that it was not the truth. How terrible for Istnofret if she thought I wished she had been the one to lose her life, and she must think me the most ungrateful person in the world. When Istnofret spoke again, her voice was gentle.

"Sadeh was broken. She never recovered from the assault she suffered. She spoke many times of wanting to die. I watched her constantly for fear that she would try to send herself to the West. If only one of us could live, I know she would prefer it to be me. I have things to live for. She did not."

"I didn't realise she was so unhappy. She told me once that she wanted to die, but I thought she got over it. I thought she…"

My voice trailed off. Anything I said would be merely an excuse. I knew Sadeh had never recovered from Ay's assault, but since she continued to undertake her tasks and ate when someone reminded her to and usually answered if someone spoke to her, I had let myself pretend she was well enough.

"I should have tried harder. To connect with her. To help her find something to live for."

"Mayhap. But Sadeh only wanted to live for you, not for herself. Being in service to the queen gave her a level of status she never expected to have, and she wanted to prove to her parents that she did not need to marry some old man to make a life for herself."

"What happened to her body?"

Even as I asked, I wasn't sure I wanted to know. If she had been tossed onto a rubbish heap somewhere and left for the jackals and the vultures, it would only hurt even more.

"Nenwef was going to see that she was embalmed. I know only that he had found out where her body had been taken. We left before he could retrieve her, but he promised Intef he would see to her. Sadeh will have her chance to get to the Field of Reeds."

"Intef arranged for Nenwef to look after her?" My eyes suddenly filled with tears and I blinked them away before they could fall.

"Intef would have done it himself but he feared Ay would keep him close and he might not be able to get away if he stayed too long. He desperately wanted to go after you. Nenwef was staying anyway so he promised to look after Sadeh."

"What will happen to Nenwef?" How selfish of me to not have enquired after the rest of my squad. With no queen to serve, would they even have positions in the palace anymore? Would they be thrown out and left destitute? Or imprisoned? "And Tuta? Woser?"

I hadn't noticed Intef approaching until he spoke.

"They were going to wait until things calmed down a little and then slip away, one by one," he said.

I looked towards the shore, my feelings too convoluted to share. He had killed Sadeh, but he did it to save her from a worse death. Sadeh had known she would die, but she did it to save me. Intef arranged for Sadeh to be embalmed. Had he done that for her or for me?

"Where will they go?" I asked, not directing my words at anyone in particular.

"Most of them have family elsewhere," he said. "They will go to them when they can."

"Will nobody go after them? Will they be safe?"

"Nobody other than they know where their families are. My men have always been cautious in case one day they needed a secret place to retreat to. We may have talked about our families from time to time — it would seem strange if we didn't — but we were always careful to say they were somewhere they were not. Take my father, for example. Anyone who has asked after him believes he lives somewhere on the outskirts of Memphis, that he followed us there from Akhetaten."

I could barely imagine what it must be like to live that way, always watching everything you said so as not to give away some secret that you might regret later.

"Where is he really?" I asked.

"Thebes. We will pass by there on our way to Behdet."

It was on the tip of my tongue to suggest we should stop at Thebes so he could spend time with his father, but his next words sharply reminded me once again that it was no longer my place to decide what we did.

"We will stop in to see him," Intef said. "I need to say goodbye in case I cannot return again."

"But we will be coming back." My heart already pounded in alarm at the suggestion and I finally let myself look at him.

"We have to. Once we find the Eye, I must return and take back the throne."

Intef looked at me evenly. "You surely realise that we might not find the Eye. It is possible — perhaps even probable — that such an artefact does not exist."

"It must exist," I whispered. "Hemetre believes it does. And I have no other options if it does not."

"You could go to your sisters. Forget about politics and dynasties. Live with them, wherever they are. You could be free of it all."

If I let myself think too long on the possibility of seeing my sisters again, I would throw everything else aside and rush to them. Maybe one day — once I had found the Eye and made things right again — maybe then I could go to them.

"That is not an option." Even as I spoke, my heart whispered the opposite.

He looked at me for a long moment and I felt the pity in his gaze, even though I looked out at the water.

"We go to Thebes first," Intef said. "And then to Behdet. We will figure out our next move after that."

SEVEN

I lost track of the days as we sailed towards Thebes, although Renni had said it would take around two weeks. With every breath I inhaled the familiar marshy scent of the Great River, transporting me back to my beloved desert city. I spent much of the journey silently reminiscing about my childhood.

My sisters, my father. Learning to read Akkadian on the missives sent by our allies. Meketaten and I running away from our nurses, giggling and holding hands as we raced through the palace. Sneaking into our mother's pleasure garden to swim in her lake. Watching Merytaten sit beside our father on the throne that had once belonged to our mother. The memories were bittersweet and it had been a long time since I had allowed myself to think of such things.

I shed more than a few tears during that journey while those around me pretended not to notice. Likely they thought I mourned the life I had left behind. They were correct, in a way, but my thoughts were not on my sudden lack of status, or being surrounded by servants who had somehow become friends, or the sudden absence of the luxuries I had always taken for granted. I grieved for secrets shared with my sisters. A fond smile from my father. Catching a whiff of my mother's perfume — a spicy blend of lily, myrrh and cinnamon — as she passed me in the hallway. Running barefoot through the palace with no worries or burdens. As a child, these things had been commonplace. Now they seemed idyllic.

Ramose let us off at Hebenu and we quickly secured passage on a boat that looked much sturdier than his. It was, at least, less crowded and it was a relief to be able to stretch out my legs when I sat down. A few days later we sailed past Akhetaten. I recognised the landscape as we approached and made sure that I looked at the opposite bank until long after we had passed. It had been more than five years since we had left and the mud brick buildings were likely crumbling by now. I didn't want to see that, nor did I want to see whatever remained of the palace or its twin jetties.

The weather was starting to change as the season edged from *akhet* to *peret*. The days grew cooler and noticeably shorter. After being immersed in my own thoughts for so long, it was a shock to reach Thebes and once again be surrounded by crowds. Some half dozen boats were already at the port and we had to wait until it was our turn to dock.

As I stepped onto the shore, the ground swayed beneath me and Intef was quick to grab me around the waist when I stumbled. I pretended not to notice, either that he had aided me or how he recoiled. I had been avoiding him for days because I didn't know what to say. I could hardly blame him for not wanting to touch me.

The harbour was filled with folk pushing and shoving in all directions. I kept my head down, lest someone recognise me, and followed Renni. Behind me, Mau yowled from her basket and Behenu promised her some tasty treats if she would just stay quiet for a little longer.

At length we reached a house which was small but well made and neatly maintained. A tiny vegetable garden had a crop of lettuce ready to be picked and a date palm that looked like it was thriving. Intef knocked on the door and the old man who opened it bore a clear resemblance to him.

"Intef!" the man cried, his face lighting up. "Why didn't you send a message to tell me you were coming?"

"I didn't know until it was too late."

They embraced and I looked away as tears filled my eyes. Their joy at being reunited was clear. Would anyone ever be that pleased to see me?

The man turned his attention to the rest of us and his jaw dropped when he spotted me.

"My lady." He dipped into a low bow. "I never expected you to grace my doorstep."

"I am surprised you recognise me."

His face would not have been familiar to me except that it was an older version of Intef's. He had to be at least forty, but he still stood with the straight back of a soldier. It shamed me that I could not recall his name. He waved us inside.

"Come in, come in. My knee does not tolerate standing for long periods so come and sit down. Intef, what brings you this way? How long are you here?"

"Just briefly, Papa," Intef said.

Inside was as neatly maintained as the outside. The furniture was sparse but well made, the floor neatly swept, and the man's belongings put away on shelves and in chests.

Intef introduced us and Setau, his father, beamed with delight.

"Sit, sit." He gestured to the mats on the floor. "I will bring refreshments."

"We cannot stay long, Papa," Intef said. "I must speak with you privately."

He followed his father into the other chamber. Their quiet conversation was punctuated by the noises of Setau preparing a meal while the rest of us sat on the mats and stared around the chamber. I strained to make out their words but they kept their voices low.

When they finally returned, Setau passed around mugs of beer while Intef set a tray in the centre of the mats. A hastily prepared meal of dates, little onions, and bread awaited us.

"Eat, eat," Setau urged.

I took one of the little onions and popped it into my mouth. It was as sweet and crunchy as I had anticipated. I accepted a mug of beer and felt myself start to relax a little.

"You have a very fine home, Setau," Istnofret said.

He beamed at her so proudly that I regretted I hadn't thought to compliment him first.

"Intef paid for it." Setau bestowed a fond smile on Intef, who was sitting beside him. "He sends me whatever he can spare. The palace pays him well."

"I am afraid there will be no more," Intef said. "At least not until I find work again."

Setau patted him on the leg. "By the gods, I have been fortunate that you are so generous to your old father. Few men are as lucky as me. But tell me, how was your journey here? I assume you sailed?"

I busied myself with nibbling on the little onions and left the others to answer his questions.

"I shall not ask where you travel to next," Setau said, with a pointed look at me. "Better that I don't, for I cannot tell what I don't know. But, of course, I know why you are here."

He jumped up and hurried out to the other chamber. There was the sound of furniture being moved and then he returned bearing a large basket, which he offered to me.

"They are all here," he said. "Every one."

I accepted the basket with no understanding of what he so proudly presented to me. When I looked inside it, my heart felt like it stopped. Hundreds of scrolls, all neatly rolled up and secured with a seal. I already knew whose seal they would be, but I lifted one to inspect it, hoping I was wrong. My hands trembled. Yes, those were my seals.

"My letters." My voice broke. "Are these my letters to my sisters?"

"None of them have been opened." Setau's face creased into worry. "I swear by Montu, I never read any of them. They went into this basket here as soon as I received them, each and every one."

"But why do you have my letters?" I looked across at Intef and caught the pained expression on his face. "You promised me. You said my letters would get to them."

"I didn't know," Intef said. "I swear to you. We put certain measures in place to assure your sisters' safety and one of those things was that I didn't know where they were going. I thought there was a trail, though. I honestly believed that if your letters reached the first messenger, they would be passed on and eventually they would reach your sisters. I would not have offered to take you to them if I didn't think the first messenger could aid us."

"And Setau was the first messenger?" I turned to Setau. "Why didn't you forward my letters?"

"I didn't know where they had gone," he said. "Nobody

did. I led Intef to believe I had more information than he did, though, so that he would not have to lie to you. You were fragile at the time and we thought it best you didn't know that there would never be any possibility of retrieving your sisters."

"So where are they? Somebody must know."

He gave me a sorrowful look and shook his head. "I don't know, and that is the truth."

"But you know who went with them."

He and Intef shared a look and I was sure he would lie to me.

"I know who went with them," Setau said. "That knowledge gives no clue as to their destination, though."

"Tell me who. Give me at least that much."

He shook his head. "I have sworn I will never tell. For their protection and that of the one who went with them."

I turned back to Intef. Desperation rose within me. I would never know where my sisters had gone. "Who is it? Tell me. I know you know."

"I cannot." He looked far less sorrowful than his father. "And you vowed you would never ask."

"I vowed I would never ask where they had gone, and I have kept that promise. I am asking you who went with them."

"I will not tell you," he said. "It is better you don't know. It is better that those of us who know, forget."

I was on the verge of tears but I fought to hold them back. I was so close to finding out something, anything, about my sisters. I couldn't give up now.

"Please," I whispered. "Tell me. Just give me the name of the person who went with them. That is all I ask."

"Maybe it is all you ask today," Setau said. "But knowledge

is dangerous. Once one has a little knowledge, one always wants more. Today you might think this will be enough for you, but tomorrow there will be another question and another the day after. It will never be enough and it will not make you happy, for neither of us can tell you where they went. And I assume that is what you really want to know."

"You assume too much." My tone was frosty now. "I demand to know the name of the person who went with them."

"Are you still in a position to make such a demand?" Setau asked. "Intef led me to believe you are no longer the queen."

I couldn't answer. I looked away, towards the floor. I took a deep breath and held it for a long time. Eventually I had to let it out, but I still had no answer. They all waited in silence and when I looked up again, their faces were more sympathetic than I had any right to expect after the way I had behaved. Setau was correct. Even though I had said such a thing myself only a few days ago, it was confronting to hear it from someone else's mouth.

"Forgive my rudeness," I said.

Setau nodded and gestured to the basket of letters. "I understand you may be travelling for some time. Do you wish me to keep these for you? You could collect them on your return."

I stared down into the basket. So many letters, each one written with love and hope. With the earnest need to share my feelings with someone. With the certainty that my sisters would receive them. With the belief that I shared my life with them.

"Burn them," I said. "Please."

"It will be done as soon as you leave."

I was glad that he didn't intend to do it immediately. I

didn't think I would be able to watch my letters being destroyed.

"Thank you for keeping them all these years." I fumbled in my little bag until I found one of the finger rings Istnofret had put there. I withdrew a carnelian stone set in a band of gold and offered it to him. "Please take this as payment for your services."

His eyes widened. "I cannot accept such a thing. Perhaps if I was in need, but Intef sends me more than enough."

"Take it. If Intef is not able to send you anything more, this will ensure you are fed well for some time."

Setau slowly reached out and plucked the ring from my palm. "Thank you for your generosity, my lady. This will feed me for the rest of my days, not just some time."

Was such a small item really so valuable? Once I would have worn a dozen such trinkets at a time and not spent a moment wondering how much they were worth. Now I had only what wealth I carried in my bag. I had three finger rings left.

"When do the boats heading south usually arrive, Papa?" Intef asked. "We must be on the next one going to Behdet."

"Every day or two," Setau said. "You will stay here, of course, until then. There is not a lot of room, but we will make do well enough."

"I don't want to arouse suspicion about why you have a houseful of strangers if someone comes looking for us," Intef said. "Better that we slip out as soon as it is dark. I am sure we will find somewhere to sleep."

Before Setau could reply, a voice came from outside.

"Setau, are you home?"

"It is my neighbour," Setau said. "I will go out and speak with him. Be quiet."

He slipped out the door and closed it behind him. I heard a cry from Setau that might have been *run* followed by a muffled thud. My little spell bottle was suddenly burning hot.

"Get in the corner," Intef said.

"What happened?" I asked.

"Silence." His voice was terse.

Istnofret, Behenu and I gathered in the corner. Intef and Renni positioned themselves in front of us, their daggers drawn.

"Check the other door," Intef said, very quietly.

Renni slipped away. He returned in moments.

"They are on that side as well. We cannot get out without being seen."

"Then we stay and fight," Intef said.

Had Setau's neighbour spotted us going into the house? Had someone been snooping around, offering a reward for news of strangers? We didn't have to wait long, for very soon the door burst open and a full squad entered. If Intef and Renni fought, it would be two against ten. Hardly a fair fight. Two against four, I had no doubt they could manage. Perhaps even two against six. But they were well outnumbered.

EIGHT

"Stand down," I said. Intef didn't respond and nor did he put away his dagger. "You cannot fight so many."

"I will not let you be taken," he said. "These are Ay's men."

"I would rather be taken than see you die on the floor of your father's home."

"Renni, please," Istnofret said. "Make him see sense."

Intef and Renni exchanged a glance. No words were spoken, but I saw the way their hands twitched. They were communicating even if none of us knew what they were saying. They both tucked their daggers away at the same time.

"On the floor," one of the intruders said. "Both of you. Toss your weapons into the centre of the room."

Intef's hand was on the dagger at his waist. He was still wondering if he could take them. I held my breath, but eventually he threw his dagger so that it landed, tip first, in the floor. Renni's dagger landed right beside it.

The intruders were wary, staying well out of reach until both men were lying on their bellies. Then they pounced on Intef and Renni, and tied their arms behind their backs, handling them with unnecessary force given that neither man was resisting. They paid little attention to the rest of us until they were satisfied that they had subdued Intef and Renni. I recognised none of these men and assumed Intef's reputation had preceded him.

"Come here then, sweetheart," one of them said to Istnofret. He leered at her and licked his lips. "I am thinking you and me can come to an arrangement. No need for you to be hauled off and imprisoned with these traitors."

Istnofret gave the man a haughty glare. "I would prefer to eat donkey dung."

His face changed. "That could be arranged if you don't watch your tongue."

"That the queen?" one of the others asked with a nod towards me.

They looked me up and down.

"Dinna look like much," one said.

"Eh. She can probably still give a man a good time. I hear Pharaoh had her on her back."

Intef snarled. He almost managed to get to his feet and it took three men to subdue him again, even with his hands tied.

"She the queen?" one of them asked Istnofret.

She pointedly looked away and didn't respond.

"Now don't be too haughty." The man stalked towards her. "You can answer nicely or I can make you answer. Your choice."

"I am the Queen of Egypt." I spoke before he could hurt her. "And your actions here today will not be forgotten."

"Bind her," one of them said. "I am not taking any chances. I want my reward."

"What did Ay promise you for your treachery?" I asked. "I will double it if you all leave immediately."

The man laughed. "As I understand it, you have nothing. You are in no position to offer me anything other than your own body. Still, I might—"

"Knock it off, man," one of his companions said. "The reward is for all of us. It is not your place to bargain with her. We take her back and we get our reward. That was the deal."

The man sneered at him. "Nobody said we couldn't have a little fun first."

"I don't want any trouble," one of the others said. "I want to get the job done and get my reward. Then I will pack up my family and move them to a nice little seaside village somewhere well away from here."

"I am quitting my job as soon as my reward is in my hands," another said.

"You really think Ay is going to give you anything?" I forced out a laugh I didn't feel. "He sends you off to do his dirty work and you go back to him, expecting rewards and promotions. More likely, you will be reassigned to some undesirable position, like guarding the slaves in the Nubian mines. Or he will kill you. After all, a dead man cannot tell what he knows."

"Shut your mouth," one of the men said with a snarl. "Pharaoh said you were trouble."

"Let's go," said the one who seemed to be the captain. "The sooner we get this lot secured, the sooner we can find somewhere to have a beer."

"Come on, then." One of the men kicked Intef in the ribs with his sandalled foot. If it hurt, Intef gave no sign of it. "On your feet, dogs."

With their hands bound behind them, Intef and Renni were allowed to stand. More rope was tied around each of their ankles, the other end of which was secured around the waist of a guard. If Intef or Renni made any attempt to escape, it would be easy for the guards to sweep them off their feet. For a few minutes, nobody watched us women. Istnofret eyed the two daggers still sticking into the floor.

"Istnofret, no," I said, very quietly. "You will get yourself killed."

"I know what to do with it," she whispered. "Renni showed me."

"There are too many of them. Be patient. Intef and Renni probably already have a plan."

"Are you going to dawdle here all night, ladies?" one of the men asked, his voice scornful. "Or have you forgotten you are prisoners?"

It was only as we were shoved towards the door that I realised Behenu still stood silently in the corner. It seemed nobody had noticed her. I met her eyes and saw the question there. I shook my head very slightly and hoped she would understand. There was no point her being captured with us. Better that she stayed here. Setau was a good man from all that I knew. He would ensure she found a position somewhere. I looked around for Mau, but she had disappeared. It saddened me that I might never see Sadeh's cat again.

Outside, we were hustled past Setau who lay face down on the ground. He was motionless and I couldn't tell whether he was dead or alive. It grieved me that Setau may have lost his life in order to help me. It seemed he was one of those who had helped to shepherd my sisters to safety, and I owed him a great debt for that.

NINE

They herded us through the streets of Thebes and folk turned to stare as our captors rudely ordered them out of the way. I waited for Intef and Renni to make their move.

The soldiers didn't bother to tie up Istnofret and me, despite one of them suggesting earlier that we should be bound. I guessed they considered us no threat. Maybe I shouldn't have told Istnofret not to grab the daggers. She said she knew how to use them and I knew a little myself. I had, after all, killed a man in my own bed with Intef's dagger. But as we walked, I came to the conclusion that I should do as I had for the last four years. I should be meek and compliant. Allow them to underestimate me. Then when Intef and Renni finally struck, I might actually be of use to them.

So I watched the path we took and tried to remember landmarks that might help me find the way back to Setau's house in case we were separated. Intef would want to know his father's fate, and we needed to go back for Behenu and Mau anyway. But I quickly realised the task was hopeless. I was too unaccustomed to having to find my way anywhere. Hopefully Istnofret was more proficient at remembering the way.

We walked for a long time before we were ushered inside a building which seemed to be some kind of administrative centre. The guards locked Intef and Renni in a chamber. At least they hadn't been thrown into a prison pit.

For a few moments, I wondered whether Istnofret and I should try to escape while the guards' attention was focused elsewhere. But we couldn't leave Intef and Renni behind any more than we could leave Behenu, and we knew nobody in Thebes other than Setau. So if Istnofret and I were to provide any help, we would have to stay here. The men locked us women in a chamber together and departed with much merriment about the reward they expected to claim.

The chamber was bleak — mud brick walls with not so much as a mural on any of them. A bucket in the corner, which I assumed was intended for us to relieve ourselves in. No bed or reed mat. Not even a blanket on which to sit.

"At least we are together," Istnofret said, quietly.

"I am surprised they have given us that much."

She sank down onto the floor where she could lean back against the wall. I sat beside her, hesitant for the floor was none too clean.

"Do you think Setau is alive?" she asked.

"I didn't see him move."

"I hope he is. For his sake, and for Intef's."

I didn't know what else to say and we lapsed into silence for a while. My mind was blank. I should be using this time to plan. To try to come up with a way we could rescue Intef and Renni. A way we could get back to Behenu. But I couldn't think at all.

"Do you think Renni is well?" Istnofret asked, eventually. "And Intef?"

"I don't think they were badly injured, even though the soldiers were rough with them."

"I hope not."

"I didn't realise you and Renni were so close." Now didn't seem like the time to discuss her burgeoning relationship but the words were out of my mouth before I could stop them.

Istnofret blushed furiously. "I am sorry I kept it from you."

"I didn't mean that as a reprimand. I was just... surprised. But I can see that he makes you happy."

"He is a good man. I always intended to tell you, but the moment never seemed right."

The conversation felt too intimate and I didn't know how to retreat gracefully so I said nothing. Despite all we had been through together, we had never really talked of private things like this. What was one supposed to say in a conversation with a friend such as Istnofret?

"And what of you and Intef?" she asked, when it became clear that I wasn't going to comment further.

I studied my fingers. Without the perfumed oils that my ladies used to rub into my hands every day, my skin had roughened and was beginning to peel in places.

"What of it?" I asked.

"It is clear you have feelings for him. Do you think—"

"He is servant." My tone was brusque. "And one who has betrayed me. There is nothing between us."

"Have you asked him?"

"Asked what?"

"About whether he betrayed you."

"Of course not. I was there. I heard the words that came out of his mouth. I don't need to hear whatever lies he might tell to excuse his actions."

"What actually happened?" she asked.

"You don't know?"

"Of course not. You have said little about it. Intef told me about Sadeh but that is all."

Somehow, my bitterness about Intef's role in Sadeh's death had lessened. I believed him when he said he had done it himself to ensure she didn't suffer. But I couldn't forgive him for humiliating me and it was hard to speak about those moments.

"Has Renni said nothing?" I asked.

"We don't gossip about you." Her tone was prim and almost reproachful. "If he knows anything, he has not shared it, and nor have I asked him."

"I don't know why you are so loyal to me." I continued to study my hands. It was better than looking around the empty cell. Or meeting her eyes. "I can do nothing for you. Any of you."

"We are loyal because you are our queen. And because we love you."

My eyes suddenly filled with tears and I had to swallow down a sob before it burst out of me.

"Intef loves you," she said.

"He is my servant. That is all."

"Is that really what you think?"

Having blinked away my tears, I allowed myself to glance up, very quickly, to meet her gaze.

"Of course it is."

She made a little sound, almost a huff.

"If all he feels for you is loyalty, then he must be the most loyal guard ever to live."

"Until he betrayed me."

"You still have not told me what happened."

Haltingly, I told her about what had occurred when I was summoned before the advisors. Of how Ay had demanded to know the father of my child. Of how Intef had casually admitted to having been in my bed, of doing whatever I told him to in order to "entertain" me. My cheeks burned and I blinked away more tears.

"He didn't mean any of that." Istnofret's voice held nothing but certainty. "He said what they wanted to hear."

"He was callous. Indifferent."

"He was letting them think they could trust him."

"By implying there had been so many men in my bed that he couldn't count them?"

"He didn't intend to humiliate you. I am certain of it. Intef does nothing without a plan."

"Then why has he not explained himself? He has had opportunities since then to tell me why he did it."

"Maybe he is waiting for you to ask."

"I should not have to ask. He should offer an explanation."

Istnofret laughed a little.

"This is the way things are between men and women, my lady. We think one way, they think another. If we don't talk with each other, we don't understand. You will not know what he was thinking until you ask him."

"He humiliated me. In front of Ay. He must have known how that would make me feel."

"And yet he did it anyway. Doesn't that tell you he was striving towards some higher goal? Something he thought was more important in that moment than your feelings?"

It was my turn to laugh, although scornfully. "You think he was trying to show Ay he could be trusted?"

"He wanted Ay to believe he was loyal to the throne, not to you. He said what Ay wanted to hear."

I suddenly remembered Intef telling me that I shouldn't put much weight on the odd things I might hear his men say from time to time. That they did it for a reason. Had he thought I would remember and realise that there was more to the situation than I understood?

"Have faith in him, my lady," Istnofret said.

I shook my head. My heart was still resentful and the words that came to my lips too bitter to be said.

"What do you think they mean to do with us?" she asked, when it became clear that I didn't intend to reply further.

"I expect they are making arrangements to return us to Memphis. Or me, at any rate."

"We must not let them separate us. I suppose they will keep Renni and Intef here, but you and I must stay together. If Intef cannot protect you, I will be your guard."

"You?" I might have laughed if our circumstances had been a little less dire. "What can you do to protect me?"

"Like I said, Renni taught me a few things. I will do what I can. But for now, my bladder is about ready to burst."

Istnofret got to her feet and inspected the bucket in the far corner of the chamber. "Whew. They didn't even bother to empty it."

I averted my gaze as she hitched up her skirt and crouched over the bucket. As she finished, we heard footsteps from the hallway. The door opened and a guard entered carrying two bowls.

"Dinner time." He stopped to look us both over. "My, it is not often that we have such fine ladies staying here."

Istnofret picked up the chamber bucket and took it to him.

"So fine that you couldn't even be bothered to empty the bucket after your last guests? Go empty this."

"I think you misunderstand your situation here." He gave her a cold glare.

"I disagree."

Istnofret tossed the contents of the bucket into the man's face. He gasped and the bowls clattered to the floor. She swung the bucket and slammed it into his face. He dropped to the ground.

"Dear Isis." I didn't know whether to be amazed or horrified.

"Quickly." Istnofret crouched over the man. She opened a pouch that hung from his waist and removed the contents. "I have the keys."

I got to my feet, feeling slow and clumsy after Istnofret's startling display. She closed the door behind us and locked the man in.

"We need to find Renni and Intef," she said and took off down the hall.

I trailed after her, trying to shake off my bewilderment. Istnofret had said Renni taught her a few things, but I hadn't expected that she would be the one to save us.

TEN

There were only four other chambers and it took us mere moments to locate the one in which Intef and Renni were held. They were both on their feet, ready and alert, when we burst in. Istnofret threw her arms around Renni while I hung back in the doorway.

"She smacked the guard in the head with the chamber bucket," I said in response to their questioning gazes.

"There is probably at least one more guard," Intef said. "Most of them were going off to celebrate, but they are unlikely to have left only one behind. We might not have much time before someone comes to see why your man failed to return."

He led us to the closed door at the end of the hall.

"Stay back," Intef said, very quietly. "We will go first."

Istnofret and I waited with our backs to the wall. She constantly looked back in the direction we had come. So far, she had shown herself to be more competent in defending us than I had expected, so I would follow her lead. It seemed I could learn a lot from her.

Intef flung the door open with a shout, and he and Renni ran in. We heard crashes and thuds but it was all over in moments. As we crossed the chamber, heading for the door that led outside, I tried not to see the body on the floor. It was the man who had told Istnofret he could arrange for her to eat donkey dung if she wished.

"Is he dead?" Istnofret asked.

"Yes," Renni said.

"Good."

I was surprised at the venom in her voice. After all, it was me they were after, not her. But then, Ay would show no mercy for anyone caught helping me escape. We must all do anything necessary to ensure we got away safely. If I had to kill someone myself, it would be no more than I had done before.

We waited at the door while Renni slipped outside. A low whistle sounded and Intef motioned for us to go. For a brief moment, there was only the four of us, but then we rounded the corner and encountered two women chatting, baskets of shopping slung over their arms. A man carrying a large bundle swore at a dog that darted between his feet. Three naked children ran down the street, shouting and waving little wooden daggers.

"Walk swiftly," Intef muttered. "But don't run."

My legs trembled. Surely someone would realise we had escaped and would raise the alarm? But nobody even looked at us, other than one of the children who poked his tongue out at me as he ran past. We hurried past a few buildings and ducked into a narrow alley.

"Anyone watching?" Intef asked, quietly.

Renni shook his head. "Not that I could tell."

"Good. We slip through between the buildings and make our way back to my father's house."

We zigzagged through the alleys. Intef thought, at one point, that someone was following us. We slipped into a nearby house and waited in the dark, hearts pounding. But the person walked right by without pause, so maybe it was just someone else who happened to be trying to avoid notice. We finally came to the house next to Setau's. I leaned against a wall, breathing shakily as much from the exertion as the fear of discovery.

"I will go," Intef said.

We waited in the shadows while he ran up to the house. He listened at the door for a few moments, then slipped inside. Setau's body was gone. Either he wasn't really dead or someone had taken him away for embalming. I hoped, for Intef's sake, it was the first.

Moments stretched into minutes. I tried to stand still, but my feet itched to move and I found myself clenching my fists, then releasing them, only to clench them again, just for the sake of being able to move some part of my body.

"What is taking so long?" Istnofret whispered.

"Patience," Renni said. "Just because we cannot see what is happening doesn't mean we should assume the worst."

"A good soldier follows orders and waits patiently," she said, as if repeating a lesson long learned. "But what do you *do* with yourself while you wait?"

"I do nothing," Renni said. "Only wait."

"I will never be a good soldier," she said.

Setau's front door opened and Intef emerged with our bags slung over his shoulders. Behenu was close behind him, carrying Mau's basket.

"Thank you, Isis," I whispered.

They hurried to us.

"We must go." Intef handed out our bags. He passed Renni his dagger. His own was already stuck through the waistband of his *shendyt*.

"Is Setau well?" I asked.

Intef shook his head.

"They killed him?" Istnofret asked.

He nodded once, briefly, and didn't look at us.

"I dragged him back into the house after everyone was gone," Behenu said, quietly. "A woman came to check on him. She had been watching out of her window and saw what happened. She said she would make arrangements for Setau to be embalmed, so I took the ring you gave him from his pocket and gave it to her for payment."

Intef put his hand on her shoulder and squeezed it. I supposed it was his way of thanking her without words for looking after his father.

"Intef, I am sorry," I said, but he shook off my condolences.

"I will mourn him later, when we are safe. We must go now. They will be looking for us."

I hesitated to ask about my letters, not wanting to sound like I was only thinking about myself, but what if one of Ay's men came to search Setau's house? Intef had already guessed my thoughts.

"Behenu burned your letters," he said.

I glanced at her, surprised.

"I don't know what they are." Her gaze was downcast and her voice trembled a little. "They seemed important to you and I thought they might be dangerous. You said for Setau to burn them so when he... could not, I threw them in the oven. I am sorry if I did wrong."

I grabbed her chin and made her look up at me. "You did

very well, Behenu. If the wrong people had found those letters…"

"I saved one."

She reached into Mau's basket and retrieved a scroll. The seal was unbroken. I tucked it away in my bag. Maybe I would read it one day and see which one she had saved. Maybe I wouldn't.

"Thank you," I said.

"We must go," Intef said.

"Where?" I asked.

"To the harbour. If you have any other jewels in your little bag, we might be able to buy a boat."

I swiftly dug the three remaining finger rings out of my bag and offered them to him. They were all I had left.

"Take them. I have no need for jewels. I would rather that we were safely away from here."

He took them without comment, although he stared down at them for a long moment. Was he, like me, wondering if I shouldn't have given the carnelian ring to Setau?

"There is more," Istnofret said.

"More finger rings?" Intef asked.

"Rings, earrings, gems. Anything that was small enough to sew into my skirt."

She lifted her skirt to knee-high and showed us the hem. The stitching was finely done with not a wrinkle in the cloth, but I could see how she had turned up the bottom all the way around her skirt. The entire hem seemed to be filled with small items, each cleverly stitched into its own tiny pocket so that they could be removed one at a time.

"I didn't intend to steal them," she said to me. "Only to bring whatever I could of value. I thought they might be useful to you."

"How much do you have in there?" I asked.

"I didn't count, only stitched in as many as I could. A couple of dozen rings, a few pairs of earrings with fine gems. The stitching is not my best, for I didn't know how much time I had. I even removed the stones from some of your necklaces. I tried not to damage them," she added quickly. "If— When you return, a craftsman should be able to put the gems back in place."

"You did well," I said. "I would not have thought to do such a thing."

Once again, we followed a winding route between the houses, but when we reached the harbour, guards milled everywhere.

"We took too long," Intef said. "They have realised we escaped."

"I will find the drinking house," Renni said. "Likely the captain is whiling away his time in there."

"They might recognise you." Istnofret grabbed his hand. "It is too dangerous. If they capture you again, they will take care that you do not escape a second time."

"It has to be either Intef or I." Renni traced her cheek with one hand. "If I don't return, go with Intef. He will look after you."

"I am not leaving without you," she said.

I looked away into the crowd. This moment felt too private for me to observe.

"I can do it," Behenu said.

"Do what, child?" Intef asked.

"Find the captain. Buy his boat."

Intef and Renni exchanged glances and Intef shook his head.

"Nobody will take you seriously," he said. "You are too young."

"They don't know my face," Behenu said. "They never noticed me, and I am the only one they don't know."

He looked down at her for a long moment, then at me, as if asking my permission. I didn't want to be the one to say that yes, Behenu could go and put herself in danger, but she might just be able to save us all.

"Give her the rings," I said. "And tell her how she should go about negotiating with the captain."

"Offer him two for the boat," he said. "It is more than double what the vessel is worth and will compensate him well for his lost income while he purchases another. Once he has agreed to this, give him the other one and tell him that this is for his silence. Do you understand?"

Behenu nodded and tucked the rings away in a small pouch she wore beneath her shirt. I had never noticed the pouch before. What else did she keep in there?

"Will three be enough?" I asked.

Intef made an amused noise. "Those rings will pay for a lavish lifestyle for his whole family for the rest of his life if he sells them wisely."

"I had no idea they were worth so much."

Once I would have worn a dozen or more rings on my fingers, along with golden bracelets on my arms and necklaces set with gems. How much wealth had I adorned myself with? How many people could have fed their families with the jewels I once wore for no purpose other than my own amusement?

"Go now," Intef said to Behenu. "There is only one boat in the harbour at present. Find the drinking house and locate the captain. Buy the boat and return as swiftly as you can."

Behenu hurried away.

"Can we trust her?" I asked.

"My lady." Istnofret's tone was disapproving.

I blanched a little, unused to anyone speaking to me like that. "She is a slave, after all, and she is carrying enough wealth to allow her to go anywhere she wants. I just thought..."

My voice trailed away as I realised they were all giving me disapproving looks.

"What?" My cheeks were uncomfortably hot. "It was not an unreasonable question."

"She is loyal to you," Istnofret said. "You saved her from a horrible situation and she is grateful."

"She is still a slave," I muttered, but nobody seemed to hear me. It seemed I was the only one who thought this fact important.

ELEVEN

Darkness fell while we waited for Behenu. An official came by to light lamps, but they revealed little of our surroundings and I could no longer see either the boat or the water from where we waited. My feet were sore and I desperately wanted to sit down, but everyone else was standing. The longer we waited, the more I silently questioned the wisdom of having sent Behenu away with so much riches. Likely we would never see her again. Perhaps she had negotiated the purchase of the boat and was already making her way back to Syria. I didn't share my thoughts, though, not wanting Istnofret to rebuke me again.

"She comes," Renni said, eventually, and I couldn't conceal my sigh of relief.

"Have faith, my lady," Istnofret muttered. "You will see."

Behenu had barely reached us before she motioned for us to follow.

"Quickly. We must go."

She led us back to the harbour and we boarded the boat. It was smaller than our previous vessel but without any cargo, there was plenty of room. Intef and Renni swiftly set about preparing to leave, untying the rope that secured the boat to the harbour and making various other preparations that I didn't see the point of wasting time on. Behenu lit lamps at each end of the boat. Soon enough, Intef and Renni took up the oars and the boat slowly edged out into the middle of the river. But before we could catch the wind, the boat came to a stop. No matter how hard Intef and Renni strained, they couldn't make it move.

"We don't have enough men on the oars," Istnofret said. "I can row. Behenu too."

She pointed the girl to an oar and took up the place opposite her. As they began to row, I realised I was the only one not contributing.

"What about me?" I asked. "I can help."

Nobody replied, probably because they were all too intent on their task to pay any attention to me. Istnofret determinedly moved her oar and looked like she actually knew what she was doing. Behenu, though, was struggling. I sat beside her.

"Let me help." I placed my hands beside hers on the oar and together we strained to move it through the water.

Finally the boat began to edge further out and, at last, we caught the wind. I slouched over the oar, panting. I had never realised how hard rowing was. All those times I had watched the slaves do it and had never even thought about how hard they were working. Renni and Intef were already back on their feet and doing various tasks. Istnofret was still slumped over her oar, though, so I felt like it was acceptable for me to sit a moment longer also. But as soon as she stirred, I forced myself to get up.

"We did it," Behenu said.

I had almost forgotten the girl beside me.

"Good job." Intef slapped her on the back and she grinned up at him.

I went to stand at the bow. We were not moving fast, but it was enough for the breeze to whip through my dress. As long as we were on the river, we were safe. Somebody came to stand beside me and I knew without looking that it was Intef. It was he who finally broke the silence.

"I need to explain what happened with Ay," he said.

I breathed carefully. In and out. His words made me want to cry even before he said anything further.

"I am listening."

"I had received word of the approach of the Hittites. The advisors were unaware at that point, but I knew they would find out very shortly. Before that happened, though, I received a message from Ay, asking to meet privately with me."

"So you went?" I didn't try to hide my bitterness. "The man I hate the most asks to meet you secretly and you do it without telling me?"

"I had to find out what he wanted. He didn't know about the Hittites, so it had to be something else."

I said nothing and eventually he continued.

"He wanted to know whether you were really with child. He seemed to be trying to decide whether you were disposable."

"You think he was going to have me killed."

"Probably, although perhaps he was already considering sending you away. All I know is that he was desperate to know about the babe. He offered me gold, a position in his personal squad, a house of my own. I played along for a while, pretending I was considering his offer but was still unsure, and he kept offering more and more. It was too good an opportunity to turn down. If I was one of his personal guards,

I would have direct access to the sort of information that had only ever come to me second or third hand. I would know immediately if there was some threat to you. So I let him think I had been persuaded by his riches. I told him I had been in your bed and that although I didn't know whether you were with child, you seemed to genuinely think it."

I had thought that if I carried the heir, I might be able to use that fact to keep hold of the throne. After all, my babe would be the next pharaoh if he was a boy. If the child was a girl, the man she married would be pharaoh. I had thought an heir would ensure my own safety.

"And he believed you?" I asked.

"He seemed satisfied enough. I gave him a few nuggets of information, nothing that was exactly true, but close enough that if he discovered they weren't, the discrepancies would be explainable."

"Why did he want to know about the babe?"

"He never said. I assumed he was trying to figure out whether it was his, but I couldn't tell whether that made you more or less valuable to him."

"Why didn't you tell me? Or at least send a message. Renni could have told me."

"I couldn't risk it. Your reactions had to be genuine if we were to avoid suspicion. It would likely have meant my head if Ay realised he had been duped. If Suppiluliumas had sent a son as you asked, he would certainly be accompanied by armed guards. That is a situation easily misunderstood. Or misrepresented, depending on your motives. I wanted to be close to Ay so I would know exactly what he knew.

"Then he started making comments about wanting to be rid of you, about how it would look too suspicious if you suddenly disappeared, so you had to be publicly accused of a crime. When word came soon after of the Hittites, it was exactly the excuse he needed, but it didn't occur to me that he might send you to the mines. That seemed too low, even for him."

"So you sent Renni to the Medjay?"

"Some old friends. From back when I trained with them. They owed me a couple of favours and Ay is not well liked by any of them."

"I didn't know whether I was being rescued or abducted."

"There was no way to warn you without making the soldiers suspicious. There were none there who were not loyal to Ay."

"Hannu was kind to me."

"And yet he was still Ay's man. None of them survived. The Medjay would have made sure of that. It was part of the agreement we made."

I stared out at the water ahead of us. Of all of the soldiers escorting me to Nubia, Hannu was the only one I might have argued should be left alive. But, of course, Hannu was not the only one to have died.

"I am sorry about Setau," I said. "He did not deserve such a death."

He inhaled shakily. "He would not have died had I not taken you to him."

"I know."

I could argue that I hadn't asked to be taken to his father, but Intef was right — the men who killed Setau were looking for me. He would still be alive if I hadn't gone to his home.

"I am sorry your letters never reached your sisters."

In the rush to leave Thebes, I had almost forgotten the single letter still carefully tucked into my bag. I had no words to express my feelings about learning my sisters never knew I had written to them every week. There was grief and loss and something that felt a little like relief. If they hadn't received my letters, that meant they had been free to live their lives. Maybe it was best for them this way. I wasn't yet sure whether it was best for me also. I took a deep breath. There was something else I needed to say and it was probably the hardest thing I had ever said to him.

"I am sorry I doubted you."

"You should not have."

It was as close as he had ever come to reproaching me and I felt the sting of it.

"I know."

"Why did you?"

His voice broke as he asked. My answer was terribly important to him. I didn't want to think about why. It felt like we were veering into dangerous territory. I could feel the way he restrained himself. He was treading carefully, tiptoeing around whatever it was he wanted to say.

"After all of the intrigue and the spies and assassins, I suppose it didn't seem unreasonable that Ay might have finally gotten to someone close to me," I said.

"But me? I would understand if you had believed it of one of your other guards. Tuta or Woser or Nenwef. Renni even. But I will never understand why you didn't trust me. After everything I have done. All the years I served you."

Shame flooded through me and my cheeks heated. He was saying no more than both Istnofret and Renni had already said, but it was different to hear it from Intef himself.

"I am sorry. I don't know what else to say. There is no way I can excuse myself."

"I am not looking for an excuse. I just want to understand. To know why you were so ready to believe I would betray you." He turned to face me and I could barely bring myself to look him in the eyes. "Tell me why you believed such a thing of me."

I turned my face away and didn't answer. I didn't know what our relationship was now that we were no longer queen and servant. I wasn't even sure what I wanted it to be, but I needed to figure that out before I could let him in any further.

"Will you tell me nothing? Is this all the response I am to receive?"

The anguish in his voice brought unexpected tears to my eyes, which I didn't want him to see. I kept my face turned away and didn't respond. Eventually, he left.

I stood looking out into the dark for a long time after he had gone, letting the wind dry my tears.

TWELVE

I didn't relax until morning and Thebes was well behind us. Then I found a place to sit where I could watch the wildlife on the river bank. Istnofret often sat beside me. She seemed content with silence, which suited me well enough.

The boat contained enough supplies for the first two days of our journey. The food was simple — a sturdy, hard-baked bread, small sweet onions, salty beer — and we supplemented it with fish caught in the nets we found on the boat. When our supplies ran out, we had to dock at a village. I longed to stretch my legs and walk on solid ground but it quickly became clear that only Renni and Behenu would be leaving the boat. Istnofret didn't ask to disembark and so neither did I. When Renni and Behenu returned, they carried three large sacks of supplies.

"This is far too much," Istnofret said. "I thought you said Behdet was only a few days away? We will not be able to eat it all before it spoils."

"We had only the gemstone you gave us to trade," Renni said. "We had to be seen to be accepting a reasonable deal for it. If we took too little, folk would talk and if Ay sends men looking this far, that is the sort of thing they would pay attention to."

Intef avoided me for the rest of the journey. He said little but when he spoke, his words were directed at Renni or Istnofret or Behenu. Never at me. I didn't know how to make things right again and persuaded myself not to even try because he was grieving his father and probably wanted to be left alone.

As we sailed, we passed a number of villages.

"How will we know which is Behdet?" Istnofret asked.

Renni only shrugged and it was Intef who answered her.

"It will be larger than these small villages," he said. "We should be able to see the temple of Horus from the water."

"And if the temple is not in sight?" she asked.

"We will continue until we are sure we have gone too far, then we will turn back."

"Why don't we ask someone how much further it is?" It seemed like an obvious solution to our problem and I didn't understand why nobody had suggested this. Intef busied himself with the fishing net he was trying to untangle and it was Renni who answered.

"It makes it clear that we don't know where we are, and that—"

"Will make us stand out," I finished for him. "I understand."

He glanced at Intef who was still hunched over the net, then shot me a sympathetic look. I turned my attention back to the river bank. This part of the Great River was wild and unpopulated, by humans at any rate. I saw hippopotamuses and cows, brown ducks and a family of geese. Swallows flitted over the river and then back to shore. In the water's depths, I occasionally caught sight of something fast and silvery. Perch perhaps, or maybe eels. I saw no sign of crocodiles although they were undoubtedly there, perhaps even watching us. At night we slept on the boat, not daring to risk sharing the shore with the creatures that lived there.

I thought I had already grieved for my sisters, but that was nothing compared to the pain of realising that they were irretrievably lost to me. Learning that they had never received my letters was both devastating and a relief. Knowing that Setau had information that he would never be able to share, hurt even more. I had always thought they were just a question away, that if I broke my promise never to ask, Intef would be able to tell me. But he never knew where they had gone. My only chance of finding them had died with Setau. It felt like I grieved for them all over again.

After several days we reached a village that was larger than the others. A large temple dominated the skyline.

"Can you make out the carvings?" Intef muttered to Renni.

They both squinted against the sunlight bouncing off the stone walls.

Renni shook his head. "Cannot see anything with that glare. We will have to get closer."

"I can go," Behenu offered.

"Try not to be noticed," Intef said. "Go quickly, but not so quickly that you draw attention to yourself."

"I know how to make sure nobody sees me," she said, somewhat tartly.

Intef flashed her a grin. "I know, but it doesn't hurt to remind you. You could endanger us all if you forget."

Behenu slipped away and we busied ourselves around the boat, trying to look as though we were merely completing our chores before disembarking. Intef seemed to be moving things around, although I couldn't see that what he did made any difference. Renni sanded an oar that had developed some splinters. Istnofret and I bent over a tangled fishing net, of which there seemed to be a never-ending supply.

When Behenu scrambled back on board, I was sure she had returned too quickly to have found out anything useful.

"This is Behdet," she said. "And we are expected."

I restrained my sigh. Surely Ay couldn't have gotten his men here ahead of us?

"What did you see?" Intef asked.

"A boy watching me," Behenu said.

"Was it the same one who passed you the note in Memphis?" I asked.

All four of them frowned at me.

"Of course not." Behenu's face said clearly that she thought my question was daft. I bristled at the feeling of judgement.

"What happened?" Intef asked.

"He slipped away after I saw him. I found the temple and Horus is carved all over it, so I think it is the one we are looking for. As I was coming back, someone brushed past me and whispered in my ear. She said to return to the temple at midnight."

"What did she look like?" Intef asked.

"I didn't see her face. There were people all around and I couldn't tell who had bumped me. All I know is that it was a woman's voice."

I had rebuked her once for not paying close enough attention to her surroundings and she looked genuinely regretful that she couldn't give Intef more information.

"How old would you judge her to be?" Intef asked.

"From her voice? Old. Much older than my lady or Istnofret."

"We will find somewhere to wait," Intef said. "And then we will see."

"We are going to meet her?" I asked.

He shrugged. "Depends how the situation looks by midnight. We don't know whether she is friend or foe at this stage."

"Surely Ay would not send a woman after me. She might be a Daughter of Isis."

"Have you forgotten the time he sent Tentopet to spy on you?" he asked. "Some women are trained as well as men. He might assume you would trust a woman more quickly than a man. That it would be easier to get close to you."

"I have never seen a woman trained as a guard." The mere thought was ridiculous. "No woman is permitted to do such a thing, even if she wanted to."

He gave me a dark look. "There is much of the world you don't know, my lady. I would suggest you should not be so quick to make assumptions about things you have not seen."

"You have seen a woman trained as a guard?" I asked. "A soldier?"

"I knew a woman once who was better trained than I am," he said. "She could bring me to my knees almost as fast as she could look at me."

I wanted to ask where this woman was now, but the look on his face said quite clearly that he wasn't in the mood for questions.

"Where can we wait?" Istnofret asked. "We are too conspicuous here."

"She is right," Renni said. "We need to move, and I would not say no to a meal."

We left Mau in her basket with a sail cloth strung over her for shelter. We disembarked and the dock swayed from side to side as I adjusted to being on solid land. Intef stopped a young woman carrying an infant.

"Excuse me, lady," he said. "We are visitors to your city and the person who was supposed to meet us is not here yet. Is there somewhere we could rest for a few hours?"

The woman looked us up and down.

"We can pay," he added. "We have plenty of supplies and would be happy to exchange some for a place to rest."

"See that you do," she said. "My husband will be none too happy if he finds you all there when he gets home from work. Follow me."

"We are much obliged," Intef said.

The woman walked swiftly and led us to a small house. It was plain and a little shabby, but the walls were solid and that was all I cared about. It consisted of only one chamber, with a couple of bed mats stacked neatly in one corner and a threadbare rug covering most of the floor. Shelves on the walls displayed the family's meagre belongings.

"I am Neferet," the woman said stiffly. "And I will thank you to pay me now."

Intef gave her a brief bow, although he was clearly of higher status.

"I am Intef, and my companions are Ren, Ist, Be and Samun." He pointed to each of us in turn as he gave the names Renni had used previously. They would be obvious for anyone who knew us, but at least they were easy for us to remember. "I will go to fetch some of our supplies for you."

"Would you like me to hold the babe?" Istnofret asked Neferet as he left.

Neferet gave her a suspicious look. "She is hungry," she said, curtly, then sat down on the rug, pulled out her breast and began to feed the babe.

I wondered whether I looked as awkward as I felt as we stood beside Neferet. She had made it clear that we weren't exactly welcome in her home and I wasn't sure what she expected us to do while we waited.

"Sit," Neferet said, eventually. "You are making me nervous standing over me like that."

I sat down with a sigh. Even such a short walk had tired my legs after sitting on the boat for days.

Neferet kept her gaze on her child. With nothing else to do, I watched her feed the babe but my eyes quickly began to droop.

"Have you travelled a long way?"

I didn't realise Neferet was speaking to me until Istnofret poked me with her elbow.

"Oh, yes, quite a way."

"You should lie down," she said. "Sleep while you can."

"Thank you."

I glanced at the rug, which didn't look clean enough to sleep on, but quickly decided that I could no more afford to be picky about where I slept than I could afford to offend our unwilling host. I lay my head on my hands and closed my eyes. I must have only slept for a few minutes because I woke when Intef returned. Neferet inspected the contents of the basket he presented to her and frowned.

"I said you could only stay for a few hours," she said.

"You did indeed," he answered, easily.

"There is enough in here to feed all of you for a week."

"I said we could pay you."

She looked from him to the basket and seemed undecided. Was she going to turn us out just because he had given her more provisions than she had expected? But at length, she took the basket over to the shelves.

"I will make you a meal." She sounded a little less begrudging. "Rest while you can."

She served us bread and cheese from our supplies, and a salad of cucumbers and lettuce from her own garden with some of our small sweet onions. With a mug of beer in my hand and my stomach pleasantly full, I felt more content than I would have expected in such surroundings. I watched through the open doorway as the light faded from the sky and the stars emerged. Was one of them my brother looking down on me tonight?

Neferet began shooting us dark looks.

"My husband will be home soon, and he would not be pleased to find his house full of strangers."

Intef got to his feet and gave her a swift bow.

"Thank you for your hospitality. We need to be moving on."

"Will anyone come looking for you?" she asked.

"Perhaps," he said. "And if that happens, I trust you will remember that large basket of provisions."

She looked at him for a long moment before she nodded. As we walked away, I glanced back to see Neferet standing in the doorway staring after us.

We returned to the harbour so that Behenu could retrace her path to the temple.

"That way," she said, pointing.

"We should split up," Intef said. "If anyone is looking for us, they are likely looking for a group. Renni and Istnofret, you walk ahead of us. When you reach the temple, go around it to the right and wait for us at the back."

They set off and quickly disappeared into the darkness. Intef, Behenu and I lingered for a few minutes, trying to look as if we waited for someone.

"They are far enough ahead of us," Intef said, at last. "Let's go."

As we walked, I became increasingly uneasy. Were we heading straight into a trap? Intef was obviously thinking the same thing, for as the temple came into sight — a great stone building lit up by torches — he stopped.

"You should wait here," he said to me. "Behenu and I will go on alone. Anyone who sees us will think we are merely a father and daughter going to the temple to worship. Stand against the wall and keep to the shadows. I will return for you as soon as I know it is safe."

"Don't leave me here alone," I said. "What if they come looking for me?"

"They will expect you to be with me," he said. "They are unlikely to pay much attention to a woman on her own."

"At least leave Behenu with me."

They exchanged glances.

"I will stay," she said.

"She might not reveal herself to us if you are not there. I need you to come with me." He offered me an apologetic shrug. "I am sorry, but we have to leave you alone."

I sighed. "Just go."

I leaned against the mud brick wall. It was still warm from the sun and was pleasant against the tight muscles in my shoulders. There were enough people walking past that I didn't feel too alone and nobody seemed to see me standing there in the shadows. Intef finally returned.

"Come," he said. "But keep your head down."

He took my arm and we walked swiftly. My heart pounded so loudly that I wouldn't have heard anyone sneaking up behind us. From between the buildings, the temple came into sight. It was a massive, stone structure with carvings of Horus in various poses all along its front wall. We hurried around to the back where the others waited. Renni's hand rested on the dagger stuck into his *shendyt*.

"Anything?" Intef murmured to him.

Renni shook his head. "All quiet."

Even as he spoke we heard the whisper of feet on the hard-packed dirt path. Intef pushed me behind him, against the wall, and slid the dagger from his waistband. The familiar act of Intef putting himself between me and danger was reassuring. Despite the tension between us, it seemed I was still his first thought.

A boy emerged from around the corner. He was perhaps eleven or twelve, with short dark hair and bare feet. He halted at the sight of us and although his gaze flicked down to Intef's dagger, he didn't seem alarmed. He pointed at me.

"You are to come with me."

"Who are you?" Intef asked.

The boy looked at him steadily. "I am not here to answer questions. My task is to find her." He gestured towards me.

"If she goes, we all go," Intef said.

The boy shook his head. "I am to take her only. The rest of you wait here. I will bring her back to you."

"No," Intef said. "The others can wait, but I go with her."

"I was given specific instructions," the boy said. "Her only."

"Who wants to see me?" I asked.

"I can tell you nothing," the boy said. "Only that you must come alone."

"She is not going alone," Intef said.

The boy shrugged. "Your choice. I will leave then. Good luck with your search."

"What do you know of our search?" I asked.

He looked at me but didn't answer.

"Does the one who has sent for me know about it?"

Again he didn't answer.

"I know what you are thinking," Intef said to me, quietly. "But no."

"This might be our only chance to get information."

"It is more likely a trap."

"I am going."

"Not without me."

"Intef, you are being ridiculous." I couldn't keep the exasperation from my voice. "He has made our options clear. I am not going to lose our first real chance of help."

"It is a trap."

"Then I will expect you to rescue me."

He held my gaze for a long moment, but eventually he slid his dagger back into his *shendyt* and stepped back.

I turned to the boy.

"Can you assure me that I will be safe?"

"You are safe with me," he said. "Past that, I cannot say, but I don't think she has any intention of hurting you."

"That will have to be good enough," I said.

THIRTEEN

I ntef said nothing as the boy led me away. I shot him a look, trying to tell him with my eyes that he needed to trust me, but he looked only at the boy.

"My companions might try to follow me," I said.

"You had better hope they don't," the boy replied.

He led me to a hut which was just a short walk away. No lamps shone from within.

"I am expected, am I not?"

"Ssh."

He put his hands to his mouth and made a sound like an owl. Footsteps behind us made me jump. I started to turn, but the boy grabbed my arm.

"Just wait," he whispered. "They are checking we weren't followed."

I prayed to Isis that Intef had had the sense to stay at the temple. At length came the returning call of an owl and the boy led me up to the door. It opened.

"Return in an hour," a female voice said.

The boy slipped away into the darkness.

"Well, do you intend to enter or did you come all this way to stand on the doorstep?" she asked.

"Who are you?"

"If you want information, come inside. Otherwise, I can call the boy back and he will return you to your companions."

"I want to hear what you have to say," I said, quickly, before she could send me away.

She chuckled a little. "Oh, it is not me who sent for you. But hurry up and come in."

As I stepped into the dark chamber, my heart pounded and my knees trembled. The door closed and somebody took my arm.

"Come this way," she said.

I took a few shuffling steps. The darkness was absolute and I could see nothing.

"Wait a moment," she said.

The air around me shifted as if somebody had opened a door. She led me forward and then the door closed again. A flame flared and a candle shed light on the chamber.

It was empty other than for a rug on the floor and two women. The woman standing beside me was perhaps my age, with dark braids dangling to her shoulders. The woman who sat on the rug was Maia.

"I didn't expect to see you again," I said.

Years ago, she had been my brother's wet nurse. More recently, she had been a Daughter of Isis and the one Hemetre told me to find if I needed aid. But I had been attacked at her husband's perfume stall and no longer knew whether she was a friend. I suddenly wished Intef had found a way to come with me after all.

"Sit." Maia gestured at the space in front of her.

I did as she bade and waited. I was bursting with questions, but if it was she who had summoned me, she likely had specific information she intended to share. I could ask my questions later if there was time.

Maia looked me up and down, no doubt noting my crumpled gown, my lack of kohl and jewellery, and my wig-less head where my own hair had grown into a stubbly layer.

"Are you well?" she asked. "I heard about the circumstances in which you left Memphis."

"Well enough."

"You seek the Eye of Horus."

"How do you know?"

"You would not be in Behdet otherwise." She studied me for a long moment. "Why do you want it?"

"It is supposed to give its holder ultimate power."

"Mortals are not meant to have such power."

"But sometimes we need it."

"For what?" she asked.

"To allow me to control the advisors. To take back the throne. To take control of my country."

"So you desire power."

"I am trying to save Egypt."

"From what? We have a pharaoh on the throne. Chaos did not descend on us. The sun continues to rise."

"Pharaoh is an evil man who stole the throne for his own glory. He has killed the son of the Hittite king and we are on the brink of war. He worships nobody but himself. He uses fear and hatred as his tools to control the people around him."

"He is Pharaoh. It is his right to rule however he chooses. His word is law."

I was momentarily speechless.

"You cannot believe this is acceptable. Pharaoh should be a just and honest man. He should rule with compassion and wisdom, for the benefit of all of our citizens, not just a chosen few."

"And yet you married him." Her voice was placid. "It was you who made him Pharaoh."

"I didn't marry him. My signature on the marriage contract was forged."

She considered me, looking deep into my eyes as if she found a truth there that was different to my words. "And you think you can do better? You plan to make yourself Pharaoh?"

"I— I don't know. I have no wish to be Pharaoh. I have no desire for power or glory. I want to protect my people. Perhaps I need only be Pharaoh until I can find a man worthy of the task."

"And you know no men you consider worthy? You must have impossibly high standards."

"And the impossible is exactly what the Eye can do, from what I understand. Will you help me?"

"I don't know where it is."

My eyes filled with tears which I quickly blinked away before they could fall. "Then why did you ask to meet with me? I thought that meant you could help."

"I can help you, but I don't know where the Eye is."

"Somebody must know."

"There was one person," she said. "But that was years ago and he might not even be alive anymore."

"Where do I find him?"

"I don't know."

A sudden rush of fury flooded me.

"Then what exactly can you do to help me? So far, all you have done is prevented me from continuing with my search."

"But you don't know where to search, so I have not

prevented you from anything." Her tone was still placid, unperturbed by my anger.

"You said you could help. What are you offering?"

"You must go to Indou. There is a woman there who will be able to guide you on your journey."

"She will be able to take me to this person who knows where the Eye is?" My brief exultation was quickly dashed.

"I doubt it. But she will be able to guide you on the next step of your journey."

"Is the Eye in Indou?"

"Probably not."

"So I must travel all the way to Indou to find this woman who will tell me where I must travel to next?"

"Yes."

"I don't have time for this. I need the Eye now, before there is war with Hattusa."

"The gods keep the Eye well hidden. They don't intend it to be used lightly. If you cannot locate it, you are not meant to wield it."

Surely if the gods knew why I wanted the Eye, they would hand it to me, but I kept my thoughts to myself. She was trying to help, in her own way.

"How will I find this woman?"

"Go to Indou and find the place where the ocean splits into three rivers. Follow the southern-most river to the end and you will find a white house which sits on a hill. Behind the house stands a grove of bael trees. This is where you will find her."

"What is her name?"

"I was given directions, but not a name."

"You want me to go all the way to Indou without even knowing the name of the woman I seek?"

I didn't know whether to laugh or cry. This quest seemed both ludicrous and impossible.

"Truly, I wish I could give you more information, but I don't know who she is."

"How do you know even that much?"

"The Daughters have been trying to keep track of the Eye. In case it was ever needed. But information about its location is elusive and mercurial. There is a little we know and much we do not. If the gods want you to find the Eye, they will show you where it is."

"I am sorry if I sounded ungrateful." Her calm sincerity shamed me and I tamped down my frustration. "You must be taking a great risk in telling me even this much."

"There is much danger for both you and I to be meeting like this."

"Somebody has tried over the years to warn me of danger. The messages were signed by the Daughters of Isis. Was that you?"

"I was not supposed to try to communicate with you, but they were not doing enough to protect you. I spent several years with your family and remembered all of you children fondly. I would have done you a great disservice had I not at least tried to warn you."

"I was not sure I would recognise you until I saw you that day in the market, but I knew you immediately. I could even remember your scent."

She gave me a small smile. "I was very fond of your brother."

"He was very fond of you."

"I was terribly sad to hear of your mother's death. She was a fine woman."

I hardly knew how to respond to that.

"She was..." My voice trailed away.

"She loved her daughters immensely. You were very precious to her, all five of you."

"I never felt like she took much notice of us. She never saw us." My voice was a whisper. "She never saw me."

"She was trying to raise you girls to be strong and independent. Look at what she achieved."

Her observation was presumptuous, but I wasn't really offended. I stared down at my hands while I tried to think of a response. My skin was dry and peeling, and I wished I had a jar of salve. My country was in turmoil, I had lost my throne, I was on a seemingly impossible journey to locate a probably-mythical artefact and yet I worried about the skin on my hands. If nothing else, my mother had raised me to be shallow.

"Is there anything else you can tell me about the Eye?" I asked.

"The gods rarely permit it to be found. And even if they do allow it, the price they ask might be too great. I can only wish you luck. I pray that Isis spreads her wings over you in protection. I pray she gives you the courage to do what must be done and the wisdom to understand the difference between your own desires and what you must do."

"I don't seek the Eye for my own glory." Had she misunderstood everything I had said?

"You may think that now, but the Eye has tremendous power. As you draw closer to it, you might find yourself wanting it for other reasons."

I got to my feet.

"I didn't come here to be insulted. I have told you why I seek the Eye."

"The boy will see you back to your friends," she said.

I left, feeling rather disgruntled. She hadn't even apologised.

"I am not like Ay," I muttered as the boy led me back through the dark streets. "I don't crave power."

The temple came into sight and the boy hastened his speed a little, as if eager to be away.

"I know the way from here," I said.

"She said I was to take you to your friends."

"Go. I can find them from here."

He looked undecided, his gaze darting between me and the temple and then back to the dark path we had just walked along. At length he decided he had sufficiently fulfilled his duty. He gave me a brief bow and hurried away.

I had barely gone a dozen paces before my spell bottle began burning. It was only then that I noticed someone walking a little too close behind me. I darted a glance over my shoulder. Two someones. I walked a little faster, but they easily drew apace with me, one on each side.

"A fine night for a stroll, is it not?" one said to me, his tone nothing but conversational.

"I am meeting my friends." My voice was stiff and I hoped they would understand I wanted nothing to do with them.

"We have some friends you would like," the other man said. "You should come meet them."

"My friends are waiting for me." My heart pounded so loudly that they could probably hear it. "I am late and they will be looking for me any moment now."

"Your friends already left," he said.

For a brief moment, I was unsure. After all, what could I offer them anymore? They had no reason to wait around for me.

"Shame, innit," the other said. "Leaving you all alone like that. Oh well, we will keep you company."

A little voice deep inside of me said that something was wrong. Istnofret wouldn't have left without me. Not by choice.

"I will be fine," I said. "I will wait for my friends to come back."

"Oh no, they aren't coming back," one of them said. "They were going off for a drink. Likely roaring drunk by now."

Now I knew for certain they lied. Intef and Renni wouldn't leave without me just to go for a drink.

"I will wait for them." I made my tone as firm as possible.

"No, no, we will keep you company. A pretty thing like you, such a shame your friends left without you."

Then there were other footsteps behind us and suddenly there was another man on each side of me, jostling the others out of the way. A familiar hand grasped my elbow.

"Thank you for looking out for her, fellows." Intef's voice was congenial. "We will take it from here."

"I don't think so," one of the men said, his tone turning nasty. "We found her first."

"Go home," Renni said. "You don't want to be starting something you cannot finish."

The first man snarled but the other backed away.

"Come on, man," he said to his friend. "Look at them. Soldiers."

Nobody would ever mistake Intef and Renni for anything but soldiers, with their well-defined muscles and their strong limbs. Neither was particularly tall — in fact Intef was slightly shorter than me — but even a casual observer would note their strength and fitness. Someone who looked a little closer might see the way they noticed everything around them and how economically and efficiently they moved.

"Trained with the Medjay," Renni said, cheerfully. "We know a thing or two about fighting."

"Yeah?" the first man said. "So do we."

"You can stay and get yourself beat up but I am going home," his friend said and walked away.

"You would leave me to handle them both by myself?" the man called after him.

I restrained a laugh. Intef or Renni alone would have him on the ground in seconds.

"Two against one," Renni said. "Hardly a fair fight, is it? Especially one untrained man against two soldiers."

"Fine." The man threw up his hands and walked away. "You want to keep a closer eye on her in future," he called over his shoulder. "She is likely to get herself into trouble, wandering around at night by herself."

Neither Intef nor Renni responded as we quickly walked away. It was only when we stopped in the shadows between two houses that I realised how badly my legs were shaking. I leaned against the wall with a sigh. The spell bottle was cold again.

"Are you all right?" Intef asked. "Did they hurt you?"

"I am fine. Just shaken."

"Nasty creatures, those two," Renni muttered.

"Thank you." I stared off in the darkness, not wanting to look at Intef. Even now he was still rescuing me. My bitterness at his apparent betrayal and that he had been the one to kill Sadeh was still there, but it was not as sharp as it had once been. Intef had proved himself to me over and over. Would the day come when he would ask me to prove myself to him?

FOURTEEN

We went straight back to the boat and spent the rest of the night there. I didn't expect to sleep, but the lapping water and the chirps and croaks around us eventually calmed me. I woke as the boat started moving, with Intef and Renni rowing us out into the middle of the river. It was only then that I realised Behenu lay beside me.

"Are you well?" she asked. "You slept restlessly and once you cried out for Intef."

I turned my face towards the shore, hoping to hide the sudden blush that rose in my cheeks.

"Those men discomfited me. I don't know what they intended, but I am grateful that Renni and Intef were there."

"Intef wanted to go back and find them, but Renni talked him out of it. I heard them after you went to sleep."

"What was he going to do?"

"Kill them."

Surely she exaggerated, but her face was as calm as her voice.

"That is a bit much. They didn't harm me."

"Intef thinks they would have. Renni convinced him he needed to stay on the boat. They were planning to leave as soon as the sun rose and Renni didn't want to wait for Intef if he was delayed."

"At least Renni was sensible."

"He loves you. Intef. You barely notice him, but he loves you more than I have ever seen someone love."

"That is ridiculous."

I awkwardly got to my feet, my body stiff after a night on the wooden deck.

"It is a shame you don't see it."

I staggered to the other end of the boat and didn't reply.

Once we were well away from the shore, Istnofret handed out bread and cheese to break our fast, and we sipped from a jug of beer.

"Tell us what happened last night," Intef said as we ate.

I had forgotten I hadn't told them yet. They didn't even know it had been Maia who summoned me. I relayed her words about the Eye but kept what she had said about my mother to myself.

"She thinks I am wasting my time searching for the Eye. She said it was unlikely the gods would allow me to find it and even if they do, the price will probably be too high."

"The price?" Renni asked.

"She didn't say. She thinks that as I get close to the Eye, I will probably desire its power for myself."

"She doesn't know you at all." Istnofret's tone was haughty. "Or she would not say such a thing."

"Did she know where the Eye is?" Intef asked.

"No." They all sighed and I felt a little less foolish that it wasn't only me who had hoped for this. "But she said I must go to Indou. That there is someone there who can tell me where to go next."

"How will you find this person?" he asked.

"She said there is a place where the ocean divides into three rivers. I must follow the one that is most southerly. At its end, there will be a white house and behind it a grove of bael trees. This is where I will find the woman who can help me."

"Were there any other details? The name of the port? A village or one of the rivers? The woman's name, at least?" he asked.

"That was as much as she knew. Or as much as she was willing to tell me."

"Then I guess we are going to Indou," he said.

"We need a bigger boat," Behenu said.

"We need to return to Thebes," Renni said. "We will have to walk overland to the Red Sea."

He and Intef exchanged looks, no doubt both remembering how they had argued about whether to sail on the Great River or to make the trek to the eastern coast and follow it south.

Intef gave him a shrug. "At least we are only walking it once."

"How far is it?" Istnofret asked.

"Thirty-five leagues," Renni said. "Maybe a little more."

"How long will that take?" Her voice was despairing.

The men looked at each other, considering.

"We could do it in two days," Intef said. "If we were on our own."

"They will not be able to travel that fast," Renni said. "Nor to walk as long each day. Four days?"

"If we were to walk from sun up to sun down," Intef said. "Best to plan for five."

"My lady will not be able to do that." Istnofret shot me a

worried look and her gaze dipped down to my belly. I placed my hand over it. It was barely protruding yet.

"Better now than in a few months," I said.

"Take down the sail," Intef said. "We will catch the current and head north immediately."

"Why must we walk?" Behenu asked. "Could we not ride donkeys?"

"We would have to pace the donkeys," Intef said. "And we would still have to walk every few hours to give them a break. But the main problem is that five donkeys would mean we also need to carry enough food and water for them."

"That is a lot of extra baggage," Renni said. "And we would need at least a couple of extra donkeys just to carry their supplies."

"And more donkeys mean we need even more supplies," Intef said. "Better that we walk, taking only what we can carry ourselves. It is only five days. It will be over soon enough."

"I don't mind the walk," Behenu said. "I was thinking of my lady. She should not have to walk so far. Perhaps we could take a donkey for her."

"I will walk like everyone else," I said, quickly. Why should I expect special treatment? I was no longer queen and they were no longer my servants. I could not make such demands.

Intef gave me a steady look. "Are you sure you can manage it? Once we are a day or two out from Thebes, we cannot turn back if you find it more demanding than you expected."

"I can do it," I said, even as I wondered whether I really could. I had not yet forgotten that first long day when I left Memphis, expecting to walk all the way to Nubia. My feet were blistered within a couple of hours and by the end of the day, I was so exhausted that I didn't know how I would get up and do it all again.

"It will not be like it was before." Sometimes I wondered if Intef could read my mind. "We can slow down if we need to, and rest when we must."

"I said I will be fine," I snapped. "I can keep up."

He shrugged a little and turned his attention back to the boat.

When we reached Thebes a couple of days later, we unloaded the remains of our supplies. Istnofret, Behenu and I waited on the dock with Mau and our belongings. Istnofret held Renni's dagger with unexpected — to me at least — confidence, lest anyone think to steal from us while the men made arrangements to sell the boat.

"Are you sure about this?" Istnofret asked me, quietly.

"About what?"

"The walk."

"Not you, too." I sighed. "Why does everyone think I am incapable?"

"Nobody said you were incapable. It is just that you have never had to walk very far and, well, you are with child. Surely that is making you fatigued. Nobody would blame you if you said the walk was too much."

"I will manage. Even if I find it is more than I expected, I will find a way to endure."

"Speaking of the child, how are you feeling? You have been lucky to not have any of the morning sickness."

"I don't feel any different yet, but then I am not sure I know how I am meant to feel."

"Once your belly starts to grow, you will feel like you have turned into a hippopotamus. Everything will be uncomfortable and you will tire much more easily."

"Nice to know what I have to look forward to."

I knew, of course, that my belly would grow and I expected

to feel unwieldy, but I suddenly realised that I would be enduring this without the knowledge of my sisters, or even my mother. Istnofret would be by my side, of course, but she had never birthed a child and she probably knew little more than I.

My stomach felt strange and for the first time, I really missed my mother. But it was not thoughts of her that made my stomach feel so odd. I placed my hand over my belly, but the sensation was gone before I was even sure I had felt it. Was it too early to feel the babe moving? Perhaps I had imagined it. Thank Isis I was only a few months along — maybe four at the most. I had never anticipated making a journey like this while carrying a child. Best that we move as fast as possible now, while I could still keep up.

FIFTEEN

Renni sold the boat for several fat sacks of provisions. It was far less than the vessel was worth, but he thought it better not to haggle too hard.

"I told them we planned to settle here and had no further need of a boat," he told us. "We intend to build a home on the outskirts of the city, somewhere quiet where there is plenty of space for some gardens, a few fig trees, and a couple of goats."

I smiled a little at the thought of the five of us settling down and raising goats.

"My wife is a seamstress of some note and will be looking for work," Renni said. "And my wife's cousin" — he nodded at me — "is an excellent beer maker and will be setting to work brewing just as soon as we have somewhere to live."

"I am not sure so much detail was wise," Intef said. "You have made us rather memorable."

"Yes, but they will remember the seamstress and the beer maker whose husbands mean to breed goats," Renni said. "They will not think of us if anyone comes asking about a queen and her guards."

While Renni talked, he and Intef had been busy dividing our supplies up into six bags. Two of the bags contained substantially less than the others and I quickly realised that those were the ones he intended Istnofret and I to carry. The men took two bags each and slung one over each shoulder.

"Where is my bag?" Behenu asked.

"You have Mau to carry," Intef said. "She will feel heavy soon enough."

"I can still help," she said.

He placed a hand on her shoulder. "You need to look after Mau. For Sadeh. We can manage the rest."

"All right." She didn't sound entirely satisfied. "But if anyone gets too tired, I can carry their bag for a while."

"That sounds fair," Intef said. "I will tell you if I need you to take mine."

He offered her a bag and she took it gingerly, almost dropping it when he let go.

"Not yours. Yours is far too heavy. I will carry my lady's or Istnofret's if they need me to."

"You must not call me that," I said, restraining my smile at their banter. "It is the sort of thing someone will remember."

"Sorry," she said. "I keep forgetting."

"We go north first," Renni said. "To Qift. From there we will find the Valley of Many Baths. It is a dry river bed which will lead us all the way to Quseir."

"And after that?" I asked.

"We need a boat that will cross the Red Sea," Intef said. "And someone who can tell us where these three rivers are."

"What if we cannot find anyone who knows of them?" I asked.

"We will," he said. "It just may take a while."

"We cannot afford the time," I said. "Every day that Ay is

on the throne, he reinforces his power and legitimacy. Every day we delay brings us a day closer to war with the Hittites. How many innocent people will die because we took too long?"

He raised his hands in a gesture of helplessness. "This journey takes as long as it takes, does it not? Unless you can tell us exactly where this artefact is, we will have to trust that each step takes us closer."

I closed my eyes and took a deep breath. There was no point sniping at him. He was doing his best to get me there. They all were.

"Let's go then," Intef said.

As we made our way through the city, Intef set a slower pace than the soldiers who had led me out of Memphis and when the sun was directly overhead, he stopped under an old acacia tree, beneath whose wide-spread branches was a reasonable amount of shade. We sat on the dirt and Istnofret passed around bread and little onions.

Behenu let Mau out of her basket while we ate. The cat prowled around the tree, sniffing the ground and seemingly displeased at finding loose dirt under her paws. She was accustomed by now to the rope around her neck, and although she still gave a disgruntled meow every time it was fastened, she paid little notice to it after that. She had even started returning to Behenu when the girl tugged gently on the rope, and would enter back into her basket willingly enough.

Within another hour or two, we were out of Thebes and by the time the sun was setting, we had reached Qift.

"We should have sailed here," Behenu said. "It is right on the Great River."

"We could have," Intef said. "But this is only a small village and we might not have been able to sell the boat. Besides, it was but a few hours' walk."

There were only a couple of dozen houses clustered on the banks of the river. Presumably there was all of the usual buildings a village might need — storehouses, a bakery, a brewery — but perhaps they were set further back.

Intef led us along the river until we were out of sight of the houses, and then we went inland until we were out of the territory of any crocodiles or hippopotamuses who might call this stretch of the Great River home. We stopped by a dense thicket of tamarisk trees which rose almost to the top of my head. Renni set down his bags and slipped away into the darkening shadows with his dagger in his hand.

Intef and Behenu built a fire pit and she collected fallen twigs and dead leaves. Istnofret had laid out a blanket and was busy unpacking our provisions on it, moving items into various piles and frowning.

"Is something wrong?" I asked.

She answered with a shrug. "I had expected more for five days. This does not seem like much for five people and a cat."

"It is what we can easily carry," Intef said. "By the time we brought a blanket apiece and the other things we already had, plus enough beer to keep us from being too thirsty, there was not a lot of room for food. That is why Renni is hunting. We will stretch our supplies with what we can hunt or scavenge."

"But will it be enough?" she asked. "We will be very hungry after walking so far every day."

"It will suffice," he said. "You might be surprised by how much we can find on the way. And Renni and I can get by on very little for a few days if we must. It is part of our training."

"That would not be fair," Istnofret said. "We should share the provisions equally."

Behenu returned with the bottom of her skirt folded up to carry a bundle of sticks and dropped them at Intef's feet. She glanced from Intef to Istnofret and I thought she was going to say something but she only shook her head.

"Something you want to say?" Intef asked as she started to walk away.

She glanced at me as if for permission but whatever she saw in my face made her shake her head again.

"No," she muttered.

"Speak, Behenu," I said. "You don't need to be afraid."

"I am not afraid," she said, a little fiercely. "But it is not my place to comment."

I waited silently and she lowered her gaze, clearly still fighting the urge to speak. Soon enough, it spilled out.

"I wonder that if there is not enough food, you do not make me go without."

"Why?" I could make no sense of her words.

"Because I am a slave."

Her words struck me hard. Over the last few days, I had almost forgotten. I had been thinking of her as just another member of our party. As one of those that was almost a friend. But Behenu was right. She was still a slave. The thing I was less sure about was whether that should be important. After all, I too had been sentenced to slavery, and yet I didn't consider myself a slave. I had shaken off that title as soon as I was rescued. So what did that mean for Behenu? I had purchased her, after all.

"We will all be walking and we all need to eat," I said. "If there is not enough food, we all eat less. Nobody will go without."

Renni returned with a brown duck and a handful of pale green eggs, and anything else Behenu had intended to say went unsaid. He crouched beside the fire and set to work plucking the duck. Behenu sat beside him and between them they removed the feathers in reasonably short order.

I helped Istnofret to pack away our supplies. Intef's fire crackled, the duck roasted over it on a makeshift spit, and a cool night breeze swept away the day's warmth. I sat by the fire, smelling the wonderful aroma of our dinner, and listening as the others chatted. Despite our circumstances, I felt reasonably content and that puzzled me. Shouldn't I be missing the luxury of the palace? Having servants to wait on me. My soft bed, the platters of food waiting for me to pick at them, slaves to carry me when I didn't want to walk. But those things no longer seemed as important as they once were. I had a place to sleep tonight, even if it was just a blanket on the ground. I had a fire to sit by and the anticipation of a hot meal. I had company. Things didn't seem quite as bad as they should.

I watched Behenu as she chatted easily with Renni and Istnofret. When she thought nobody was looking, she pulled a few choice pieces off the roasting duck and tossed them to Mau. The cat ate with obvious relish, then sat on Behenu's blanket and groomed herself. The rope around her neck was fastened to Behenu's ankle, but Mau seemed happy to sit near the girl and not at all inclined to wander off.

The duck tasted as good as it smelled and the eggs, which Renni cooked gently in some coals, were delicious. Feeling full and a little sleepy, I wrapped the blanket around myself and wriggled around until I found a patch of dirt that was comfortable enough. With my head pillowed in my hands, I quickly fell asleep.

SIXTEEN

I dreamed about a pathway made of tiny pebbles. As I walked along the path, I breathed deeply of air that was fresh and clean. The night sky sparkled with stars. I followed the path through a grassy swathe to where a stand of trees grew. They were like no trees I had ever seen before, with very tall straight spines and many-leafed branches.

Under the trees was a wooden bench where a woman sat with her back to me. Her dark hair trailed over her back and all the way down to her waist, obscuring her form. She sat with her shoulder hunched and her arms wrapped around herself. She seemed sad, or perhaps unwell.

Then the dream changed and I again followed the pebble pathway. This time, though, it was day and I was hurrying. In my haste, my sandal caught on some pebbles and I tripped, almost sending myself sprawling, but somebody beside me grabbed my arm, steadying me at the very last moment. *I must hurry*, I said to whoever it was. *I am too late.*

SEVENTEEN

I woke, shivering and disoriented. Why was I lying outside on the ground? It took me a few moments to remember that we were on our way to Qift, intending to walk along the Valley of Many Baths all the way to the east coast.

Behenu was the only other one awake. She sat close to the fire with a blanket around her shoulders, staring into the flames. Mau's tail was draped over her leg, indicating the cat slept in the warmth of her lap. Nearby, Intef lay wrapped in his blanket. Istnofret and Renni were on the far side of the fire, presumably also fast asleep.

I edged a little closer to the fire until I could feel its warmth on my face. The night air was cold and my single blanket proved to be insufficient. Behenu started as I moved.

"Why are you awake?" I asked.

"I am keeping watch until the moon is right overhead. Then I will wake Renni."

"Oh." I had gone to sleep without even a thought of watch duty. "When is my turn?"

She turned her gaze back to the fire.

"Intef said we should let you sleep."

Even now, after so many days, they treated me differently. But I was probably also the only one to have been thinking of nothing but my own comfort as I drifted off. Behenu must have caught something of my bitterness in my eyes.

"Maybe you can take first watch tomorrow," she said. "Nobody likes first watch."

I gave her a grateful smile. "I certainly will."

"You should go back to sleep. Intef said we will walk a long way tomorrow."

I lay down again, but the cold seemed to seep right through my blanket. Soon I shivered so hard that my teeth chattered. A quiet voice near my ear made me jump.

"My lady." It was Intef. "You are cold."

"Your observation skills are as keen as ever," I said, sourly, suddenly irritated that Intef always thought he had the solution to every problem.

"If we lie close together and share our blankets, as Renni and Istnofret are doing, we will be warm enough."

"I would rather freeze."

"You may well do so. The nights out here in the desert are much colder than in the cities. Body heat is the best way of staying warm."

"Are you ready to warm my bed again so soon?" I could see him standing in front of Ay, shrugging as he said that he could hardly complain if I ordered him to entertain me in my bed.

"I am merely offering a way for us both to stay warm."

"What of Behenu? She must be cold too. Have you made the same offer to her?"

"She has Mau for warmth. It would seem that you and I are the only ones with too little sense to keep us warm."

I wrapped the blanket tighter around me and thought of hot sand beneath my toes and sunlight on my skin and the warmth of leaning against a mud brick wall. I was still awake, and still shivering, when Behenu woke Renni. From across the fire, I saw him sit up, but he didn't leave the cozy nest he had made with Istnofret. A sharp spike of jealousy prickled at me. It was not fair that she was perfectly warm and sleeping soundly, while I shivered so hard that I wondered if my teeth would crack.

Some time later, I heard movement and someone sat down behind me. I didn't need to roll over to know who it was.

"This is ridiculous," Intef said. "We are both freezing. We need warmth and sleep or we will never make it to the coast in five days."

I said nothing, but he started rustling around behind me.

"Give me your blanket," he said.

"Go away."

"You can give me your blanket or I will pick you up and dump you in the dirt."

I knew Intef well enough to know that he rarely joked. Huffing, I got up, leaving my blanket on the ground. Let him pick it up if he wanted it so badly.

He straightened my blanket, then lay down on it.

"Do you intend to join me?" he asked. "Or shall I use both blankets for myself?"

With another huff, I lay beside him, rolling immediately onto my side so that my back was to him. He draped his blanket over us both and then edged closer.

"Do not touch me," I said. "I will allow you to lie there, but do not presume to touch me."

I regretted my words almost as soon as they were out of my mouth. After all, he was still grieving for Setau. The warmth of another body beside him would probably be a comfort.

He didn't reply. It wasn't long before the heat of both of our bodies under the same blanket was enough to warm me. Eventually I dropped off to sleep. When I woke sometime later, I was pleasantly snug. It took a few moments to realise that the warmth I was so enjoying came from Intef's body pressed against my back. I was tempted to roll away so that he would be cold, but before I could do anything I fell asleep again.

When I woke next, it was dawn and Intef was already up. We ate and then broke camp. Our walk was nothing like the day I had left Memphis. Intef set a steady pace which was not too fast. I tried hard to keep up but it wasn't long before my feet dragged. Of course, Intef noticed my fatigue, even though I said nothing, and when we next came to a place with a well and the shade of a couple of dom palms, he dropped his packs.

"We will rest for a while," he said.

Renni drew some water from the well. It was blissfully cool and sweet. I splashed some on my face and over the back of my neck, and felt much better. When we set off again, I was determined to show them I could keep up.

"Ankhesenamun." My name was awkward on Renni's tongue and the look on his face said he felt as uncomfortable as he sounded. "Don't push so hard. You will tire more quickly than if you keep a steady pace. We don't need to hurry."

"I am fine." My pride bristled and my tone was indignant. "I will not slow us down."

"We have a long walk ahead and each of us will feel tired at some point. We will rest when we need to."

"You and Intef won't get tired," I muttered.

"You are not used to physical exercise the way we are. It is nothing to be ashamed of. But if you push beyond what you can manage, we cannot carry you. So slow down a little, lest we have to leave you behind."

"You would not do that," I said, alarmed and suddenly uncertain.

He flashed me a grin, surprising me as I realised he had made a joke.

"No, we wouldn't. But I am serious that we cannot carry you if you cannot walk. So please pace yourself, for our sakes as well as your own."

I felt rather shamefaced. It seemed that no matter what I did, I got it wrong. I still knew so little about being a normal person.

We walked until dusk, stopping for a couple of breaks through the afternoon. We made camp near another well and I took the opportunity to duck behind a shrubby bush for some privacy and to bathe myself in a bucket of cool water.

Renni caught a hare for dinner, although it was old and skinny, with little meat on its bones. Still, with some bread it was enough to fill our bellies. Afterwards, I sat by the fire with my blanket around my shoulders. I had not forgotten Behenu's suggestion that I should take first watch, although when I suggested it, Intef immediately said I should sleep. I ignored him and soon they all went off to bed.

I was still warm from the meal, and my toes were cozy near the fire. The air wasn't as cold as last night. I wouldn't need Intef's warmth tonight. But by the time I woke Renni to take over from me, I had started to shiver, even sitting as close to the fire as I was. I resigned myself to a long, cold night, but as I started to lie down, Intef stirred.

"Come here," he said.

I only hesitated for a moment.

"Hurry up," he said. "I need more sleep before it is my turn to keep watch."

Deciding to exchange my pride for a warm night, I draped my blanket over the top of Intef's and then crawled into a wonderfully warm cocoon.

EIGHTEEN

I t took us the full five days to walk all the way to the Red Sea. Although I was determined not to slow us down, it always seemed to be me who ended up trailing behind. I had thought that if I could survive the first day or two, it would get easier, but my fatigue only increased with each day. Every night I crawled into the bed I shared with Intef with my legs aching and my feet throbbing, and felt little better when I woke.

The babe inside me was growing and my belly had suddenly started to poke out. I wasn't feeling too uncomfortable yet, though, and could only be thankful that we would soon be sitting on a ship. In another few weeks, I might not be able to walk so far. Towards the end of the fifth day, a fresh, tangy scent arrived in the air.

"Do you smell that?" Istnofret asked.

"It is the sea." Behenu's face brightened.

"The sea has its own smell?" I asked. "Like the Great River?"

"Yes, can you smell the salt?" Behenu asked. "The freshness? Nothing in the world smells like the sea."

"How do you know what it is?" Istnofret asked.

"Where I used to live, I could smell it all the time." Her face lost some of its brightness. "I didn't realise how much I had missed it."

We finally reached Leucus Limen, so named by the Greeks for its brilliant white sand.

"I want to see the sea," Istnofret said. "Can we go straight there?"

"I was thinking we should find somewhere to sleep first." Intef shot me a look. "We could all do with a night under a roof."

"I need a bath." I looked down at my dusty feet. The sandals I wore were comfortable enough but did nothing to shield my feet from the dirt. My gown desperately needed washing as well.

"Maybe Intef could find us somewhere to sleep while we go to look at the sea," Istnofret said. "Renni could take us. You would not mind, would you Renni?"

She exaggeratedly batted her lashes at him and Renni actually blushed.

"Uh—" he stammered, but Intef laughed and waved away his excuse.

"I will look for accommodations and then come find you. Don't go too far."

Istnofret and Behenu set off. I followed, although not quite as eagerly. I wanted to see the sea, but I was tired. I wouldn't have minded waiting until tomorrow. But when the water came into sight, it took my breath away.

A vast expanse of shimmering blue. A breeze that was

somehow both refreshing and sticky. My ears filled with the roar of the waves. Beside the water was a wide strip of the famous white sand. I took off my sandals and let my toes sink into it. It was different from desert sand, cleaner but slightly sticky like the air.

I shielded my eyes as I stared out at the water. The motion of the waves fascinated me with their hypnotic dance, drawing teasingly away from the shore only to rush back towards it moments later. The water stretched as far as I could see, all the way to the horizon. I knew this was what the sea was, but until I saw it I didn't truly comprehend its vastness. Sea birds wheeled through the sky, occasionally dipping down to snatch some unfortunate creature from the waters. I tasted salt and freshness, and had sunk up to my ankles in the sand.

Laughter finally dragged me from my thoughts. Istnofret and Behenu had tucked up their skirts and were almost up to their knees in the water. My breath caught as the waves rushed back out again, tugging at their legs, wanting to drag them away from the shore.

"Be careful," I called to them.

"Come in," Istnofret called back. "I cannot tell you how wonderful it feels."

The water rushed back in, rocking both women as it surged towards the shore. Something about the waves made me uneasy.

"I think I will stay here," I said.

"No, come in," Behenu said. "At least come up to your ankles."

Once again, the waves surged back out. The water called to me, urging me to sink down into it, to go with it as it roared away from the shore, to lose myself in its cool depths.

"Ankhesenamun." I didn't realise Istnofret was standing in front of me until she grabbed my arm. "Whatever is wrong?"

I caught my breath with a gasp. For a few moments, I had indeed been lost in the water. I had almost lost myself. I shook my head, trying to dislodge memories that couldn't possibly exist.

"Nothing," I said. "I would just prefer to stay on the shore."

She looked unconvinced.

"Go back to Behenu. I would like to sit in the sand and enjoy the breeze."

As she left, I found a spot far enough back from the water that I wouldn't get wet. I sat and wiggled my feet into the sand. It was hot on its top layers but cool underneath. I closed my eyes, breathed deeply of the salty breeze and let the rumble of the water fill my ears. It didn't call me in the same way if I didn't look at it. It was only as Renni sat beside me that I realised he too hadn't ventured into the water. He set Mau's basket down in front of us and removed the lid. The cat poked her head out but took one look at the roaring waves and retreated back inside.

"I am not terribly fond of the water myself," Renni said.

"I cannot swim," I admitted. "I don't understand how they can go out so far and be so calm."

"Istnofret has been longing to see the sea. It is a lifelong dream for her. And Behenu grew up near the sea."

I didn't tell him that I hadn't known those things. It shamed me that I still knew so little about the people who had given up their lives to come with me.

"What do we do next?" I asked.

"We wait for Intef to find us, then we spend a pleasant night under a roof, and as soon as we can find a boat to take us to Suakin, we will be on our way again."

"Suakin? I have never heard of it."

"It is in Kush, which lies on the other side of the Red Sea in which Istnofret and Behenu are splashing."

"How long will it take?"

"I have never travelled so far before. Maybe a couple of weeks if we have good weather."

"Everything takes so long," I said, with a groan. "And we still need to travel even further from there. Why couldn't the Eye have been kept in Egypt? Surely this is where it came from. It belongs here."

I waited for Renni's response, but he said nothing. Of course, I could hardly expect him to have such an answer. How could anyone other than the gods know why the Eye had been taken so far away?

"Maia did say the gods would put obstacles in front of anyone who sought the Eye," I said. "I suppose this is no more than I can expect."

"Here comes Intef and he looks like he is in a hurry." Renni got to his feet and brushed the sand off his *shendyt*.

Intef jogged towards us, waving for Istnofret and Behenu to come out of the water.

"There is a boat departing for Suakin within the hour," he said as he reached us. "There are no others expected for at least a week. I have made arrangements with the captain and provided they don't have to wait for us, we can sail with them."

"What are they running from?" Renni asked.

"Running?" I said. "Why would you think that?"

"Because no captain would willingly depart at dusk for such a journey." Intef's tone was grim. "At worst, he might want to leave at first light and order his men to spend the night on board so he doesn't need to go looking for any of them in the morning. I didn't ask why he was leaving so quickly, but he knows that we seek as speedy a departure as he does."

"How do we know they are not criminals?" I asked.

"We are considered criminals by most people," Istnofret said, and her tone was a little gentler than her words. "We cannot afford to be picky about our transport. If Intef thinks we will be safe, we must go with them."

"I cannot be sure without knowing what they flee from, or why, but we must take the risk," Intef said. "If the next trade boat is not due for a week, anyone pursuing us will be at least that far behind. By the time they reach Suakin, we will be long gone."

"But we don't know if it is safe to travel with them," I said. "What if they are..." My voice trailed off as I searched for the worst possible type of person for us to be throwing our lot in with.

"Slavers." Behenu's voice was grim.

The word struck me to my core. I knew about slavers, of course. Men who sailed up and down the coasts, searching for unfortunate souls who could be stolen away and sold for profit. And slaves taken as spoils of war was both common and accepted as the right of the winning army by almost everyone. I had never before thought about what Behenu must have felt when Horemheb took her from her homeland. The terror of not knowing where she was going. The difficulty of learning a new language with no one to teach her. The fear of wondering whether her new master would be kind or cruel. The helplessness of knowing she no longer had any control over her own fate. That for the rest of her life, she would be subject to her master's whims — over her living circum-stances, her actions, her body.

"I would kill myself before I let someone take me as a slave," I said.

Behenu flinched, probably taking my words as a criticism. That I was saying she should have killed herself when Horemheb took her. I opened my mouth to apologise, but Istnofret spoke first.

"You are considered a slave now by some," she said to me, very quietly. "We must never forget that."

"I am sorry, Behenu," I said. "That was thoughtless of me."

Behenu accepted my apology with a nod, although she didn't look at me. It was clear I had wounded her with my insensitive comment.

"We stick together," Intef said. "Every moment. Nobody wanders off alone on that boat until we know what manner of people they are. Understood?"

We nodded.

"Right then." He turned to Istnofret. "We will need one of the jewels you carry. Renni, go with Behenu and Istnofret and buy as many supplies as you can. We need food that will travel well and not spoil. The captain has agreed we can share their beer but has made it clear he will not feed us."

"Food for thirty days, do you think?" Renni asked. "Allowing a few days for bad weather or in case we lose the wind."

"Go, quickly," Intef said. "We don't have much time. I will catch up with you."

Istnofret was already using Renni's dagger to unpick one of the little pockets in her hem.

"I will need one as well," Intef said. "As payment for the captain. Nothing too fancy, though. I don't want him to think we are an easy target carrying much wealth."

"This one?" She handed him a plain band of silver. I didn't

recognise the ring and couldn't recall ever having worn something so simple.

"That will do fine."

"What can I do?" I asked.

"Stay here. Mind our bags and Mau."

"I can help. There must be something I can do."

"Someone needs to stay," he said. "We cannot leave our things on the beach and expect them to still be here when we return. I will go to get some supplies but will be back as soon as I can."

I opened my mouth to object but closed it again, the words unsaid. It was true that somebody had to stay, but it seemed it was always me who did the watching and never the contributing.

"Take this." Intef held out his dagger. "We cannot afford for anything to be stolen. There will be no time to replace what we lose before the boat sails."

I took the dagger from his hand. It was warm from being tucked into the waistband of his *shendyt*. I turned it over, studying its plain handle and bronze blade. It was the same dagger I had killed Thrax with. I knew, of course, that Intef still carried this blade. It had been his favourite long before the night he loaned it to me. But this was the first time I had touched it since then. Memories flashed through my mind. Thrax's skin parting easily for the well-honed blade. His warm blood pouring over my lap. A sudden rush of nausea left me retching and I thrust the dagger towards Intef.

"Take it back. I cannot."

He took it silently and tucked it into his *shendyt*.

"I will be back as soon as I can." He left at a jog.

I considered the pile of bags at my feet. Was it better to stand over them or sit beside them? Perhaps I should put some sand over them to conceal them somewhat? I eyed the people around us but nobody seemed to be paying me any attention. Three children — young enough to be naked — splashed in the water. A man and woman walked along the shore, their hands clasped. A group of boys played some sort of chasing game through the sand. I felt awkward standing beside our bags so I sat down. I stared out at the water, trying to look relaxed, as if I was merely passing my time sitting here in the sand.

Intef returned before the others and dropped an armload of packages beside me. I couldn't fathom how he had managed to carry so much by himself.

"Any trouble?" he asked.

I shook my head.

"That is good," he said. " I was…"

"Was what?" I was looking down at my toes in the sand as I spoke and it was only when he didn't reply that I glanced up at him. The look on his face made my heart ache in a way I didn't quite know how to explain. He shook his head a little, as if banishing an unwanted thought.

"I was worried something would happen to you," he said and looked out to sea.

I swallowed the sudden lump in my throat. There was always a wall between us these days. It was undoubtedly my fault but I didn't know how to get past it. I wanted things between us to be easy like they used to be, before the events with Ay and Sadeh. Before Intef had ever come to my bed.

NINETEEN

We waited for Istnofret, Renni and Behenu to return. Mau was tired of being confined and began yowling to be let out. I poked my fingers into her basket, trying to soothe her, but she swiped at me so I left her alone. Intef paced up and down along the shore, constantly checking the sun.

"The captain will sail without us," he muttered.

Finally they came, moving as fast as they could while bearing so many bags and packages.

"We had a bit of trouble," Renni said in response to Intef's curt query.

"We should go," Intef said. "You can tell us later."

Intef and I picked up the rest of our bags, as well as Mau's basket, and he led us to a dock where a large sea-faring vessel waited. It was far bigger than the boats that had ferried us along the Great River although I was not convinced it looked any more sea-worthy. Swarthy men loaded crates and swarmed over the deck. They were from a variety of nations, although none appeared to be Egyptian other than the man who stood at the ship's bow, watching as the last of the crates were brought aboard. He raised a hand in greeting to Intef and motioned for us to hurry. Surely he was too young to be the captain.

"I would have left without you," he called, as we hurried up the ramp that connected the ship to the dock.

"I would not have expected anything else." Intef's tone was easy, but his gaze darted around the ship. He was clearly not as comfortable as he wanted the man to believe.

The man looked us each up and down, lingering over Istnofret in particular.

"You can call me Achilles," he said. "Take your things down below. We sailors tend to be superstitious about women on board. You should keep them out of sight."

I opened my mouth to object, to say that surely he didn't intend for us to spend the entire month-long journey confined below the deck, but Intef bumped me with his armload of bags. I met his eyes and saw a warning to keep my mouth shut.

"That way." Captain Achilles gestured towards the hatch. He turned his attention back to his men and it was clear we had been dismissed.

I held my tongue as we made our way down a ladder into the depths of the ship. It was dark down here, lit only by such light as made its way through the hatch. It stank too, a sour mix of unwashed bodies and gods only knew what else. In the very furthest corner, where almost no light at all reached, we found a spot that didn't have anyone's belongings piled in it. There we set down our bags.

"Is his name really Achilles?" Istnofret asked. "He looks Egyptian, but his name is not."

"I doubt it," Intef said. "Likely all the men we meet on this journey will be using names that are not their own."

"Who are these people?" I asked.

"I don't know," he said. "But the captain has been paid well for our voyage and I don't think they will bother us."

"Unless they think we have more riches than sense and intend to steal all our valuables and dump our bodies overboard," Istnofret muttered, darkly.

"We will keep a close eye on them," Intef said. "Renni and I will be working with the crew. If there are any whispers of robbing us, we will likely know, but I did suggest to the captain that the trinket I gave him was the only thing of any value that we possessed amongst us."

"Do you think he believed you?" Istnofret asked.

"Hard to tell, but if he thought we had other riches, he would likely have looked more thoroughly at you women to see if you were wearing them."

The boat began to creak and shift.

"You had best find somewhere to sit," Intef said. "Renni and I will go see what we can do to help."

They hurried off, leaving Istnofret, Behenu and me in the almost-dark.

"May as well get comfortable." Istnofret's tone was the brisk one she used when faced with a distasteful task. "Aten knows we will be here long enough."

The floor was surprisingly clean, but we still spread out a couple of blankets to sit on, being mindful that we didn't encroach on the space claimed by our absent neighbours. Behenu released Mau from her basket. The cat prowled as far as the rope around her neck allowed, then returned to sit beside Behenu and began cleaning her paws. The ship lurched suddenly and I was knocked off balance, flung against Istnofret and cracking my skull against hers.

"Ow." She rubbed her head.

"Sorry."

Around us, the timbers creaked and moaned as if they were in pain.

"Do you think this ship is sound?" Istnofret asked. "It is making an awful amount of noise."

"Maybe it is supposed to sound like that." I wasn't any surer than she, but my spell bottle was cold so I could only assume we were in no immediate danger.

"Big ships always make a lot of noise." Behenu spoke with unusual authority.

"How do you know?" Istnofret asked.

Behenu face was shuttered. "I have been on big ships before."

Recalling Renni's comments about how Behenu used to live near the sea, I wanted to ask what else she knew about ships, but her face said clearly that she regretted having said anything.

We sat in silence. The ship continued to make alarming noises but when it didn't break apart and there seemed to be no water coming in, I eventually relaxed. Istnofret lay down and went to sleep. Behenu absently stroked Mau who had curled up in her lap.

"She likes you," I said.

Behenu started, as if she had forgotten I was there. Or maybe she had been absorbed in her thoughts and forgot where we were. She looked down at the cat in her lap.

"She just wants someone to be kind to her."

Her words felt like a criticism, and I wasn't entirely sure whether she was talking about Mau or herself. It wasn't that I had ever been unkind to Mau, but I rarely paid her much attention. I had tried, at first, but the cat never warmed to me and didn't seem to like me patting her. I could count on one hand the number of times she had tolerated sitting on my lap. So eventually I gave up and we shared my chambers while rarely coming into direct contact with each other. She was Sadeh's cat anyway, not mine. A gift from Thrax which, I suspected with cynical hindsight, was probably aimed at making me fall for him.

As the ship began to pick up speed, my stomach rolled with the waves. Istnofret was awake now, looking rather green and with a hand pressed to her belly. Only Behenu seemed unaffected by our transport.

It was impossible to tell how much time had passed in the dim light below the deck but it felt like hours before our men returned. By then both Istnofret and I were lying down, clutching our bellies and groaning. Behenu had set a bowl between us in case we vomited.

"Are you sick?" Intef gave us each a careful look. He and Renni were drenched in sweat and Renni was rather pale. It seemed the waves didn't agree with him either.

"Will it pass?" I asked. "Or will we feel like this for the entire voyage?"

Intef shrugged. "I have never sailed on the open sea before."

"Why aren't you sick?" Istnofret's tone was unusually curt. "Any normal person would be on their knees in front of a bucket by now."

"I feel a little queasy," he said. "But clearly not as much as you."

Renni dropped down onto the blanket beside her. "It is not as bad above deck. The fresh air helps."

"Captain Achilles has agreed you can go up on deck when the men go to bed," Intef said.

"I doubt we will live that long," Istnofret said.

"It will pass within a day or two," Behenu said.

"How do you know?" Istnofret asked. "I would rather die than endure a whole day of this."

"I have sailed many times," Behenu said. "There is always someone on board who gets sick from the sea, but I have only once known a man who didn't improve after a couple of days."

"What happened to him?" Istnofret asked.

"We sailed for ten days and he was sick the whole time," Behenu said. "When we finally disembarked, being on solid land made him even sicker, but he eventually recovered."

"That will be me," Istnofret said with something that sounded like a sob. "I will be the person who is sick for the entire journey. If I die, please don't throw my body into the water. Take me somewhere I can be embalmed."

"Nobody dies from seasickness," Behenu said.

I mustered up enough strength to speak. "Is that true?"

"Well, I have never known anyone who died of it. There are always stories, but they are probably not true."

"Do you not feel even a little unwell, Behenu?" Renni asked over Istnofret's groans.

"Not at all," she said. "If we encounter a storm, or particularly rough seas, I might feel uneasy, but otherwise the water doesn't bother me."

Istnofret spat out an obscenity, surprising me for I had never heard such a word from her. It wasn't clear whether she directed it at Behenu or if it was merely a comment on our situation. Behenu didn't seem bothered, though, and I felt too unwell to converse any further. Intef and Renni only stayed a few minutes and then returned to their work.

The wait until we could go up above deck was interminable. I tried to sleep, but every time I lay down, the nausea increased and I began gagging. Several times I grabbed the bowl Behenu had set down for us, only to find myself retching with nothing coming out. The babe seemed as unhappy as I and gave a few tentative kicks. I rubbed my belly, hoping to calm her. She stopped kicking so perhaps it helped.

Istnofret was finally asleep, curled on her side with her arms wrapped around her belly. At least she had stopped groaning at any rate.

Behenu sat silently beside us. Mau had crawled onto her lap and the girl was slowly rubbing her spine. I could just hear Mau's purrs above the ship's creaks. It was a soothing and familiar noise, and eventually I dropped off to sleep.

TWENTY

At last we heard footsteps and somebody lit a lamp. The light barely reached our corner, for which I was thankful because the flickering flame made me feel even worse. Men poured in, bringing with them the odour of sweat and a hard day's work.

"Let's get you above."

Intef reached down to help me up. I let him drag me to my feet and support me as I stumbled towards the ladder. His hands were warm and his familiar scent made me suddenly homesick for easier times.

Renni lifted Istnofret and carried her. The crew stared as we made our way out and I heard more than one unsavoury comment. I was suddenly thankful the captain had not wanted us to have any contact with his men.

The ladder seemed an unconquerable obstacle. My legs trembled and my hands could barely grasp the rails. Intef was right behind me, only one step below me, holding me up with his own body. I had thought that nothing other than the cessation of the waves would make me feel better, but as soon as I inhaled the fresh air, the nausea began to settle. The moon was close to being full and gave more than enough light to see by as I made my way across the deck.

Intef helped me over to where I could lean against the rail. There was probably a special name for this part of the ship, but I knew little other than bow and stern.

"Look at the horizon," Intef said. "One of the crew told me that if you suffer from the sea sickness, it helps to look at something that doesn't move."

I did as he bade. Beside me, Istnofret too stared out at the place where dark waters met the dark sky. Renni fetched some supplies and began handing out bread and cheese. I shook my head when he offered me some.

"You should eat," he said. "It will be more pleasant to eat here in the fresh air than down below."

I took the bread and nibbled at it. My stomach suddenly growled in response and I realised I was indeed hungry.

"We will sleep up here," Intef said, "and return below deck at dawn when the crew awakes."

Behenu brought my blanket and I lay down. There were only a couple of crew up here this late and they all seemed to be occupied with their tasks and paying us no mind. My gaze wandered up into the sails and found a man up there, looking out to sea. Maybe he had overnight watch duty? The water wasn't as rough as it had seemed from down below, or maybe it had calmed since we first set sail, and eventually I drifted off. I woke when Istnofret shook my shoulder.

"It is time to go back down below," she said. "The crew is starting to come up."

The nausea had passed while I slept and I felt remarkably well for having spent the night on the deck. I didn't relish the thought of returning to the dark, stuffy chamber below.

"Couldn't we stay up here?" I asked. "We could find somewhere to sit out of the way."

"It is not just a matter of being out of the way," Intef said. "The captain wants you out of sight. There are many who believe women have no place on a ship. If we encounter bad weather, they might blame your presence for having offended the gods. The captain worships Poseidon, apparently."

"I have never heard of him," I said.

"He is one of the Greek gods," Istnofret said. "Charis mentioned him once or twice. He carries a trident and is quick to anger."

"Perhaps we should go below." My father had believed that his god could only see him when he worshipped if the temples had no roofs. Perhaps Poseidon's vision couldn't penetrate the ship's deck.

Despite trying not to look at the men we passed, I was acutely aware of being stared at. They weren't even trying to pretend otherwise and their insouciance sent a shiver through me. Thank the gods for Intef and Renni. Nobody was likely to hassle us with those two nearby.

The days passed with the same monotony as when Ay had confined me to my chambers. With little light and nothing to do below deck, we women mostly slept during the day while Intef and Renni helped the crew. Our only relief was the time spent above deck at night and although I was still uneasy with the water, I grew to enjoy watching the waves as the ship made its way through them. Our menfolk slept at night, although up on the deck so as not to be too far away from us.

The babe within me had become quite active since we set sail. He tended to be quiet during the day while we were below deck but kicked and wriggled when I emerged into the fresh air at night. I placed a hand over my belly, hoping to soothe him. He was, as best as I could figure, maybe five months along now. My belly was larger than a *kathal* fruit, and preceded me when I walked. Navigating the ladder seemed to become more awkward every day.

"Captain says we are less than two days out from Suakin," Renni said one evening. We had just been released from our confinement below deck and I leaned against the rail, breathing deeply of the fresh sea air. I was becoming so accustomed to its scent that I could barely remember what the Great River smelled like.

"It will be a relief to stand on solid ground," Istnofret said.

Renni yawned.

"Go get some sleep." She nudged him with her shoulder and he stumbled off to where their blankets lay.

"I will be sorry to return to land." Behenu's tone was wistful and her eyes distant as she stared out into the dark. "I feel free here."

I should release her. The thought was so sudden and unexpected that it took my breath away. I gasped and choked on nothing more than air. Istnofret pounded me on the back as I coughed.

"My lady?" Behenu asked.

I waved away her question. "I keep telling you not to call me that."

"Habit."

Her words about feeling free were still echoing through my mind. I wanted it to be more than just a feeling. I wanted her to really be free, but I didn't know how to go about doing such a thing. I owned Behenu. I had bought her from Horemheb for a gold bracelet. I couldn't even remember which one. I had acted quickly, with memories of an old dream in which I had seen Behenu cowering in Horemheb's bed. Her other fate had been to sit in my chambers with Mau on her lap. I had once heard of a slave who bought their freedom by reimbursing their master for their purchase price, but Behenu was hardly in a position to do that.

"Do you ever regret that I purchased you from Horemheb?" I asked.

Behenu seemed to consider her words carefully. "It is not my place to regret my mistress's actions."

"Speak freely." My tone was curter than she deserved, but I had to know how she felt before I could make my decision.

She gave me a long, assessing look and shook her head. "I don't know what you want me to say."

"What I want is the truth." The words came out louder than I intended and Behenu took a step back away from me.

"I didn't mean to offend." Her eyes were downcast as was appropriate for a slave. "If my lady would tell me what she wishes me to say, I will gladly say it."

"Behenu." I softened my tone and reached for her. She flinched when I put my hand on her shoulder. "Behenu, I am asking you to tell me how you feel. If I hadn't purchased you, you would still be living in the palace. In luxury. You would be sleeping under a roof every night. You could have a hot meal whenever you wanted one. Water for bathing every day."

"No, my lady. When I belonged to Horemheb, I slept out in the hall so that I could hear him if he called for me. I ate the leftovers of what he didn't want, but only when he thought to offer them to me. He never once gave me water to bathe. When you purchased me, you took me into your chamber and gave me a soft couch to sleep on. Your ladies gave me a cushion for my head and a blanket for cold nights. They bathed me and gave me new clothes."

"Surely some of Horemheb's servants were kind to you."

"They treated me as what I am: a slave. You were the first one who treated me as a person."

My throat was choked and for a long moment I couldn't speak.

"What would your freedom be worth to you?"

She looked down to her feet. "Please do not taunt me with such questions. I didn't expect such a thing from you."

"It was an honest question. I am not teasing you."

"How do you expect me to answer that? My freedom would be worth anything you could ask, but I have no means of payment."

She was right. I could hardly free her if she couldn't pay.

"My lady," Istnofret said. "Ankhesenamun. I have other jewels of yours sewn into my hem."

I shot her a quizzical look. "I know, and we all thought it best if they stayed there until we need them."

"May I have one? To keep for myself?"

"Why?" I was frankly puzzled as to why in Isis's name she would ask such a thing at this moment.

"I have served you for many years and I have never before asked for anything. I thought you might be inclined to grant me one of your finger rings. A plain one would do."

I waved her away. "Go ahead. Choose the one you want. I do not care." I turned my attention back to Behenu. "So what am I to do with you?"

"I am your slave," she said. "You may do whatever you wish."

"This one, my lady." Istnofret held up a gold band. It was fashioned in a simple design and was not particularly to my taste. "May I have this one for myself?"

I barely glanced at it. "If you wish."

"Thank you." Istnofret held the ring out to Behenu. "Behenu, you are my friend. I wish to gift you this finger ring."

Behenu stared at Istnofret. Her jaw dropped. I was still confused as to why Istnofret thought this was an appropriate time to do such a thing.

"You would do that?" Behenu asked her. "You would really give me your finger ring? It is much more valuable than I am."

"You are my friend," Istnofret repeated. "If I may do something to help you, I want to."

Behenu's eyes shone with tears as she accepted the ring from Istnofret. I was only just starting to realise what Istnofret had done when Behenu offered the ring back to me.

"My lady, is this finger ring of sufficient worth to purchase my freedom?"

I watched a tear track down Behenu's cheek and felt like crying myself.

"It is."

As I took the ring from her, both her hand and mine were shaking. I slipped the ring onto my finger. It shone prettily in the moonlight. I had never before realised how beautiful a plain band of gold could be.

"Is that it?" Behenu asked. "Am I free?"

"I don't really know," I said. "I have never freed a slave before."

"She has repaid her purchase price," Istnofret said. "As long as you accept her payment, she is free."

"Then free you are," I said to Behenu.

Her chin wobbled and she swallowed hard before she was able to speak.

"Thank you. Thank you a million times. I thank Baal for your generosity."

"Is Baal one of your Syrian gods?" I asked.

"He is the god my family has worshipped for many generations," she said, a little fiercely as if she expected me to chide
her for not worshipping Isis or another of our own gods.

"Then I thank Baal I was able to free you," I said.

"What will you do now?" Istnofret asked. "Do you intend
to leave us?"

"I can hardly leave right now," Behenu said. "Unless I wish
to swim. But no, I will travel with you awhile yet. I wish to see
my lady complete her quest."

"You should call me Ankhesenamun like the others do," I
said.

Behenu smiled. She seemed taller than she had previously,
as if being freed had encouraged her to draw herself up to her
full height. She was actually about the same height as me.
When she held her head high and looked me in the eyes, I
realised that she was really rather pretty.

"You may travel with us for as long as you like," I said.

We didn't speak much after that. I passed the night looking
out over the dark waters and thinking about what Istnofret
had done. The ring she had chosen could have funded a lavish
lifestyle for her, and for Renni if she chose, and yet she gave it
to Behenu. She didn't pause for even a moment before handing
over her newly gained wealth. I had not realised Behenu
meant that much to her. If a slave and a free woman could be
friends, what reasons did I have left to think they couldn't be
my friends too?

TWENTY-ONE

I woke feeling disorientated. As always, the area below deck was too dimly lit to tell the time other than that it was day. The air was still and warm, and increasingly odorous. For a moment I wondered if the babe had kicked and that was what had woken me so suddenly, but then the shout came again. Footsteps running. Something above us clattered to the deck. The spell bottle was a hot coal against my chest.

"What is happening?" Istnofret whispered.

"I don't know," I said. "Should we go up and see? Perhaps we have hit something and the boat is sinking."

"Somebody would come to get us if that was the case," Behenu said. Although her words were calm, she was already coaxing Mau into her basket. "Renni and Intef would not leave us down here to drown."

"So what then?" I asked. "It sounds like something is wrong."

There was more shouting, voices I didn't know and a language I didn't recognise. We listened as men ran across the deck. A heavy thud.

"They are fighting," Istnofret whispered. "And I don't think it is just our own crew up there."

"Pirates." Behenu's tone was matter-of-fact. "They ply the coastline and wait for ships carrying valuable cargo. Then they board those ships, kill the crew and steal their goods."

"No," Istnofret said. "Renni and Intef are up there."

"We must stay here," Behenu said.

"We could help," I said.

"We would get in the way," she said. "We need to stay here and wait. They will come for us when the fighting is over. If they can."

"And if they cannot?" I asked. "What happens to us then?"

"As women, we will be of value to pirates," she said.

I stared at her in horror. "Do you mean…"

"They may sell us as slaves. Or they might keep us for their own." Her voice was still calm, despite the awfulness of her words.

"I would rather die," Istnofret said, then shot Behenu a guilty look. "I mean—"

"They may well give you that option." Behenu spoke quickly, cutting her off. "Or they might choose for you."

"Then we need to be prepared." Istnofret got to her feet. "Start searching. We need weapons."

In Intef's bag, we found a dagger and not the one he usually carried. I felt slightly better at knowing he had his dagger on him. If Renni also had a spare dagger, we couldn't find it. We searched the crew's beds next and returned to our blankets with an assortment of weapons. Several blades, most of which were too heavy for any of us to wield comfortably, something that looked much like a mallet but heavier, and another item I had no name for. It resembled a hammer with a spiky head. Behenu reached for that one with a grim smile and gave it an experimental swing. Istnofret took a dagger that was small enough to conceal in her hand.

"What do you intend to do with that?" I asked.

"Hide it until someone gets close enough to me. Then stab him."

I had killed a man before. She hadn't.

"Don't think too hard about it," I said. "Think only about where the dagger must go and then drive it in."

"If it comes to it, I will be able to do it. Have no doubt."

I reached out to touch her arm. "It changes a person. To kill a man."

She looked at me evenly. "I will do what I must to protect us. I will not let any of us be taken by pirates."

"Me either."

"Or me," added Behenu.

I examined the remaining blades, trying each until I found one that felt comfortable in my hand and was not too heavy. The babe began kicking and I rubbed my belly.

"Not now," I whispered to her. "Please don't distract me."

The fighting up above seemed to take a long time. Once or twice I thought I heard Intef's voice raised in a shout. Someone screamed. Right above us, a man was groaning. It went on and on. I could hardly hear him above the sounds of the fighting, but he seemed to take a very long time to die. Eventually the shouts and thuds and cries faded away. We could hear men walking on the deck, and sometimes they spoke, but I couldn't make out either Intef or Renni's voices. Eventually we heard someone approaching the ladder.

I gripped my dagger tightly. My palms were sweating and the dagger felt like it was going to slip right out of my grasp. The babe had stopped kicking and I hoped she slept now. My heart pounded so loudly I could barely hear the man as he came down the ladder.

He reached the floor and headed towards us. I swallowed hard and readied myself. If he attacked us, I would stab him. I would aim for his belly, but if he took up a defensive posture, I would slash whatever I could reach — his arms, his face, his thighs. Between the three of us, we could disable him. We should have been discussing tactics instead of waiting in the dark like scared children.

Istnofret suddenly made a noise like a sob, then dropped her dagger and flung herself at the man. Renni embraced her and they stood together for what seemed like a long time. I looked behind him, back to the ladder, waiting for Intef to appear.

When Istnofret finally peeled herself off Renni, she was smeared in blood. There was a large cut above his eye and blood still dripped down his face. I looked back to the ladder again. Renni caught my glance.

"My lady," he said.

"Where is he?" I was embarrassed at the way my voice trembled.

Renni hesitated. I gripped my dagger so tightly that I almost expected it to crumble in my hands.

"Where is he?" My voice was louder this time.

Renni reached for me. "Be calm."

I flung my dagger to the floor and raced towards the ladder. My useless skirt tangled around my legs and I almost fell off. The fabric tore as I impatiently thrust it out of my way. I emerged onto the deck and stopped short at the scene that greeted me there. Dead and dying men lay everywhere. Blood coated the deck and when my gaze focused on something small that looked out of place, I realised it was an ear. Where the man who should be attached to that ear was, I had no idea.

"Intef?" I called.

Somebody nearby groaned and I dashed towards the sound.

"Intef!"

But the man who stared up at me blearily was not one I recognised. He was pale skinned and dark haired. He lay in a pool of his own blood, which poured from an artery in his leg. I didn't know much about battle wounds, but he surely didn't have long to live.

"Help me," he said weakly between groans.

I left him lying there. He was not Intef.

As I turned around, I crashed into Renni.

"Ankhesenamun." He grabbed my arms. "Let me explain."

"Where is he?" I shouted.

"Please."

"Intef!"

I stepped over the outstretched arms and legs of dead men, trying not to slip in their blood lest I fall and injure the babe. At last I spotted a familiar figure, propped up against a mast. He was pale — far too pale — and there was so much blood that I couldn't tell where it was coming from.

"He is gravely injured," Renni said. "I wanted to tell you before you saw him."

I crouched in front of Intef. My eyes blurred and for a moment I could see nothing. I tried to speak, but my mouth was too dry and no words came out. Renni crouched beside me and put his hand on my back.

"It is his arm," he said. "It has been sliced clean through to the bone."

My mouth still wouldn't work. I opened and closed it a few times and finally something came out.

"What can we do?"

"I already asked the captain if he has a physician on board, but near half his crew is dead and he doesn't know if there is anyone left alive who might be able to help us."

"How far from land are we?"

"Almost a full day."

My eyes finally seemed to be working properly and I watched the blood running down Intef's arm. Somebody had tied a strip of fabric above the wound, although it didn't seem to be having any effect. I could see nothing of his injury through the blood.

"Will he last that long?" I asked.

"I think it unlikely."

Renni's words hit me hard and I found myself gasping for breath.

"You should sit down," he said. "Perhaps go back below. Intef wouldn't want you to see him like this."

"I cannot leave him," I said, suddenly fierce. "After all he has done for me…"

"Does that mean you have forgiven him? He did what he thought he must to keep you safe."

Looking at Intef — pale and bloody and barely conscious — I realised my anger was gone.

"The thing he would most want to hear before he goes to the West is that you have forgiven him," Renni said.

"He is not going to the West." I got to my feet awkwardly, for my expanding belly left me off-balance, and wiped Intef's blood off my fingers with my skirt. "Where is the captain?"

Renni pointed and I marched away.

"He has his own men to tend," he called after me.

I ignored him.

I found Captain Achilles crouched in front of a corpse. He seemed to be praying. I didn't have time to wait for him to finish.

"Do any of your men have butchery experience?" I asked.

He started at my sudden interruption but paused to close the dead man's eyes before he got to his feet.

"No," he said, and my heart sank. "But I do."

"Good. I need you to remove Intef's arm."

He huffed out something of a laugh.

"As you can see, I have my own men to look after. Your men are your own concern."

"You are the captain. All lives on board are your responsibility."

"Not when those lives paid to come on board and knew the risks they were taking."

"We thought we would be safe on your ship."

"You are paying passengers, not my crew. I owe you nothing."

I drew myself up to my full height and gave the man my most withering glare.

"Do you know who you are speaking to?"

Captain Achilles looked at me carefully.

"Regardless of who you might claim to be, I have work to do." He turned to leave.

"Stop right there."

To his credit, he did.

"I am the Queen of Egypt. I am daughter of the Pharaoh Akhenaten and wife to the Pharaoh Tutankhamun, may they live for millions of years. I am the Great Royal Wife of the Pharaoh Ay and if you do not follow my instructions precisely, I will have you arrested the moment we set foot on shore. All of your property will be confiscated. All of your family will be imprisoned and their property will be confiscated too. You will be transported immediately to the slave mines. If I am feeling merciful, your family will be drawn and quartered rather than being sent with you."

While I spoke, he slowly turned back around. He looked me up and down. I had never looked less royal. It had been weeks since I had bathed or even worn a clean gown. My feet were bare, my once-shaved hair was barely as long as my thumb, and I wore no wig or jewels or makeup. Still, I had been raised a princess and I knew how to carry myself.

At length, Captain Achilles bowed.

"Forgive me. I did not realise."

"I can be merciful, Captain. If you give me reason to be."

"I will need a very sharp sword, or a large knife. You can —" He stopped and reconsidered his words. "Perhaps one of your companions could get a fire going? I will also need a flat blade, well heated."

"You have firewood?"

"Only such as we needed for cooking and we have used all of that, but there are some woven baskets that should be suitable and I suppose you will have to take some wood from the ship."

Renni spoke from behind me. I hadn't realised he was there.

"I will look after that, my lady." He had not called me that in a long time. "One of the men who attacked us had a sword. If it is well sharpened, it might serve for the captain's purposes."

Then Behenu was there as well. "I will sharpen it. Show me the sword."

Renni led her away, leaving me alone with Captain

Achilles. I felt as if I should express sympathy for his fallen crew but didn't know what to say.

"It does not need to be said, my lady," he said. "We all suffer loss. My men know that this might be their fate. We will tend to their bodies as soon as we have dealt with your situation."

"I thank you."

I left him standing beside the body of his dead man and returned to Intef. He looked even paler than before, if that was possible. Beside him, Istnofret was drenched in his blood. She had torn a strip off her own skirt and fashioned a second tourniquet on his damaged arm.

"Is he conscious?" I asked.

"In and out. I am not sure he knows what is happening, other than that he is wounded."

"Perhaps that is for the best. The captain has some butchery experience. He is going to remove Intef's arm."

Istnofret sucked in a sharp breath. "Do you think that is a good idea?"

"He will die if we do nothing. Renni doesn't think he will last until we reach Suakin. If we can take off his arm and cauterise the wound, we have a chance of saving him."

"He will be disfigured for the rest of his life. I think he would rather die."

I looked at Intef. Did I have the right to make this decision for him? With my anger gone, other feelings were emerging. Feelings that were deeper and stronger than mere obligation towards a dutiful servant. Whether it was my right to decide if he lived or died, or not, I couldn't let him go. Not now, when I was just starting to realise how I felt about him.

"We will give him a chance to live whether he wants it or not," I said. "It will be up to Intef what he does with it."

TWENTY-TWO

R enni used an axe to cut away a small section of the upper deck. He had found a large bronze bowl and carefully started his fire within it, before setting the head of the axe in the flames.

"I wish we had something to ease his pain," I said.

Intef's face was so pale and blood continued to flow down his arm, despite the tourniquets. Istnofret was crouched beside him, her hands pressed over the wound in an attempt to stem the bleeding. She had almost as much blood on her as he did.

"Do you still have the bag I gave you before you left Memphis?" she asked.

"Of course."

"The bottle. It contains a tincture of poppies."

So that was what it was. I hurried down below and found my little bag. I feared the bottle might have broken, or perhaps leaked, but the cork seemed to be stoppered as tightly as ever. I took it back to Istnofret.

"I have it," I said.

"I don't think he is aware of anything right now, so you will have to hold his head up and pour it into his mouth," she said. "Try not to spill it. It is all we have."

Intef's skin was cold — far too cold — as I tipped his head up. His head lolled to the side and I couldn't find a way to hold it up while also removing the stopper from the bottle. But then Behenu was beside me, taking the bottle and tipping its contents down Intef's throat.

"Slowly," I said. "Or you will choke him."

She didn't respond, but the competent way she emptied the bottle into his mouth made me think it was not the first time she had cared for a dying man.

"How quickly will it work?" I asked.

"Quickly," Istnofret said. "It was the strongest tincture I could get my hands on. I am not sure it is even safe to take all of it at once."

"I already gave it all to him," Behenu said. "Was that wrong?"

"Not necessarily," Istnofret said. "If it doesn't kill him, it will knock him out. It will be better for him if he doesn't know what is happening."

Thank Isis I hadn't tried to drink from the bottle when I first found it. Intef's frame was all muscle and he was far more solid than me. Something strong enough to kill me might only send him into deep unconsciousness. As we waited for the tincture to take effect, I wondered what Istnofret had thought I might need it for.

Then Captain Achilles came and we lay Intef down on his back with his injured arm stretched out.

"Hold him steady," Achilles said. "If he wakes, he must not move or he might lose more than his arm."

Renni took hold of Intef's legs, and Istnofret and Behenu grasped his shoulders.

"My lady, hold his head," Renni said to me.

I knelt behind Intef and put my hands on either side of his face. My belly was an awkward obstacle between us. Achilles readied his sword and as he brought it down on Intef's arm, I closed my eyes. Bone crunched. Intef groaned and stirred. Something splattered on my face. Intef began to writhe.

"Hold him still," Achilles said, tersely.

I gripped Intef's head tighter even as I kept my eyes closed. I was betraying him by not watching. Surely it behooved me to bear witness to what was being done to him, given it was me who insisted we try to save him, but I couldn't watch.

At length Captain Achilles finished his grisly task and Renni fetched the axe which had been heating in the flames. There was a sizzle and the smell of burning flesh when Achilles pressed the axe against what remained of Intef's arm. Intef groaned but didn't wake. The poppy tincture must have been strong indeed.

"It is done," Captain Achilles said, eventually. The axe clattered to the deck and he walked away.

I started to open my eyes.

"Don't look, my lady," Istnofret said. "It is… not pleasant."

"It is not as bad as what Intef has endured," I said.

But when I saw it all, I wished I had taken heed of her words. The deck was awash with blood. His arm lay beside the sword, discarded as if it was merely an unneeded tool. The captain had taken it off midway between shoulder and elbow. There was little more than a stump remaining and that was so bloodied that I couldn't even see whether the cut was clean or if what was left had been mangled. I swayed as I tried to get to my feet. The air suddenly felt terribly warm and I couldn't get a full breath. My back ached with unexpected intensity.

"My lady?" Behenu took me by the arm. "Perhaps you should stay seated."

I shook her off, barely even comprehending her words. Intef was paler than I had ever seen a living body. He breathed so shallowly that we would probably not notice if he stopped altogether.

"We should take him down below," Istnofret said. "See if we can clean him up a bit before he wakes."

"Is it safe to move him?" I asked.

"We cannot leave him lying here in his own blood," she said.

There was little space on the deck that was clear of blood, regardless of whether it was Intef's or someone else's.

Between the four of us, we managed to lift him, but then my stomach spasmed with a wave of pain and I almost dropped him.

"Perhaps you should sit down," Renni said. "We can manage."

"I am fine," I said. "And we should hurry."

We shuffled towards the hatch.

"What about his arm?" The mummification priests had always said that every part of the body must be retained in order for a person to be resurrected. Did that include limbs removed prior to death? I had never heard of such a thing being embalmed, but perhaps we shouldn't take the chance.

"I will come back for it," Renni said. "Let's just get him below first."

Awkwardly, with much tripping over bodies and sliding on

the wet deck, we managed to carry Intef to the hatch. Another wave of pain gripped me on the way, and it was all I could do to keep hold of Intef's shoulder and not scream aloud.

It was only as we reached the hatch that we realised how difficult it was going to be to manoeuvre him through it and down the ladder. We set him down while we considered our options.

"I don't think we can do it," Istnofret said. "He is too heavy."

"We can wrap a blanket around him," Renni said. "It will be easier to hold the blanket than Intef."

"But how do we stop it from touching his arm?" she asked.

"If we do it quickly while he is still unconscious, it makes no difference," he said.

"I will fetch a blanket." Behenu disappeared down into the dark.

When she returned, we laid the blanket down, managing to avoid any blood, and shifted Intef onto it. Another wave of pain sent me doubling over. I could barely breathe through it and hardly noticed Istnofret clutching my arm.

"My lady, whatever is wrong?" she whispered. "Are you ill?"

"No." I could barely speak through the pain. "My stomach hurts. I will be fine. We need to finish moving— Argh." I doubled over and wrapped my arms around my stomach.

"We need to move fast before he wakes," Renni said. "Can you manage?" The last was directed at me.

I wiped my sweaty brow and nodded. We swaddled Intef in the blanket.

"Take a corner of the blanket each and hold tight," Renni said. "I will hold his other arm. My lady and Istnofret, go down the ladder. Behenu and I will pass him to you. Then just hold him steady until we get down there."

Somehow, we managed to get Intef through the hatch. We knocked his head once or twice, and I was almost certain we banged his ruined arm against the ladder, but he remained blissfully unaware. I was gripped by another wave of pain just as we set him down in our corner and let him fall a little too heavily. Then I knew nothing else, for I was lost in the haze of my pain.

When I came back to myself I was sitting on the floor with my arms wrapped around my belly. Intef was still very pale, but he was breathing. Renni had disappeared, presumably gone back above deck to retrieve Intef's arm and help the crew clean up.

"My lady?" Istnofret offered me a dampened cloth. "You have blood everywhere."

It was only then I noticed the splattering of blood on my arms and chest. I wiped the cloth over my face and it seemed there was blood there too. When the cloth needed to be rinsed, Istnofret tried to take it from me.

"No, I can do it," I said.

Laboriously I got to my feet and staggered over to the cask of water.

"My lady?" The horror in Istnofret's voice stopped me short. "There is too much blood."

The pain of moving had made my head fuzzy and I couldn't quite make sense of her words. My stomach cramped again, although not as fiercely this time.

"There is too much blood on you," she said.

I looked down at myself. We were both covered in blood and she had just as much on her as I did.

"I haven't finished cleaning up yet."

"Look." Istnofret pointed to the pool of blood where I had been sitting. "It is all over the back of your skirt. It cannot all be Intef's."

I reached around behind me, but my fingers were too cold and numb, and I could feel nothing.

"I don't understand."

"The pain. It is in your belly, is it not?"

Her tone was gentle and at first I was puzzled, but then I realised.

"The babe?" I whispered.

"I think so."

"It is too soon."

"Much too soon," Istnofret said. "Either the babe intends to be born or your body has decided to rid itself."

I knew little other than pain and blood for some time after that. When the babe was finally delivered, he was still and far too small. I cradled him and tried to memorise his face. For he was indeed a boy. This was not the child I had seen in my dreams.

This babe was from my own body, but my feelings about him were conflicted. I didn't know whether he had been fathered by Intef or by Ay. I searched his face, looking for some sign of either man. I had expected to fall wildly in love the moment I held my babe in my arms, but all I felt was emptiness and exhaustion. My stomach still hurt, as did other parts of me, and I was covered in blood, both Intef's and my own. Perhaps it was best that the babe had not lived, for I was obviously not fit to be his mother if I didn't love him immediately.

Beside me, Intef groaned. Istnofret was by his side before I could move. She crouched down and rested her hand on his shoulder. Not the shoulder that had just lost an arm.

"Intef?" Her tone was gentle. "Are you awake?"

He groaned again and said something incomprehensible.

"You are back down below deck. I don't know if you remember what happened, but there was a battle. Pirates boarded the ship. You and Renni fought with the crew. I haven't been able to speak with Renni yet so that is all I know."

Intef tried again to say something.

"Renni is well," Istnofret said. "Don't fret. He is up above helping the captain. Half the crew was lost."

Intef finally opened his eyes. His gaze came straight to me and I knew the moment he saw the blood all over me. His eyes widened and at last a recognisable sound came out of his mouth.

"Samun."

"It is not all mine," I said.

His gaze went to the tiny body in my arms. His mouth opened and closed.

"The babe came too early." Again I searched the babe's face for any indication of his father. "I don't think he is yours."

Intef seemed to swallow hard. I couldn't read the expression on his face. Had no idea whether he was relieved or disappointed to hear such a thing. I hoped he would never realise I had lied. Intef moaned and closed his eyes.

"I hurt." There was a long pause before he spoke again. "Am I injured?"

Istnofret, Behenu and I looked at each other. When nobody responded, Intef opened his eyes. The looks on our faces must have answered his question. He tried to sit up but gasped and fell back down. It was then that he noticed his arm. He stared at the bandaged stump for a long time.

The silence went on and on. I looked up at Istnofret. She

opened and closed her mouth without ever saying anything. It was Behenu who finally spoke.

"It was Ankhesenamun's idea," she said. "You would have gone to the West otherwise."

It was a very long time before Intef replied.

"You should have let me."

TWENTY-THREE

Time stood still as the boat crept towards Suakin. I noticed nothing but the babe in my arms. I was empty. Devoid of feelings or even thought.

Beside me, Intef was silent. I glanced at him once to find him lying there with his eyes closed. I couldn't tell whether he was asleep or awake.

Istnofret offered me food and beer, but I shook my head.

"You must," she said. "I will hold the babe while you eat. It will give me a chance to wash him."

I made no reply, refusing even to look at her. Eventually she went away. Some time later, Behenu crouched beside me.

"My lady, perhaps it is time to set the babe down. Look, I have a blanket ready for him. We can wrap him in it until he can be embalmed."

I didn't acknowledge her presence and eventually she, too, went away.

I examined the tiny hands and feet, counting each finger and toe. His nose, his mouth, his ears. I wished I knew whether his eyes were as dark as mine or tawny like Intef's.

"Samun." It was Istnofret again. No matter, I would ignore her as I had each time and she would go away soon enough. "We are arrived. It is time to leave."

It was only then that I noticed the ship was no longer moving.

"Where are we?"

"Suakin. Here we must find another ship to take us to Indou."

I finally remembered why we were on a ship. They would take my babe away from me here. I couldn't let that happen. I needed to hold fast to him until I found a way to love him. He couldn't go to the embalming priests without being loved, at least by his mother.

Renni poked at Intef with his sandal.

"Time to get up. Can you walk or do I need to carry you?"

Intef grunted at him.

"Go. Leave me here."

"Captain's heading back out to sea again shortly. He is only stopping long enough to take on supplies and hire some new men."

"I will stay here."

"Get up."

"I told you to go away."

"You are not my captain anymore," Renni said. "You have no right to order me about. Now get on your feet or I will pick you up and carry you."

Intef finally opened his eyes. He glared hard, but Renni simply shrugged.

"Your choice," he said. "You want to be carried off the ship like a sickly woman?"

Intef managed to sit up, although not without a groan and a long hiss of pain.

"Need a hand?" Renni asked.

"Get out of my way," Intef snarled.

Renni stood back and watched as he slowly got up. He almost fell over at one stage, but Renni didn't move to help him. At last, panting and ashen-faced, Intef was on his feet.

"Good man," Renni said. "Get yourself up above."

Then he turned to me and his tone was much gentler this time.

"Your turn."

"I will not let you take the babe," I warned.

"I don't intend to. Behenu has gone ahead to find us some lodgings. We will stay here in Suakin for a few days until both you and Intef are fit to travel."

He and Istnofret helped me to my feet without trying to take the babe from my arms. As I waited for them to gather our belongings, I overheard their quiet discussion.

"Will he ever forgive us?" Istnofret asked.

Renni exhaled in a way that was more sigh than breath.

"I don't know. In truth, I am not even sure we did the right thing. Perhaps we should have let him die. He has made it very clear that would have been his preference."

"He doesn't know what he is saying."

"I think he does, but he is also angry."

"He is probably in a terrible amount of pain," she said.

"As soon as she finds us somewhere to stay, Behenu will look for a healer."

We had eaten almost all of our supplies and what was left could be easily carried by the two of them.

As I emerged into the fresh air, my head started to clear and I looked down at the babe in my arms. His little body had stiffened and I knew it was time to hand him over to the priests.

We stepped off the boat onto a sandy shore that didn't look all that different from the one at Leucus Limen. Once past the shore, though, it was clear that we were no longer in Egypt. I hadn't realised that Suakin was an island. We had sailed down a canal and into a ring-shaped harbour with Suakin at its centre. The mainland was visible just a short distance across the water. The buildings of Suakin were very different from those of Egypt, tall brick things with high arches. The sky was overcast and a cool wind had swept any warmth away.

We had barely set foot on the shore before we spotted Behenu hurrying towards us, followed by a tall black-skinned woman who held herself like she was of noble birth. She carried a woven basket.

"This is Diang," Behenu said. "She is named for a goddess."

"You are a healer?" Renni asked the woman.

"She speaks no Egyptian," Behenu said. "But I found a man who did and he took me to her."

Diang's gaze flicked between Intef and me. I was being judged, or maybe assessed.

"Come, I have lodgings for us," Behenu said.

She led us to a tall building, where we went up a flight of stairs and along a hallway.

"This is one of our chambers," Behenu said as she opened the door. She pointed to the next door. "And that is the other."

"What is this place?" Istnofret asked as she set down her bags.

"There are other chambers," Behenu said. "And a woman who seems to be in charge. I think she runs a business of sorts, letting out the chambers to travellers in exchange for payment. She was quite happy to accept the earring you gave me. She said its gemstone was particularly fine. I offered Diang the other earring, but she gave me a strange look and didn't take it. I think she was offended."

A girl of perhaps ten years waited in the first chamber. She was as dark-skinned as Diang and from the brief conversation between them, I understood the healer had expected the girl to be here. Perhaps she was an assistant or apprentice. The chamber was neat, with three reed mats, each with a blanket that looked to be reasonably clean and a soft cushion for our heads. There were a couple of low stools, a small table which bore a bundle wrapped in cloth, and several buckets of water.

Diang set down her basket and pointed at Intef, indicating that he was to lie on one of the mats. He collapsed onto it with a groan. Diang then turned her attention to me. She gestured towards the babe in my arms.

"No." I clutched him tighter.

Her face was sympathetic as she reached for him.

"You cannot take him."

"Samun." Istnofret touched me lightly on the back. "You must let him go. He needs to be embalmed before it is too late. You know it must be done quickly."

I looked down at the tiny figure. This would be the last time I ever saw him, I knew that. I held him to my chest for one last, long moment, then kissed his face. Even as Diang was taking him from me, my fingers continued to grasp him.

"Let him go, my lady," Istnofret said. "You know you must."

I finally gave him up. Diang held the tiny babe carefully. Her lips moved in silent prayer and she made a symbol in the air above his head.

"What is she doing?" I asked.

"She is blessing him," Behenu said.

"What did she say?"

"I cannot understand her language, but I have seen that symbol before. It is a blessing to ease the babe's path to the afterlife."

Diang handed the child to her assistant, issuing a stream of instructions in a language that was harsh to my ears. The girl cradled the babe to her chest and hurried away.

"No," I said softly as she left.

Istnofret wrapped her arm around my shoulders. She said nothing, only let me lean against her as I cried.

Diang busied herself with unwrapping the bundle, which turned out to contain a stack of neatly-folded cloths. She offered one to me and pointed towards the buckets.

"I think she wants you to wash," Istnofret said. "I will help you."

It was only then that I became aware of just how much blood was on my gown. Had anyone noticed as we walked here from the boat? I had been so absorbed in my babe, that if anyone had been staring, I didn't see them.

Diang then turned her attention to Intef. While Istnofret helped me take off my blood-stained gown, Diang inspected the remains of Intef's arm. She removed the soiled bandages, soothing him with gentle noises when he groaned. I couldn't tell whether she was pleased or displeased by what she saw beneath the bandages. She took a bucket of water and a handful of the cloths and began to wash him.

I hadn't noticed until then that Intef was covered in as much blood as I. Why had nobody tried to wash him before now? Perhaps they had thought it better to let him rest. Intef submitted to Diang's ministrations with disinterest. He hissed in pain once or twice but otherwise barely seemed to notice.

When I had finished washing all the blood from my body, I wrapped myself in one of the larger pieces of cloth while

Istnofret scrubbed my gown. Eventually she tossed it on the floor.

"It is ruined," she said. "We will need to find you new clothes."

I was about to suggest that Behenu go when I realised Diang's young apprentice had returned and my babe was not with her. My heart suddenly hurt and my eyes filled with tears. I took a deep breath to steady myself. I would never see him again. We couldn't afford to wait here for the seventy days his embalming would take.

Diang spoke sharply to her apprentice and the girl responded in a conciliatory way. The healer seemed satisfied and pointed towards the basket. The girl began unpacking the contents, seemingly looking for a particular bottle, which she presented to Diang.

Diang showed Intef the bottle, talking to him in a tone that was far gentler than she had used with her apprentice. Then she unstoppered the bottle and held it to his mouth. Intef turned his head away.

"No," he said. "I don't want it, whatever it is."

She murmured to him, pressing the bottle to his lips.

"Let me die," he said.

Still Diang held the bottle to his mouth.

"Oh for Isis's sake, Intef, just drink it," I snapped.

"I said I don't want it."

"She is trying to help you."

"Look what happened the last time someone tried to help me." He turned to look at me finally. His cheeks were reddened and his eyes fever-bright. "You took my gods-damned arm off. I don't need any more help. Just let me die like you should have back on the ship."

"I have had quite enough of this nonsense," Istnofret said.

"If he will not take it for Diang, I will pour it down his throat myself."

She marched over to him. Intef glared up at her but she merely held his remaining arm down with her foot and pinched his nostrils closed. He struggled weakly.

"Go on," she said to Diang.

Diang obviously understood well enough, for she was swift to pry open Intef's mouth and pour in the bottle's contents. She held his mouth closed.

"Swallow," Istnofret said.

He glared up at her defiantly.

"Isis help me, but I will hold your nose until you either swallow or pass out."

Intef's face was bright red and his eyes were beginning to bulge.

"You are an idiot," I said. "Son of a dung-covered dog."

Intef finally swallowed. Istnofret released his nose with a satisfied *ha*.

"This is how you repay me?" he asked me.

At his side, Diang was closely inspecting his ruined arm. She asked her assistant to fetch something else from the basket, then made a peculiar motion at me with her hand.

"I think she means for you to keep him talking," Istnofret murmured. "Distract him while she tends to his arm."

I allowed the rage I had held inside for so long to bubble over. After all, Diang wanted him distracted.

"How are you going to protect me now?" I taunted him. "You will barely be able to take care of yourself. I will be the one protecting you."

He glared at me, even more furiously than he had glared at Diang, but then the fight seemed to go out of him. He turned his face aside and didn't respond.

"So that is it? I realise you can hardly fight in your own defence, let alone mine, but you cannot even speak up for yourself? Is this what you have become?"

He blinked quickly and I saw the way he deliberately calmed himself. He slowed his breathing, relaxed his facial muscles. He was as impassive as he had been before and I found myself suddenly unreasonably irritated. He flinched as he finally noticed Diang who was wiping a foul-smelling ointment on his ruined arm. He pulled away from her, almost rolling off the mat in an effort to get away. Diang shot me a pleading look. I was going to have to work much harder to distract him.

"Are you to spend the rest of your life as a cripple?" I asked. "What am I supposed to do with you? How do I keep one as useless as you in my employ? I suppose you could follow Behenu when I send her on errands. You could watch her and report back to me if she does anything she should not. I can hardly think of anything else you might be useful for in your present condition."

Intef finally reacted. "I will not spy on Behenu for you. I am the captain of your guards and I can still perform my duties adequately."

"With one arm? How will you defend me when the next assassin comes? You are useless now and you are right — we should have let you die."

"You." He glared at me, so furious that he could hardly spit out the words. "You are a spoiled princess who has never done a day's work in her life. You have spent your whole life sitting around, waiting for others to do everything for you. You wouldn't survive an hour without me. You need me, even if you are too stuck up to admit it."

"Stuck up?" I suddenly noticed the shrillness of my voice

and lowered my tone. I had to remember that I was only picking a fight in order to let Diang do her work. But it felt like Intef had just said what he really thought about me. "You didn't think I was so stuck up when you came to my bed all those times."

Diang spoke before Intef could reply, something encouraging that ended with her patting him on the shoulder. She had finished, it seemed, for now.

I inhaled a little shakily and turned away. My legs wobbled and I needed to sit down before I fell over.

"So you intend to walk away?" he said. "You think you can say something like that and just walk away?"

"I was only trying to distract you. I was helping Diang."

"No, you come over here and talk to me properly. For once in your life, face the truth and have a real conversation with somebody who cares about you."

"Who? You?"

"Of course me, you damned fool. Why else do you think I would be here?"

"Because it is your duty," I stammered.

"Are you really as obtuse as you seem to be sometimes?"

"You…" I was dumbfounded for a moment. "You are being extremely rude."

"No, I am being human. I am trying to connect with someone I care about. You might try it sometime."

He turned his face away and said nothing further. I went to sit on one of the mats, intending to sulk and console myself with thoughts about his rudeness, but Diang came to stand over me. She motioned for me to lie back. It seemed it was now my turn to be subjected to her ministrations.

TWENTY-FOUR

D iang tended to us well. She used a variety of pungent ointments on Intef, who passively accepted her ministrations. As we spoke no language in common, she could tell us nothing about her treatments or Intef's prognosis. We communicated by nods and hand gestures.

Her young apprentice was constantly by her side, anticipating her mistress's needs and fetching buckets of water, clean cloths and various ointments. Diang often used a word that sounded like *sada* when she spoke to the girl, so we took to calling her that, although we didn't know whether it was actually her name or a word that meant something like *girl* or *helper*. It was close enough to Sadeh that I thought of her every time I heard it.

The days were pleasant with cool nights. I figured we must be well into *peret* by now, when the land emerged from the Great River's floodwaters. The chamber we occupied had two small windows which let in little fresh air, but it was more than we had below deck on the ship.

For the first two days, Diang made me lie on the reed mat. I didn't sleep much, but she seemed satisfied as long as I lay there. I passed the time thinking about my babe. Worrying that I hadn't given him a name. The name was one of the essential components of a person. Could he even be resurrected in the Field of Reeds if he didn't have a name?

Sada fed me watery broths and a foul tea that was so bitter I could barely swallow it. Diang nodded with satisfaction every time I managed to take some. After two days, I could lie down no more and took to prowling up and down the hallway. I had seen little of Istnofret and nothing of Renni since the day we had arrived, although the sounds that came from the chamber next door indicated they were finding ways to occupy their time.

Behenu seemed to have struck up a friendship of sorts with Sada. I heard them speaking together on the occasions when Sada was permitted a short break from her duties. They conversed haltingly in something that seemed to be a mix of both of their languages. When I asked Behenu how she knew Sada's language, she shrugged.

"I tell her words for things in my language and she does the same."

"Is her name really Sada?"

"Close enough. It sounds different when she says it, though."

Indeed the language Sada and Diang spoke seemed both harsh and melodic at the same time. I was familiar enough with Akkadian to comprehend how different one language could sound from another but it was my first experience of listening to people conversing at length in a language I had no understanding of. At first, I found it entirely too strange, but eventually their conversations flowed over me like a breeze moving over desert sands. I still understood nothing of what they said, but the sounds became familiar enough to send me to sleep. My peaceful doze was interrupted when Renni burst in with Istnofret on his heels. He stopped and shot a look towards Diang and Sada.

"They speak no Egyptian," Behenu said to him.

"Are you certain?" he asked.

"As certain as I can be."

"Fine, then. We have been followed. A squad arrived by ship this afternoon and have been asking about a party of four Egyptians. Looking for their fellow soldiers who have taken up with some women they recently met, apparently. They are saying that the fellows are probably lying low somewhere with their new sweethearts."

"I suppose they could have come up with a worse story," I said.

"We are five," Behenu said. "Six if you count Mau."

"I heard no mention of a cat," Renni said. "Or of you."

"How do you know this?" I asked.

"Ist and I went for a walk. We saw them strolling along the street, stopping passersby, and I managed to get close enough to hear what they were saying."

"Was there any description of us? Did they say who we are?"

"No names, at least not in the brief exchange I overheard."

"I keep telling him it might not be us they are looking for," Istnofret said.

"You think it likely that another group of Egyptians are so recently arrived in Suakin?" he asked. "With two of them being soldiers?"

"Perhaps if you looked a little less like a soldier, we would not be as noticeable," she said.

Renni looked down at himself. He was dressed, as most

Egyptian men did, in a white *shendyt*. He and Intef had taken to wearing sandals and linen shirts on our overland trek. They still wore their daggers tucked into their waistbands but with a shirt over the top, the weapons were hardly noticeable. Their once-shaved heads sprouted dark hair, although they both still removed the hair from their chins, and none of us had worn kohl for weeks. Still, Istnofret was right that Renni looked every bit the soldier. He walked with his back straight and his head held high. Every step was taken with a self-assurance that most men didn't display.

"You could slouch a little," Istnofret suggested. "Maybe stop looking around you quite so much."

"I cannot cease being alert to our surroundings." His voice was stiff.

Istnofret placed her hand on his chest. "I am not suggesting you should not be alert. Only that you look a little less like—"

"A soldier?" He stepped back away from her and she let her hand drop. "It is what I am. I can no more stop being a soldier than I can stop breathing."

"That was not what I meant," she said, softly.

"We need to move as soon as we can," he said. "Intef, can you travel?"

Intef took so long to reply that I thought he must be asleep.

"Leave me here," he said.

"Don't be ridiculous." Istnofret stood over him with her hands on her hips. "You have been lying around feeling sorry for yourself for a whole week. Now, tell us frankly. How much longer do you need before you can travel?"

"Ist." Renni pulled her aside and spoke to her softly, although not so quietly that I couldn't hear him. "Let me handle this."

She glowered up at him. "Like you have been handling it

for the last week? Someone needs to slap him out of that bed before his moping around sends him straight to the West."

He stared down at her for a moment and she glared up at him. Eventually he nodded towards Intef.

"Have at him," he said. "I heard of a trade vessel leaving for Indou in two days. We need to be on that ship. With or without Intef."

TWENTY-FIVE

A fter the length of our journey so far, two days should have seemed like no time at all. Instead it was endless. Renni found the captain of the trade ship and secured passage for us. Behenu slipped out a couple of times to purchase supplies and our pile of bags and baskets waiting in the corner grew. Other than that, we remained in our chambers, keeping out of sight of the men who searched for us. Mau prowled around and meowed occasionally. Once she had lived her life entirely indoors, but now that she had had a taste of the outside world, even if it was with Behenu's rope around her neck, she was increasingly intolerant of being inside.

At first, I was anxious that we would be found, that at any moment soldiers might come bursting in and cart us back to Memphis, but as the hours passed and my spell bottle remained cold, my fear subsided. I was still weak from having lost so much blood and secretly wondered whether I had the strength for another lengthy boat journey.

Intef had stopped even responding when Istnofret berated him. It was clear that she tried to stir him into action, that she sought to raise his fury enough that he would find the will to live, but she seemed to have little success. He drank when Diang put a mug to his lips. He ate when she placed food in his mouth. He allowed her to help him up to use a chamber pot, at which times we women would wait in the hallway. But he made no move to do anything for himself. When Istnofret stood over him and harangued him, he closed his eyes and pretended to sleep.

"What will we do if he won't walk to the ship?" I asked Renni as we wandered up and down the hallway. I was still weak, but my frequent short walks seemed to be helping. "He is too heavy for us to carry so far."

"He will walk," Renni said. "Istnofret will make sure of it."

"It doesn't seem to be working so far."

"She is a very determined woman. She will get him on his feet."

I had to concede that Renni was right. This was the woman who followed me from Memphis. Who travelled in secret to the Medjay to arrange for my rescue. Who insisted on being at my side as I searched for an artefact I wasn't sure even existed. When Renni announced that it was time to leave, Istnofret marched over to where Intef lay.

"On your feet then, you lazy dog." She stood over him with her hands on her hips. "You have laid there long enough."

"Leave me be." His words were slow and disinterested, his eyes closed.

Istnofret kicked him in the leg and it didn't look like she was being all too gentle.

"I said, get up."

He opened his eyes long enough to glare up at her.

"Are you trying to get yourself hurt?"

She laughed scornfully.

"By who? You? You cannot even get off your mat, let alone keep up with me long enough to hurt me."

"Go away. Go get on your ship and leave me alone."

She kicked him again, harder than before.

"What will it take to get you on your feet? You might only have one arm, but you still have two good legs."

Intef breathed rapidly. Istnofret was getting to him.

"You call yourself a soldier?" she taunted. "Weakest soldier I have ever known. One little injury and you lie in bed for a week, moaning as if you will die."

"One little injury?" He glared up at her, his face reddening. "You let her cut off my gods-damned arm."

"You would have died."

"You should have asked."

"You were barely conscious, you damned fool," she yelled. "We did what we had to in order to save your life. You should be thanking us, not moaning about how terrible your lot is."

"You had no right to make that decision for me."

"No right to save your life? Dear Aten, you are even more of a fool than I thought you were."

Intef thrashed around on his mat. At first, I thought something was wrong, but then I realised he was trying to sit up. Istnofret moved to help him and he pushed her away, no more gentle with her than she had been with him. At last he was sitting, his chest heaving and his eyes furious.

"Did nobody think I would not want to live like this?" He glared around the room, including all of us in his fury. "How am I supposed to fight like this? How can I protect—" His gaze landed on me and his voice broke. "How can I protect anyone with one arm?"

"It is not even the arm you wield your dagger with." Istnofret's tone was scornful. "A proper soldier would have been back on his feet long before now and learning how to move without his arm. But you, you just lie on your back feeling sorry for yourself."

Intef was trying to stand and my heart ached to see his struggle. I looked towards Renni, wondering why he wasn't helping, but Renni caught my glance and shook his head slightly. If Intef was going to get to his feet, it would be on his own.

It took him a long time. Even once he was standing, he swayed a little and his knees seemed to buckle. I thought he would fall down, but he got his balance and glared around at us. Before he could speak, Renni was already moving.

"Get the bags." His words didn't seem to be directed at anyone in particular. "We have wasted too much time."

In very short order, he had passed out various bags and packages for each of us to carry. Intef took his share without comment. His fury seemed to have already dissipated. Istnofret cast measuring looks at him, no doubt wondering whether she needed to provoke him again in order to keep him on his feet. But he noticed that Renni had kept the largest share of the bags for himself and motioned at him for more. Renni handed them over without comment.

When we were ready to leave, Intef could barely stand up straight for the load of bags slung over his shoulders. There was even one hanging around his neck. But his face was defiant and it was clear that he intended to carry his share. I bit my tongue and didn't offer to help him. After all, I too had insisted on doing my share on our journey. I couldn't deny Intef the same, even injured as he was.

In our rush to leave, we had forgotten Diang and Sada. Sada was packing away the various bottles and jars, but the healer was watching us.

"Thank you," I said, hoping she would understand my intent, even if she didn't know my words.

Diang came to stand in front of me. She placed one hand on my still-swollen belly and spoke in her own language.

"What do you think she is saying?" I didn't expect a reply, but Behenu answered.

"She is blessing you. Or blessing your womb. She is offering good wishes of some sort."

"You can understand her?"

Behenu had been spending as much time with Sada as the girl's duties allowed, but even so, I was surprised she had picked up so much of their language in such a short time.

"Not word for word, but I can make out enough to guess at the meaning."

"Thank you," I said again to Diang. "Truly."

Diang went to Intef next. He turned his head away, but she took his face in her hands and made him look at her. She spoke to him, a longer speech than the one she had made to me. She placed her hand on his forehead as she spoke and as she finished, moved her hand to his chest and poked at the place where his heart was. She seemed to be asking a question.

"She wants you to promise you will live, I think," Behenu said. "That you will not give up."

"I don't make promises I cannot keep." His words were stiff although he at least looked at Diang as he spoke.

Diang shook her head at him and spoke again, more forcefully.

"She wants you to promise," Behenu said. "Promise or... I am not sure of what she said next, but I think it is something like if you don't promise, she curses you."

"She is supposed to be a healer," I said. "She cannot curse him."

"We know little of these people's customs," Istnofret said. "Perhaps if Intef seems ungrateful for the treatment she has given him, the curse is a punishment. Fair enough, I think."

"I would have thought he has suffered enough," I muttered to myself.

Diang shot me a sharp look, as if she had not only heard me but understood.

"We need to be away from here," Renni said. "Intef, just do as she says."

"Fine." Intef's tone was as close to sulky as I had ever heard him. "I promise. Does that suffice?"

The last was directed at Diang who nodded in satisfaction. She said something else and made a motion in the air in front of his face.

"It is a blessing," Behenu offered. "I can understand no more than that."

Intef reached for Diang's hand.

"Thank you for treating me." He sounded more sincere now.

She smiled and patted his cheek, then hurried out of the chamber, issuing instructions over her shoulder to Sada, who by now had collected up all of her things and was at her heels. Then they were gone and the chamber suddenly seemed so much emptier.

TWENTY-SIX

The ship was larger than any I had seen before. I had thought the vessel that bore us from Leucus Limen to Suakin was big, but it was nothing compared to this. And now that I had some experience of ships, I could see how well organised it was. The crew moved swiftly and with purpose. Most of the men walked in the same efficient and deliberate way that Intef and Renni did, which left me speculating that they, too, were trained soldiers. The captain of this ship was not relying on butchers and farmers to guard his cargo.

"We sail around the Persian Gulf," Renni said, as we waited to board. "And then across to Indou."

"How long?" Did I really want to know? The journey to Suakin had taken almost a month, and Indou was much further away.

"A couple of months," he said. "It depends on the weather."

"It gives you time to rest," Istnofret said. "You are still weak, even if you are trying to pretend otherwise. And Intef needs to heal."

"I will be helping the crew." Intef's tone was stiff. "Renni and I must be seen to be sharing the work."

"Not this time, old fellow." Renni slapped him on the back, although the action was far gentler than usual. "You need to rest."

"I do not intend to sit below deck with the women while you work," Intef said. "I will do my share."

Renni shook his head.

"I was very specific when I made arrangements with the captain. It will only be me working. You will rest and learn how to move properly again."

"I have no time for sitting around," Intef said. "Nor the patience for it. There is nothing like honest work to help a man heal."

"Intef," I said. "You will do as Renni says. You will rest and heal. Once you are fully recovered — once we all agree that you are recovered — you can work with the crew. Until then you will do as you are told."

I was in no position to command him anymore, but I counted on his many years of service. Habits formed over the course of more than ten years are hard to break. His face revealed his internal battle, but eventually he lowered his head in what I took to be agreement.

"Now that is settled, we should board," I said.

"We didn't pay Diang," Istnofret said. "Behenu said she tried to pay her when we arrived, but she refused. I meant to try again before we left."

"I gave Sada the earring," Behenu said. "She will give it to Diang later. That way she cannot refuse again."

"Well done," Renni said. "It would not have been right for her to receive nothing in exchange for her time and care for us."

The captain — a brown-skinned man wearing ankle-length pants and a loose shirt — raised a hand in greeting as we walked along the ramp that connected the ship to the dock. At his heels trotted a boy of maybe ten years who had the distinct look of an Egyptian, despite his chin-length hair which was not shaved in the sidelock of youth as it should have been at his age.

The captain bowed respectfully to us and spoke. At first, I thought I was having difficulty understanding his accent, but eventually I realised he wasn't speaking in Egyptian or even Akkadian. He spoke and then waited. Before I had time to wonder how he expected us to respond, the boy spoke in Egyptian.

"His name is Kanta. He is the captain and I will translate his words that you may understand them. He says there are rules to be established. You will follow all directions given by the crew, however insignificant the order may seem. This is for your own safety."

We nodded in agreement, and Kanta continued. Once again, the boy translated his words.

"The women will stay well away from the crew. There is a chamber in which we usually store the most valuable cargo. We have cleared this for your use. You will remain in this chamber until we reach Indou.

"You will not wander amongst the cargo, nor open any of the crates or packages. You will share our supplies, as this is what you have paid for, but there will be no special requests. You will eat what the crew eats. If any of these rules are broken, you will be put to shore at the first opportunity."

His speech complete, Kanta gave the boy a brief order and left.

"You are to follow me," said the boy. "I will show you the

chamber that has been readied for you. Once we have put out to sea, then you" — he pointed at Renni — "will return to help the crew."

He turned on his heel and hurried across the deck. We followed him down some steep steps and along a dark passage. He stopped in front of a door and gestured for us to enter. The chamber was small, not much more than the length of two men. I supposed it would accommodate all of us lying down, but there would be no room to spare. Nevertheless, it was a more private space than I had expected and the floor even looked freshly swept. I dropped my bags with a sigh.

"What do we call you?" Istnofret asked the boy.

He barely glanced at her.

"You call me nothing. I answer only to the captain."

"Your mother would be shamed to hear you say such a thing in front of a lady," she shot back.

He gave her a bewildered look and she tipped her head toward me. Despite my exhaustion and my very urgent need to sit down, I shot him my steeliest glare. The boy bowed from the waist. I doubted he recognised me, but he at least knew a noble woman when he saw one.

"Forgive me, lady. Captain calls me Pawah."

"Is that your real name?" I asked.

"The name my father gave me is Patenemheb, but Captain finds it too difficult to say. He generously allowed me to choose another Egyptian name and that is why he calls me Pawah."

So generous that he doesn't even try to say the boy's real name. And yet was this any more than we had done to Behenu? Had I ever asked her real name? Perhaps I had, back when we first met. I wasn't sure. I could only remember that when I asked if she had been named after Queen Behenu, she had not known who I meant. I had accepted the name she was given and had likely never questioned it again.

"Meals are served when the bell rings," Pawah said. "Captain said you" — he pointed at Renni — "may eat with the crew if you wish. The rest of your company will eat here. Captain does not want the crew thinking of things they cannot have instead of focusing on their work." He directed a meaningful look at both Istnofret and I. "When you need water for washing, I will show you where to find it. You are permitted one bucket per day, which you will share amongst you." Then he left.

"Well," Istnofret said. "I suppose we may as well get settled."

She began arranging our bags, stacking them against the wall.

I looked around the tiny chamber. The bare timber walls suggested it was not intended for occupation for any length of time. A clay pot had been left neatly in a corner, likely intended for our toilet needs, but otherwise the chamber was entirely bare. There was not even so much as a rug on the floor. I hadn't expected windows or murals, but we would be occupying this chamber for the next several months and already it felt even smaller than it had a few minutes ago. I would lose my mind if I had to stay down here for the entire journey.

It seemed to take a long while before the ship was ready to depart. By the time the timbers began to groan and the sloshing of water reached our ears, I itched to get out.

"Be still, Samun," Istnofret said, quietly.

We three women sat side by side with our backs against the wall. Behenu had released Mau from her basket and the cat prowled around, looking thoroughly displeased with her new lodgings and likely longing for fresh air as I was. Renni sat against the wall opposite us. Only Intef was still on his feet, pacing the short length of the chamber, although he had to step over our outstretched legs to do so.

"I cannot stay in here," I whispered to her. "I will go out of my mind."

"It is not so different from when you were confined to your chambers," she said. "Sure, it is smaller and not as comfortable, but you were still confined just the same."

"It was different back then. Or I was different." I paused to gather my thoughts. "Then I knew nothing of what it was like to be alone in the desert or to walk for hours without seeing anyone else. I was always surrounded by my guards and servants. It is different now. After walking as far as I have, and sitting on a boat for days at a time, with nobody but the four of you around me, I am not the same person I was back then. I would not tolerate being confined to my chambers now."

Mau sat on one of the blankets and gave an unhappy yowl.

"I am like Mau," I said. "Once I knew nothing but captivity. Now it stifles me."

Istnofret inhaled but said nothing. When I glanced at her, her face was pensive. She shot me a sidelong look.

"Speak freely, Ist. You are no longer my servant and I am not your queen. Speak your mind. Not that you ever held back much anyway."

If I had thought my comment might make her laugh, or at least huff at me, I was mistaken. Eventually I nudged her with my knee.

"Go on. What do we have if we cannot be honest with each other?"

She sighed. "I was merely thinking that it is too bad you didn't learn these things about yourself back then. Things might have been different if you had been more willing to stand up to Ay from the start."

It was the closest she had ever come to criticising me and her words stung. Tears blurred my eyes, briefly, until I dashed them away.

"Do you think I don't feel guilty?" I hissed. "If I had been stronger, if I had spoken out more, if I had insisted on seeing my brother more when he was young and new to the throne. If I had gotten myself with child when I first promised to. There are so many things I could have done differently. I might have been able to save him."

My voice broke and I suddenly wasn't sure whether I meant my brother or Thrax.

Istnofret took my hand. "I should not have said such a thing. I don't blame you. You did the things you did for reasons that made sense at the time. But it is hard to look back at it now and wonder..."

"I know. I wonder too."

TWENTY-SEVEN

Once again, our days became a monotonous blur. Renni left at daybreak to work with the crew, although how he knew that dawn had arrived from within our dark chamber, I never knew. He lit the lamp before he left, but the rest of us went back to sleep for as long as possible. After all, the longer we slept, the less hours there would be to occupy ourselves by staring at the walls.

Renni had asked a couple of the crew if they knew of Achilles and had discovered he was a well-known smuggler who traded in a variety of goods, including gold bars, precious gems, and fine fabrics. No wonder he had been targeted by pirates. How different things might have been had we waited for another ship to be leaving for Suakin.

Day blended into day. I had little sense of time sequestered away in our chamber where the only light came from the carefully-guarded oil lamp. We ate when we rose in the morning and again after Renni returned to us at night, bearing a tray which contained our meals for both that evening and the following morning. The captain worked his crew hard, and

Renni even harder. Fortunately Renni was fit and hale, and able to keep pace with anyone.

We also had the extra supplies Behenu had procured before we left Suakin and they gave us some relief from the crew's monotonous diet of salted meat and dried legumes cooked into a watery stew. It was served with hard-baked bread which became increasingly stale as the weeks passed. Thanks to Behenu, we had cheese, a variety of dried fruits and berries, and dom palm nuts. Behenu took charge of rationing these out and it was a good thing she did or Istnofret would have eaten all of the berries in the first week.

With so much time to sit around, I could no longer keep myself from thinking. Why hadn't I dreamed about Intef's arm? I had always thought my dreams represented significant decisions. Things that would change either my fate, or someone else's. The decision I made about Thrax ended his life. The one I made for Akhetaten resulted in the city's abandonment. My dream about Behenu had undoubtedly changed her life. Time after time, my dreams had shown me big things. Significant events.

I could understand why I hadn't dreamed about my babe being born too soon. After all, that was not a result of a decision I had made, but purely a matter of accident. But surely Intef being gravely wounded after our ship was attacked by pirates was something I should have seen? At the time it had seemed that the only possible alternative for him was death, but was that true? I spent far too much time morosely pondering whether my dreams might have shown another fate for Intef, one that didn't result in either his death or the loss of his arm.

I found some playing pieces and a set of sticks in the bottom of one of our bags. We scratched a rough playing board into the floor — a game of *senet* didn't require much, just three columns of ten boxes — and we women passed our time playing against each other. Behenu invited Intef to join us but he ignored her, too occupied in lying on his back and staring at the ceiling.

I was starting to worry about him. He didn't look ill or feverish, even when the rest of us were green for the first day. He changed his bandages every second day and applied an ointment Diang had given him, a mix of honey and resin from its smell. He refused any help, and from the quick glimpses I managed to snatch, the wound was healing nicely. But the damage done inside of him did not heal as readily as the physical did. I began to wonder whether we should have let him die after all.

When we tired of *senet*, we played hounds and jackals, although we lacked the correct playing pieces. Behenu scratched a new playing board into the floor and taught us another game, which she said came from the ancient city of Ur.

Eventually even the new game could no longer amuse us and then we shared stories. Istnofret told us about the creation of the world, when the god Atum made himself and then his son Shu and his daughter Tefnut. I told the tale of when Osiris, the mighty god of the underworld, was killed by his brother Seth and chopped into pieces. Osiris's sister-wife Isis searched through all of Egypt to locate the parts of his body. That tale had given me some measure of comfort in those first days after my brother had gone to the West. Knowing that Isis had experienced the same thing and that she had emerged stronger than ever had reinforced my determination to survive.

Behenu told a tale I had never heard before, of a great Syrian king who had no heirs. He promised a sea goddess much tribute if she aided him in a campaign against another country which he intended to make provide him with a bride. He learned the folly of making deals with gods, though, and was left bereft of both country and wife in the end.

"Intef, you have yet to share a tale with us," Behenu said when we women had exhausted all of the tales we knew.

"Indeed, I have a tale for you," he said.

We all sat up a little straighter. This was the first time he had willingly interacted with any of us. Perhaps he was finally starting to recover.

"There was once a soldier. He was captain of the queen's guards and was very good at keeping her safe."

My heart sank. This was no folktale.

"After many trials and assassins and spies, through every one of which he kept his queen safe, came a battle that would turn out to be his last. He was mortally injured, but instead of letting the loyal soldier begin his journey to the West, his queen cut off his arm. She turned him into a cripple and forced him to keep living against his will. He begged his friends to let him die, but they turned their faces away and would not listen."

He drew in a ragged breath. I wanted to say something, to reassure him that his life was still worth living, but I couldn't find the words. They had to be the right words or I would only make things worse. Istnofret was the one who broke the silence, her voice barely more than a whisper.

"What happened to the soldier?"

"He spent the rest of his days as a useless cripple, no longer able to defend his queen, unable to make a living or do anything a useful man might do. He could still feel his arm, even if he could no longer see it or use it. He became a burden to the friends who had refused to let him die."

It was clear that his tale was finished, even though he had given us no real ending. I took a deep breath and continued.

"Eventually, after a long period of darkness and despair, the soldier began to heal. His physical wounds were mended and the emotional trauma he had been suffering began to ease when he realised why his friends wanted him to live."

I paused, searching for the right way to continue. Intef stared at me, his eyes so bright that I wondered if he had a fever.

"Why did she want him to live?" he asked. "He had made it clear that this was not his wish. Why did his friends, if they were really his friends, not give him the thing he most desired in the world?"

"Because his friends knew him better than he knew himself," I said. "He was too lost in his despair to see all of the reasons he had to keep living. He didn't see that once he was healed, he would learn how to be a soldier again. He didn't see that the loss of his arm didn't mean he could no longer do the things he wanted to. He just needed to figure out how to do them with his new body. He didn't see that his friends needed his alertness, his knowledge, his strategic brain. Even without his arm, he was still the strongest man they knew and they needed him to help them complete their quest. Because without him, they would surely fail."

I ran out of words. Intef still stared at me, but his face was no longer quite as distant as it had been. I was getting through to him. I searched for a way to continue the tale, but my mind was suddenly blank. It was Intef who spoke next.

"But there was something the soldier wanted even more than all of that. He heard the things his friends wanted him to live for, but they were not things he wanted enough to live as a cripple. There was something else, something he had never dared to think might be his, something he had longed for since he was seven years old and he first met a princess who stood up to a bully. He told her that day that he loved her, but she didn't believe him.

"As the years passed, it became clear that she had forgotten his words. The soldier didn't mind so much. He had never expected she would return his love. As long as he could be near her, and watch over her, that would be enough for him. Or so he told himself. But then the day came when the princess, now a queen, invited the soldier to her bed and he began to think about things he had told himself he would never think about.

"One day, while trying to protect his queen, the soldier had to do something that hurt her terribly. He knew it would hurt her and he believed that once she learned the truth of it, she would forgive him. But she didn't. She punished him relentlessly, day after day, even after he had given up everything to continue to serve and protect her. She never let him forget the thing he had done in order to save her life.

"Then when he was mortally wounded, she punished him again and refused to let him die. The soldier had no future anymore. He had given up everything for his queen, and now she had taken away the last two things he had: his ability to protect her, and his secret hope that one day she might learn to love him."

"He might have thought she had forgotten that first day they met, long before he became a soldier." My voice was ragged. "But she hadn't. He was also wrong when he thought she didn't believe him when he said he loved her. He might have only been a boy, but his words were fervent and even back then she believed he meant them."

"Then why did she allow his arm to be cut off?" His voice

was little more than a whisper. "If she knew how much he loved her, could she not have let him die? Would that not have been a suitable reward for all his years of service?"

"She could not permit that." I hardly realised I was on my feet until I found myself kneeling at his side. "The solider had been loyal and true. He had served her faithfully, faultlessly, and very, very well. How could she let him die there? On blood-soaked timbers surrounded by strangers. Not on Egyptian soil. Not even where he could be assured of being embalmed so he could be resurrected in the Field of Reeds."

"It would have been a soldier's death and that would have been enough for him."

"But it was not enough for her," I whispered, fiercely. "How could she let him die thinking she didn't love him?"

I hadn't realised until that moment that I was gripping his hand — his one remaining hand. I tried to let go, but he held me fast.

"If he thought she loved him, he would have a reason to go on living." His eyes bored into me. "But how could he know whether she did, or if she was merely saying what she thought he wanted to hear in order to convince him to live?"

I wanted to run away. Away from Intef. Away from the way he looked at me. He wanted something from me that I didn't think I could give. I tried again to withdraw my hand from his grasp, but he only held on tighter.

"Tell me." His voice was a whisper. "Tell me how the story ends. Tell me whether she loves him truly."

Run. Get away. Find somewhere to hide. This was too close. I was not supposed to let anyone get too close.

"Tell me," he said again.

My mind was blank. I couldn't remember what he wanted me to tell him.

"Tell. Me."

At last, I remembered we were telling a story. About a soldier and the queen he loved.

"She—" My voice was an unintelligent croak.

Still he fixed me there with his stare.

"She... needed him."

His stare dulled and he abruptly released my hand. I had said the wrong thing. But I couldn't say the words he wanted to hear.

"She needed him to help her. On her journey. She knew she couldn't do it without him. How could she achieve her goal without her loyal soldier by her side? And what would it mean without him anyway, even if she succeeded in her improbable quest? He could help her save Egypt—"

"You couldn't even give me that much?"

I wanted to hide my face in shame at the sorrow in his voice, but I couldn't say what he wanted me to. It was too definite, too final. I would be too vulnerable. A statement like that couldn't be taken back. Once it was said, it would be out there forever.

"After everything, you couldn't toss me even the tiniest scrap of hope?"

"I do need you, Intef," I said. "Every word I said was true. I cannot do this without you."

"You have other companions." He turned his face away from me. "You do not need me, not like this."

TWENTY-EIGHT

I fled the chamber, hardly knowing where I headed. I barely made it out before the tears came. The area out here was filled with the crew's belongings, as well as one or two men who seemed to be sleeping. There was no privacy anywhere. Leaning against the wall, I let myself cry big, gulping sobs. I sank down to the floor and drew my knees up so I could rest my head on them. My skirt was soaked through with my tears.

At last, I could cry no more. My nose was blocked and my eyes were swollen, but the tears at least seemed to be gone. I had never cried like that before, not even when Meketaten died.

It was only when Renni returned that I realised how long I had been out there.

"Samun?" he asked. "What are you doing? You aren't supposed to be out here. Quickly, get up. Let's get you back into the chamber before anyone sees. The crew will be down in a moment."

He helped me up, hauling me to my feet when my legs

didn't seem to work. He gripped my shoulders and studied me in the dim light from the hatch.

"Have you been crying? What happened?"

I shook my head. "It doesn't matter."

"Is it Intef? He will come around, Samun. You must not worry. He is fit and strong. He will recover, even if he isn't yet sure that he wants to."

"It is…" I stopped, suddenly realising there was nothing I could say. No explanation seemed adequate for why I withheld the words Intef wanted to hear. Besides, Renni had Istnofret and he would probably think me a fool for pushing Intef away. "We should go."

Confined to our chamber and with Intef steadfastly ignoring me, I began to feel like I was going out of my mind. Day after day, week after week, the meals that Renni brought for us were the only indications that time really did continue to pass.

Intef began to heal, both in body and mind. I knew he had decided to live when he stopped spending the entire day lying flat on his back. At first, he would sit up for very short periods and always with his back propped against the wall. But as he grew stronger, he would sit up for longer and soon he no longer needed the wall behind him. A few days later he started to get back on his feet to pace briefly around our chamber. Then he risked Captain Kanta's wrath by walking through the lower deck where the crew slept.

He pretended I wasn't there when he could and if he couldn't, he spoke briefly and avoided my eyes. He began to interact with the others more, though, and Behenu even convinced him to play a few rounds of *senet* with her. She won every time and accused him of losing deliberately.

Time passed as it always does and eventually the months of our voyage came to an end.

"Land has been sighted," Renni said when he brought our morning meal. "Captain says we are not much more than a day away."

"Truly?" Istnofret asked. "I was beginning to think I would be stuck in this chamber for the rest of my life."

"I will believe land still exists when I have my feet on it," I muttered.

"This will surely be the longest leg of our journey," she said.

"How can you say that when we have no idea where we are going next?" I asked.

"I believe the Eye will be found in Indou. The gods would not have sent us all this way for nothing. Besides, surely there are no inhabited countries which are further from Egypt than Indou."

"Maia said the gods would put obstacles in our path. Would not sending us on an endless chase around the world be an obstacle?"

"Have we not already faced obstacles?" she asked, very quietly. "We have already lost more than I ever expected."

"We are all alive, and we are together. I think the gods have barely begun to make us pay for our arrogance in thinking we might find the Eye."

"If you think it is so arrogant, why do we persist? Why do we not give up and find somewhere to live? I would like a quiet place by the sea."

"Have you so quickly forgotten the situation at home? Ay will not give up the throne unless he is forced to. He will provoke war with the Hittites, if he hasn't already. He will continue to sow fear and division. He will act in nobody's interest but his own."

"But there is no guarantee that whoever is pharaoh next will be any better. What if you find the Eye — if such a thing actually exists — and use it to remove him and then the next pharaoh is even worse?"

"Could anyone be worse?" I suddenly realised what she had said. "You still don't think the Eye exists? Why do you stay with me then? You could leave. Take Renni with you. Find yourselves a seaside village to live in. You do not have to share this burden."

"We cannot leave you," she said, a little fiercely. "At least not until your quest is complete. Whether you find the Eye or not, we will stand with you until it is done. But then, maybe then we will find ourselves a quiet place to settle down."

It saddened me to realise that she was making plans for after she left me. Did she and Renni talk about this late at night after the rest of us were asleep? Did Behenu join in with their planning? Did they motivate themselves to keep going with thoughts of what they would do after it was all over? But of course I had no right to expect that she would stay with me forever. I was no longer queen and I could offer her nothing.

"What do you actually intend to do with the Eye?" Istnofret asked.

"I will take it back to Egypt and..." I suddenly realised that this was where my hopeful plans ended. I couldn't see a path forward after that. "I don't know. I have no idea how it works, what it can do. All I have ever thought is that I will take it home and it will help me to bring down Ay."

"You intend to kill him?" Her voice was little more than a whisper.

"No."

That was a lie. He had tried to kill me after all. He had known I wouldn't survive the slave mines, if I even got that far.

"You don't need the Eye for that," she said. "We would have helped you."

"I am trying to save us. Save Egypt. Restore my father's dynasty. We need a legitimate pharaoh, not one who stole the throne with a forged signature on a marriage certificate. To do those things, I need..." I floundered. My thoughts were confused. I wasn't even entirely sure what my aim was. "I need power. Ay controls the military. I cannot hope to defeat him with mere men. I need something more. I need the power of the gods."

She looked at me steadily.

"Never forget Maia's words, that as you get closer you might want to possess the Eye for your own purposes."

"Will you tell me if you think I have begun to want it for myself?"

She hesitated.

"Speak freely, Ist. I need to know if I can trust you."

"I will tell you, I can promise you that. But I think it unlikely you will pay heed to my words."

"I promise I will listen."

"You think that now, but when the time comes, when the Eye twists your fine intentions into acting for your own good, you might not."

"Then you must make me listen."

"How?" she asked. "Has anyone ever been able to make you do something you do not wish to?"

Her words stung and it was a little while before I could admit their truth, even if only to myself. I had been a queen. I was not accustomed to doing anything I didn't want to.

"I swear I will listen if you tell me."

She tried to hide her doubt, but I could still see it.

"I am not a bad person, Istnofret."

"I never thought you were, but I think you underestimate the power of the Eye."

TWENTY-NINE

We docked at a port called Krokola. I had never heard of it but Renni assured me we were close to our destination. Pawah had told him that Captain Kanta said there was a man, one who had a smaller boat, who could take us in search of the three rivers Maia had spoken of.

"Does Kanta know of these rivers?" I asked.

Renni shook his head. "But he believes this man will."

I didn't like trusting in the knowledge of strangers, but it was no more than we had done through the rest of this journey.

Emerging onto the upper deck was a blissful experience. The sun dazzled me, even though it barely peeped over the horizon. The air was fresh and full of so many scents that for a few moments, I could do nothing other than stand there with my eyes closed. My nose tingled and the air was so clean I could barely stand it. I had to breathe a little more shallowly while I accustomed myself to it.

I had grown used to the confines of our chamber and had stopped noticing how stale and still the air was. I could smell it on myself now, even though I had bathed only yesterday. I carried with me the odour of still air and confined spaces.

I stumbled as I stepped foot on solid land for the first time in months. The air no longer had the crispness of *peret* and I guessed the year had edged into *shemu* — harvest — while we sailed. It was disconcerting to discover the season had changed and I hadn't known. Istnofret clutched my arm, as unsteady on her feet as I was. Even Renni and Intef stumbled a little. Only Behenu seemed unaffected. She had said she grew up by the sea, but I suspected she spent more time on the water than beside it.

The man Captain Kanta sent us in search of was younger than I had expected, perhaps only fifteen or sixteen. He drove a bargain that seemed unnecessarily hard, but when I opened my mouth to object Istnofret nudged me sharply with her elbow and my protests went unsaid. Instead I spent my time wondering how a young man of his age spoke such flawless Egyptian. He shot Behenu a number of admiring glances. She blushed a little and pretended not to notice.

Trishira — for that was his name, or as near as I understood — took us to his boat, which seemed hardly worthy of such a title, being little more than a few planks nailed together with a mast and a much-mended sail. He was in constant motion as we travelled, adjusting the ropes fastened to the sail, straightening our course, and other things that were still a mystery to me after so many months at sea. He and Behenu chatted animatedly.

Jealousy rose within me and I puzzled over why. I had no wish for Trishira to look at me the way he looked at Behenu, and I had no personal interest in the young man. So why did I feel so envious at watching him and Behenu? Because he looked at her the way Intef used to look at me.

Trishira was around the age that Intef had been when I became queen. Years before that, while we were just children, Intef had told me that one day he would be the captain of my personal squad. I had laughed and told him that only the queen had her own guards, but he had insisted.

Over the years, I saw how hard he worked, the way he followed the more experienced soldiers, copying everything they did. If they ran a lap of the city, Intef would run it twice. If they hiked out into the desert to train themselves to survive in that harsh environment, he would do it with half their rations. If they stayed awake for two nights to learn to stay alert without sleep, he would do it for three. Everything they did, he followed behind them and taught himself to do it better, longer, harder, more efficiently. So when I became queen and was assigned my own guards, how could I have asked for anyone other than Intef to be my captain?

My feelings for Intef had been growing for some time. Years if I was honest with myself. But I had spent just as long pushing him away with one excuse after another. He was a servant, a commoner, and bad things happened to people I cared for.

"This is the place you wanted," Trishira called to us from the stern. "Where there are three rivers. You want the southern one, yes?"

The landscape was not that different from Egypt during *shemu*. After the Great River rises up to cover the land, it retreats and leaves behind a rich, black silt in which all manner of things can be easily grown. I assumed all rivers did the same.

Trishira wore something like a *shendyt*, although it was dyed red, with a long piece of cloth wrapped around his head. We sailed past many folk working in their fields who were dressed in the same way. It wasn't until we saw a woman standing on the banks of the river that I realised even the women dressed like this. Like Trishira, she wore a brightly-coloured *shendyt* and shirt with a head wrap. Her *shendyt* was shockingly short but Trishira's lack of interest indicated her dress was not unusual for this place.

The sun was setting by the time we came to the river's end. I was keenly aware of Intef's stare as I allowed Trishira to help me from the boat, and avoided his gaze by looking at the city around us. I had expected it would be something like the little villages that sprawled along the banks of our own river but this was a great city, like Memphis or Thebes or Behdet. There was all manner of buildings although they seemed to be made of mud brick, like my desert city Akhetaten, rather than stone like Memphis. Folk bustled around, going home after work or perhaps running a few errands before sunset. Children played in the street, a game that seemed to involve much shouting and running. It was all so familiar that my heart ached for home.

"Samun?" Istnofret nudged me with her elbow. "Are you well?"

"It is not what I expected. I had thought..." My voice trailed off as I realised there was little I could say without exposing my own prejudices about how primitive I had expected such a faraway country to be. I had not expected Suakin to be very different from Egypt — after all, it was only just across the Red Sea — but I hadn't expected Indou to be so civilised. "It all looks so... normal."

"But somehow exotic at the same time," she said. "The bright colours they wear, those scarves around their heads...." Her voice trailed off as we both caught sight of something that appeared to be a market stall. The wares looked edible but like nothing I had ever seen before and reminded of the *kathal* plant from my friends Dakini, Abha and Bhumi. Istnofret was obviously thinking the same thing.

"Will we see the women you know?" she asked. "The ones who visited with you at the palace some years ago?"

"I think it unlikely." I would have liked to have seen them again. "I have no idea where they live and nor do we have the time to go in search of them."

"I think I would like them, from what you have told me."

"I think you would, too."

Meanwhile, Trishira seemed to be translating a conversation between Renni and another man. As the man left, Renni waved us over.

"There is a hill with a white house in the centre of the city," he said. "It has a grove of bael trees behind it, just as Maia said."

"Let's go then," I said.

"It is at least an hour's walk and we are already out of sunlight. Better that we find lodgings for tonight and go in the morning."

"It has taken us months to get this far," Istnofret said. "And nobody is expecting us. One more night will make no difference. Besides, after all those months at sea, I am longing for a bed on solid ground and a good wash."

Trishira helped us to secure lodgings before he left, but not before a lengthy whispered conversation with Behenu. She blushed prettily and shook her head at whatever he was saying. The man who had agreed to accommodate us led us to his home. It was spacious with a large courtyard leading into the house. He showed us to a chamber and motioned that we should set down our bags, calling all the while over his shoulder to someone else.

Two girls hurried in, carrying large tubs of water, which they set at our feet. As they did, I noticed the designs inked on their hands and was reminded again of my friends from Indou. With much motioning of his hands and shaking of his head, the man indicated that Intef and Renni were to go to another chamber while we women bathed. Then he too left. The two girls waited in the corner, whispering between themselves. As soon as we finished, they swooped in to take the tubs away.

"Do we follow them or wait here?" I asked, quietly. Even though it was clear these people spoke no Egyptian, I still felt uncomfortable that they might overhear us talking about them.

"I think we wait here," Istnofret said. "Someone will come and get us sooner or later."

Mau yowled to be released from her basket so Behenu let her out. The cat prowled around the room and, as always, seemed to judge our lodgings with dismay. I supposed that for a cat who had grown up in the luxury of a queen's chambers, anything else must be a disappointment.

One of the girls reappeared in the doorway, giggling as she motioned for us to follow her. She led us out of the house to the courtyard, where an older woman who looked too much like her to be anything other than her mother was setting out an array of bowls. The aroma was enticing, if unfamiliar, and my stomach grumbled at the prospect of a hot meal that wasn't a watery stew.

The man made noises at us, motioning for us to sit on the blanket with the food. I expected that they would eat with us, but the whole family — the man, the woman, three girls and a young boy — all stood and waited. The man indicated we should eat so I reached for a bowl.

The food was entirely foreign. There were little white

grains which seemed to have no real taste of their own, fish cooked in a creamy sauce, an orange-coloured fruit sliced into thin strips. Its sweetness made my mouth tingle and I eagerly reached for more. Even the bread tasted different and it was flat as if it had failed to rise. The girls passed us mugs of creamy liquid. Everyone else drank with enthusiasm, but I found the aroma off-putting. I sipped it hesitantly, but disliked its sweet-sour taste and set my mug aside.

"Perhaps we should go find the white house?" I said.

"Not tonight, Samun," Renni said. He sounded lazy, or perhaps just content, as he lay back on his cushion and accepted another mug of the sweet-sour drink. "I will go with you first thing tomorrow."

"But we have travelled so long to get here," I said. "Don't you want to know whether we can find the person Maia said would be there?"

"I am not going anywhere until I have had some sleep," Istnofret said. "And I want another bath and a change of clothes. I feel like I am still crusted in salt."

I didn't want to wait when we could possibly have the answer tonight, but I could hardly go searching through a strange city on my own after dark. I reached for another slice of the orange fruit. Tomorrow would be soon enough.

THIRTY

R enni was true to his word and when I woke shortly after dawn he was already up and waiting.

"We can go now and be back in time for breakfast," he said.

Istnofret had just woken and still lay on her bed mat.

"Wait a few minutes and I will come with you," she called.

She stretched and yawned and didn't look like she would be ready quickly.

"Stay here," I said. "There is no need for you to hurry. We will be back soon."

"We don't know the customs of the people here," she said. "It may not be appropriate for you to be escorted only by Renni. What if women should be accompanied by their waiting lady?"

"Since I have no ladies these days, that will not be possible," I answered, rather tartly. "If we sense that it is not appropriate for me to be out with Renni, we will return to fetch you. In the meantime, stay here and rest. It would be best if Intef were not left alone yet. Where is he, by the way?"

"Outside in the courtyard," Renni said. "Don't worry. He is well. He wanted to sit in the sun."

"I will go sit with him." Istnofret tossed aside her blanket and began rising from her mat.

"Behenu is with him," Renni said. "She took Mau out for some fresh air."

"So I am not needed." Istnofret sat back down. "Well, that is something I never thought to hear."

"Will you rest for a while?" I asked. "How often do you get a chance to lie in bed after the sun has risen?"

She lay down but rolled onto her side, putting her back to Renni and I. Renni motioned for me to follow him out.

"Let's go," he said, once we were out of earshot. "Leave her be for a bit and she will be fine."

"I didn't mean to offend her."

I had meant to be considerate in suggesting she stay in bed a while longer.

We made our way through the city and soon enough I saw ahead of us a hill. The white house that perched on its plateau must command a fabulous view. This had to be the house we had come to Indou in search of.

"Go to the place where the ocean splits into three rivers," I said quietly to myself. "Follow the southern-most river to the end and you will find a white house which sits on a hill. Behind the house stands a grove of bael trees. This is where you will find her."

"I have gone through it a hundred times myself."

I hadn't thought I spoke loudly enough for Renni to hear.

"I am certain this is the house we seek," he said.

"It is not the house we need but the trees."

"Find the house and you will find the trees."

It took longer than I expected to reach the hill. The walk left me far too fatigued after having spent the last couple of months sitting in a ship. I should have spent that time keeping up my strength. I could have asked Renni to show me some exercises to keep myself strong in such a small space. Instead I had whiled away the days playing games and telling tales. I was panting by the time we reached the top of the hill.

"I suppose we should go up to the house," Renni said. "Introduce ourselves and see if we can figure out who we are looking for."

Off to the side of the house, I spied a familiar pebbled path and my dream from months ago suddenly came back to me, the one where I ran along that same path. I stared at it for a long moment. The dream was hazy in my memory, but I remembered thinking I was too late.

"No," I said. "We need to find the trees."

Despite my tired legs, I raced along the path. The sense of urgency was building. Why hadn't I come last night? My sandal caught on the pebbles and 'I tripped, saved at the last moment by Renni grabbing my arm.

"Slow down," he said. "The trees will still be there if you walk."

I shook him off and hurried on. It was not the trees I had come for.

I rounded the corner and there it was: a grove of tall, many-leaved trees growing closely together. Beneath the trees stood a woman. Her back was to us and all I could see was the bright colours of her skirt and her long, dark hair. It was all wrong, though. She was supposed to be sitting on a wooden bench. That was what my dream had showed me. This was not the woman I was meant to find.

She must have heard us approaching, for she turned. Her face was swollen and streaked with tears, but I still knew her.

"Ankhesenamun?" She wiped the tears from her face and spoke in Akkadian. "I must be delusional."

"Dakini." I stopped just in front of her. "I am sorry to arrive unexpected."

"You are too late, I am afraid." Dakini stepped aside and I saw behind her a long pit heaped with dirt. "We buried her this morning."

I looked from Dakini to the pit. My mouth opened and closed, but I couldn't force out any words.

"You did not know?" she asked. "I thought that must be why you are here. But of course not. There is no way word could have reached you. You were already on your way here before it happened."

"But who?" I asked. "Who is it?"

"Bhumi. She bore a child not ten days ago. She seemed well enough, if fatigued. But two days ago she became ill and late last night she died. I thought she was improving, right up until her last moments. She asked to come out here, to sit under the trees and the stars. This is where she died. We do not normally bury our dead, but it was her wish to lie here beneath the trees."

"Bhumi."

Grief filled me as I stared down at the pit. I didn't know the three sister-wives well — Dakini, Bhumi, Abha. They had visited Memphis once and I had entertained them for lunch. We had written letters since, but I had not seen them in person again. But my dream had shown I would be too late. It was Bhumi I was meant to find. Bhumi as she sat on a bench beneath the trees in those last moments before she went to the West.

"I am sorry I did not arrive earlier."

Dakini would make her own assumptions from my words and she would be at least partly correct.

"Come." She seemed to shake off her grief as she leaned in to hug me. "You are not here to watch me cry. Come into the house. We will have some refreshments and you will tell me why you are here."

I followed her back along the pebbled path. The house was large and airy, clearly the home of a wealthy man. I couldn't remember the word the sister-wives had used to describe him, but he was something like a king, or an important leader of some sort. Dakini called out in her own language and servants came running to offer me plump cushions and a mug of the same sweet-sour drink our hosts had offered last night. Renni sat on a cushion beside me and drank from his mug with relish. I took a sip or two to be polite, then set it aside.

"It was a boy," Dakini said. "Bhumi's fourth son. She was so proud to be able to give our husband another son."

"The babe. Is he well?"

Dakini averted her face and there was a long pause before she replied.

"We buried him with her. He sickened the day before she did."

"Oh." I hardly knew what to say. "I had assumed she died from the birth."

"She died of a broken heart."

"Poor Bhumi."

When Abha entered the chamber, I hardly recognised her, her face was so pale. There were dark shadows under her eyes and she was far skinnier than I remembered.

"Ankhesenamun." Abha gave me a ghost of a smile. "I did not know you were here."

"I am sorry to arrive unexpected, and at such a sad time."

Abha sat on a cushion and a servant rushed at her with a mug.

"Dakini has told you?"

"I am so sorry. I would have liked to have seen her again."

"It is a shame you did not arrive a day earlier," Abha said. "Yesterday afternoon she seemed to rally. She was talking and was much brighter, but after we took her outside, she went quiet. She did not speak again. She sat out there for an hour, with Dakini and I on either side of her, and then she asked to lie down with her head in my lap. I did not even realise when she died. I thought she had just fallen asleep."

"Such a sad thing," I said.

"But tell us." Dakini sat up straighter. "If you did not come for Bhumi, why you are here? You must have had quite a journey."

"I have." I hardly knew where to start. Had I written to tell them about Tutankhamun? "My brother-husband has gone to the West."

They made sorrowful noises and I waved them away.

"It was months ago."

I had lost track of the days and weeks as we travelled, but he had died in early *akhet* and it must be at least *shemu* by now. Seven or eight months had passed, at the least.

I told them about that first part of my journey and how the Medjay had rescued me. About how we had gone to Behdet, then the walk overland to Leucus Limen, the ship to Suakin where we were beset by pirates and Intef was injured, and the journey to Indou.

"Intef is the chief of your guards?" Dakini asked.

"My captain, yes."

"I remember him," she said. "Very serious-faced and very handsome."

"And now sadly one-armed," Abha added, her voice mournful. "Poor Intef."

"He is recovering."

I wanted to say he was recovering well, but that would be a falsehood. Intef lived, but begrudgingly. And he would probably never forgive me for what I had done, either for cutting off his arm or for refusing to tell him I loved him. I hesitated to say more about Intef in front of Renni, but he seemed to be paying no attention to our conversation and at length I realised he probably spoke no Akkadian. Of course, a soldier, and the son of a soldier, would not have had any opportunity to learn the language of diplomats.

"Where are your other companions?" Dakini asked. "We will send for them. You must all stay here."

I hesitated to accept. Her offer was generous and much welcome, but we would be intruding at such a sad time. I jumped as Dakini called out in her own language. Several servants came running. She issued some brief instructions and they turned expectantly to Renni.

"They will help you carry your things," Dakini said. "Go now so that you can be back before nightfall. Ankhesenamun and we will spend some time catching up."

I relayed her words to Renni and he shot me a worried look. I knew exactly what he was thinking: that Intef would never forgive him if he left me here alone.

"I am with friends," I said. "Go."

He left, although reluctantly, trailed by the servants.

"Now that we three are alone," Dakini said. "Why are you here? You have spoken about being sent away from Memphis and about where you went after that, but you have not explained what possessed you to travel all the way to Indou."

"I am searching for something."

How much to tell? Could I trust them? I suddenly decided to tell them everything. After all, I had followed Maia's instructions and they had led me here. The dream, too, indicated I was supposed to be here. I had found a woman in the grove of trees, and even if she was not the woman I was meant to find, she was someone I considered a friend. Surely that was no coincidence.

"There is an artefact. It is very old and very dangerous. It is supposed to give power to the one who possesses it."

"What kind of power?" Dakini's tone gave no indication of whether or not she believed me.

"Ultimate power. There are tales of this artefact, things it has done. Strange and unexpected things."

"You do not seem like the sort of person who would crave power," she said.

"I don't want it for myself. I want it for Egypt."

They waited, watching me. I took a deep breath and hurriedly said the rest.

"I intend to use it to remove Ay."

They barely reacted other than a flicker of an eye from Abha.

"I can still save Egypt. Save my people. Keep us from war with the Hittites."

I was pleading with them to understand, but they weren't shaking their heads or telling me I wanted too much. It was Dakini who finally spoke.

"So why come to Indou? Surely you do not think this artefact is here?"

"Not necessarily, but this was where I was told to go."

"To Indou?"

"No, here. To this house. I was told to find the place where the ocean splits into three rivers. I was to follow the southern-most one to a white house on a hill. Behind the house would be a grove of bael trees and there I would find a woman who could give me the next clue."

Dakini regarded me seriously and shook her head. "I am sorry, Ankhesenamun, but I have never heard of such a thing before."

"It was not you I was meant to find. It was Bhumi. The woman was supposed to be sitting on a bench beneath the trees. I was meant to be here last night."

"If that is all true, then there is some strange magic at work," Dakini said. "Maybe Bhumi was expecting you. Maybe that is why she wanted to sit out there. Of the three of us, she was the one with the most interest in myths and other old tales. If anyone here might know of such an artefact as that you seek, it would have been her."

I made myself breathe calmly. In and out. Had we come all this way for nothing? Had Maia been wrong? My dream had warned I would be too late. I should have made the connection earlier. I should have been here yesterday. It took me some time to gather my senses and realise how rude I was being in not replying.

"Never mind," I said. "I will keep searching. There must be a clue here somewhere. But let's not talk about that anymore. Tell me what else has been happening."

Dakini spoke of mostly inconsequential things, with the occasional input from Abha. I let their words drift over me, smiling when they did, and once laughing because they did, but I barely noticed any of it. There had to be a clue. Maia had not sent me here for nothing. Surely the gods wouldn't have led me all this way only to dash my hopes at the last moment. There must be someone in Indou who had the knowledge I sought. Eventually Dakini's chatter faded away.

"Ankhesenamun, have you heard anything I have said?" she asked.

I gave her a guilty smile.

"Forgive me. I am tired and I have not eaten yet today. It is hard to concentrate."

"It has been a long day, for all of us. As soon as your friends arrive, we will eat and then go to bed. Tomorrow is a new day."

THIRTY-ONE

The others arrived soon after and I noticed for the first time how pale and quiet they were. We were all exhausted. They sank gratefully onto the soft cushions and Dakini was as hospitable to them as to me, even though she spoke no language in common with them. After a meal that was little short of a feast, Dakini showed us to the chambers that had been prepared for us, one for the women and another for the men. Reed mats and soft blankets awaited us, along with large bowls of water for washing. There was even a blanket for Mau. A girl brought in an armload of bright fabric.

"I have no doubt you need fresh clothes," Dakini said. "I will send one of my serving girls in the morning to help you dress."

She departed with many wishes for peaceful sleep.

Behenu lay down with a huge yawn.

"I am too tired to care about washing tonight. I feel like I could sleep for a month."

She seemed to fall asleep instantly. Istnofret and I stayed up long enough to wash. The water was fresh and warm, and I wished the bowls were large enough to climb into. Istnofret inspected the bundle of cloth, which seemed to be comprised of many long pieces of fabric in brilliant shades of red, yellow, blue and pink.

"They wrap these around their bodies." She held up a piece of bright cloth. "I will definitely need someone to help me with this. I am afraid I won't secure it properly and my clothes will fall right off."

I laughed a little at the thought of Istnofret suddenly finding herself naked in front of everyone.

"Sadeh definitely would have made sure hers would fall off," she said, and my laughter died.

"She would have thought it a fine joke."

I blinked away the tears that filled my eyes but not fast enough to hide them from Istnofret.

"She would have been so proud of you. Going off on this seemingly impossible quest to find a way to save Egypt."

"I have not found anything useful yet."

"But you are trying, and whether you succeed or fail, we know how hard you tried. How much you gave."

An image of Intef came to my mind, lying on his mat in our chamber in Suakin with his ruined arm swathed in bandages.

"I have given nothing so far. It is those around me who are paying for my arrogance."

"You still call this arrogance? Searching for an amulet that might save the world?"

"It is arrogance to think the gods will permit me to find such a thing, let alone wield it."

"Then why persist? There are jewels enough left that we could go anywhere you wanted. We could live very comfortably for the rest of our lives instead of going from ship to miserable ship."

"I cannot give up. I must try. If the Eye exists, I will find it."

"And that is why Sadeh would be proud."

I lay down on my mat and stared up at the ceiling. After so long at sea, it was strange to not feel the ship rocking gently beneath me or to hear water sloshing against its sides. The only sounds were of servants chattering quietly, the cricking and croaking of night-time insects, and Mau making little snuffly noises in her sleep.

"It is my fault," I said, very quietly. "If I had stood up to the advisors earlier and more often, none of this would have happened. I am no hero. I am merely trying to fix my own mistakes."

I waited, but Istnofret didn't reply. She must have fallen asleep before I spoke. I stared up at the ceiling for a long time before I too fell asleep.

I slept late the next morning and woke to find myself alone in our chamber. My heart was heavy with the knowledge that after travelling so far, we had failed to find the clue Maia sent us in search of. I lingered in bed for some time, not wanting to face the others. Would they be angry that I had led them all this way for nothing? What would we do now? Find another ship and spend months confined to its bowels as we travelled back to Egypt?

Someone had thoughtfully left a fresh bowl of water for me. I didn't know how to put on the strange clothes Dakini had left so I wore my own gown, although now acutely conscious of how stained and odorous it was.

I found the others lingering in the chamber where we had eaten last night. They all wore brightly-coloured wraps, although only Behenu seemed comfortable in the odd garments. The remains of a morning meal were scattered in front of them and the scent of fresh bread lingered in the air. Despite my misery, my stomach growled.

"Ankhesenamun." Dakini waved me over. "Come, sit. We put some food aside for you as it seemed your friends were going to eat everything in the house."

She laughed and I managed a smile. Even as I seated myself on a cushion, a servant girl was already placing a bowl in front of me and another came bearing a plate of flat bread. The bowl contained chunks of fruit that I instantly recognised as *kathal*, like the plant they had given me, with more of the tiny white grains which Dakini called rice.

As I ate, the others began to drift away. Behenu took Mau for a prowl around the gardens. Istnofret and Renni slipped away together. Intef disappeared without a word, but I was heartened by how much stronger he seemed. Dakini finally left with many excuses about needing to oversee the servants. Eventually it was just Abha and me.

"You don't have to sit with me," I said to her. "I don't mind eating by myself."

"Actually I was hoping to speak with you privately," she said.

I shot her a glance, noticing how wan she was. Her eyes were large and the dark shadows under them suggested she hadn't been sleeping much.

"Were you close to Bhumi?" I asked.

"We were like sisters. It does not always work this well when a man takes multiple wives. Sometimes there is jealousy and competition amongst the women. But for us, there has never been any of that. We were determined that if we must spend the rest of our lives together, we should at least be friends. So we worked hard at that and eventually we became sisters too."

"Bhumi is a great loss to both you and Dakini. I see that."

Did their husband feel her loss so strongly? I had seen no sign of him yet and couldn't even remember the man's name.

"Yes, but she may yet be able to give you the information you seek."

"The Eye?" I sat up straighter and set my bowl aside. "She mentioned it to you?"

"Never, or if she did, she did not call it that. But I could not sleep last night so I looked through her correspondences. She wrote many letters to people all over the world. They discussed all sorts of things: poetry, mathematics, astronomy, magic. Bhumi was the smartest of us three and she was always seeking out someone new to learn from."

"I did not know that."

How little I knew these women. I wished I had time to linger here with them.

"She was never happier than when she received a reply from a new contact and could learn about something new. A couple of years ago she began corresponding with a woman named Shala. Her husband works in an archive."

"Go on."

"Her husband, I forget his name, would often tell her about new documents they had received. Some recorded historical events. This king came to the throne in that year. This army fought that army. Others recorded stories that someone thought too important to risk being forgotten. Tales of how the world began, of the gods and goddesses that used to walk the earth with us. Of heroes who lived so long ago that nobody is even quite certain whether they were real."

I swallowed down my impatience. Trying to hurry her might only irritate her and then she might decide not to tell me after all.

"Bhumi delighted in each new story, each historical event she had never before heard of. She poured over Shala's letters for hours."

Her voice wavered a little and her eyes filled with tears.

"A new letter arrived from Shala yesterday morning. Bhumi was too weak to read it so I set it by her bed, intending to read it to her later, but then..."

Her voice had started to tremble and she paused to gather herself, then unrolled the scroll she clutched. I hadn't even noticed it until then.

"It begins with my dear Bhumi. I delighted to receive your news last week. How wonderful to hear that you will soon bear another babe. I could feel your joy through your words. Every morning I pray to Gula that you will deliver the babe safely. I anxiously await news of his birth.

"I have a new tale for you and I know you will find this one greatly fascinating. I visited my husband at his work last week and he was most excited, for he had been reading some old scrolls which had not been touched in many, many years. One was in the Egyptian language of pictures and it has taken him some months to find somebody who could read them. Eventually he found a very old man who translated the scroll for him.

"It told of a time many generations ago, before the Two Lands were united into one. There were two rival tribes who both wanted to possess the same territory. Each tribe sent their leaders to talk to the other tribe, but they could not agree on which tribe would settle on the land they both wanted, and which tribe would go somewhere else. At length they decided that the only way they would decide the argument was to fight each other. The tribe that surrendered first would find other land to live on. If nobody surrendered, they would fight until all of the men of one tribe were killed. Then the land would belong to the tribe that still had men living.

"All of the men in both tribes agreed that this would be the best way of settling their argument. The women in both tribes disagreed. They argued with their men, but the men would not listen. They cajoled and scolded, but still the men would not listen. So they decided that if their men would not cease their foolishness, it would be up to the women to solve the question of who settled on the coveted land.

"The women of one tribe got down on their knees and begged the gods to intervene. They asked the gods to do something to convince the men not to fight. That night, all of the men in that tribe sickened. By morning, they were lying on their backs, with their hands clutched to their bellies, groaning and moaning that they were going to die.

"Alarmed, the women got down on their knees again and begged the gods to stop. They had only wanted to teach the men a lesson, not to kill them. The gods listened to the women and allowed the men to recover. As soon as the men were well, they again began making plans to fight.

"Then the women of the other tribe got down on their knees and begged the gods to intervene. They promised that if the gods would stop the men of the two tribes from fighting each other, they would give over their most beautiful woman to the god who helped them. While they were still on their knees, a falcon flew down from the sky and landed in front of them. The falcon turned into a man and they knew he was indeed a god."

"Horus," I breathed.

"Shala does not name him. The god demanded that they bring out the woman who had been promised if he stopped their men from going to war. When the god saw her, he immediately fell in love and asked her to marry him. She said she would only marry him if he stopped the men from fighting.

"So the god reached up and plucked out his own eye. He handed it to the woman and said that it would bestow power on whoever possessed it. The women used the god's eye to stop the men from fighting and make them agree they would all share the land. They married the daughters of their leader to the sons of the other tribe's leader. When the god saw that peace had been restored, he took the beautiful woman away to marry her and the two tribes lived in harmony for the rest of their lives."

"How did it work?" I asked. "How did they use the Eye to stop the fighting?"

"Shala does not say. She finishes her letter there with good wishes to Bhumi and the health of her babe."

Her voice wobbled again and she drew in a deep breath to steady herself.

"Does she say nothing more about the Eye? What happened to it after the women used it?"

"That is the end of her letter. I could write to her, if you like. I need to tell her about Bhumi anyway. I could ask if she knows anything more about this Eye, as you call it."

"Where does she live? I cannot afford to wait months for her reply."

"Babylon."

The world shifted around me. I should have known I would end up in Babylon. It brought me all the way back around to Sadeh who had given her life for me, and my suggestion that she should go to Babylon.

"I must go there," I said.

Maybe Maia had been corresponding with Shala? Although how these two women on different continents could have ever met, I had no idea. And even if Maia was the source of this story, how would she know that Shala would tell Bhumi?

"Do you know a woman called Maia?" I asked. "She is Egyptian. She was my brother's wet nurse many years ago. Now she is a Daughter of Isis."

"The name is not familiar to me," Abha said. "But Bhumi used to write to an Egyptian woman. Let me see if I can remember her name."

I waited while she thought.

"Hammat, perhaps?" she said, at last.

I shook my head, disappointed, but she raised her finger to forestall any comment.

"No, wait, that is not quite right. Hemmet?"

"Hemetre?" Even as I said it, I was sure it couldn't be.

"Yes, yes, Hemetre. How could I have forgotten. She is a, uh—"

"Priestess?"

"Yes. You know her?"

I was almost speechless with the connections I was barely beginning to understand. Hemetre knew Bhumi. Maia must have known Shala. But if that was true, then Hemetre had lied to me. She had known more about the Eye than she had revealed. And how had Maia known to send me to Bhumi? How could she have known that Shala would pass on the story about Horus and his eye?

"Did Hemetre ever tell Bhumi about the Eye?" I asked.

"If she did, Bhumi never mentioned it. But then she didn't necessarily tell me about every letter she received, only the ones that excited her the most."

"You do not think she would have been excited to learn about an artefact of such power?"

Abha seemed undisturbed by my question. "Perhaps it was

not the first time she had heard of such a thing, or perhaps she gave it little credence. Maybe Hemetre never even mentioned it."

"It seems a strange coincidence that Hemetre and Bhumi were in communication and then I subsequently find myself here after following instructions from another Daughter of Isis."

"What exactly is a Daughter of Isis?" Abha asked. "I know that Isis is one of your Egyptian goddesses. Bhumi told me about how she was married to her brother who she had to resurrect after another god chopped him into pieces. But she did not mention Isis having a daughter and you use the phrase as a title."

"The Daughters serve Isis and work to protect her people. They were watching over me, trying to keep me safe. I know little about them, though. I do not even know how many there are."

"Bhumi loved secret societies. She would have particularly liked one that protected women. I am not surprised to learn she was in communication with someone from such an organisation."

"Are you sure she never mentioned it?"

"I am certain," Abha said. "But as I said, she did not share all of the contents of her letters. Bhumi had her own agenda and she never revealed it, even to her sister-wives."

"Perhaps she knew more about the Eye than she told you," I said.

"That would not surprise me at all."

THIRTY-TWO

I didn't see the others again until the evening meal. When I told them of my intention to go to Babylon, Istnofret looked despairing. Renni shook his head, Intef frowned. Only Behenu was nonplussed.

"It is not that far from here," she said.

"You know how to get there?" I asked.

"We will need another ship. It is east of here, sort of. I think."

"How do you know?" I asked.

She gave me a steady look. "It is close to Syria."

Of course. And Behenu would likely leave us soon. She would come with us to Babylon, since that would take her closer to home, but we would undoubtedly part ways there. I was surprised at how much that disappointed me.

"Must you leave so soon?" Dakini asked. "Surely there is no reason to hurry. You are not yet recovered from your journey."

She gave us all disapproving looks but reserved the longest for Intef. Did she really want to give Intef more time to recover or did she just want him around for longer? I pushed my uncharitable thought away. Dakini and Abha had been nothing but hospitable.

"We must go," I said. "We have no information about how bad things might be at home. We cannot afford to dally."

"We have had some news of Egypt," Dakini said. "I am so sorry. I assumed you already knew. There was some incident between the Egyptian army and that of the Hittites. Folk say the Egyptians killed one of the sons of the Hittite king right under his nose. That the Egyptians sent assassins to Hattusa and killed the prince in his own bed. The two countries have been on the brink of war for months."

"Do you know anything else?" I asked. "Have they fought?"

"A few skirmishes from what we have heard. Border patrol forces running into each other and clashing. There is talk of war but if it has happened, the news has not yet reached us."

"That is not what happened," I said, almost absently. "Zannanza was killed on Egyptian soil, not in his bed."

"Do you know that for a fact? We have heard from several sources that he was killed in Hattusa."

"I was still in Memphis when it happened. It was a terrible misunderstanding."

Would she think less of me if I told her that Zannanza was on his way to marry me and become Pharaoh?

"That certainly shows events in a different light," she said. "The Hittites must be spreading propaganda to make Egypt look bad."

"But why is Egypt not countering this story with the truth?"

Few people knew why Zannanza was in Egypt, but to reveal that he was on Egyptian soil showed his death in a very different light than to let people believe he had been murdered in his bed.

"Perhaps they have determined there is some strategic advantage to not revealing the truth," Dakini said.

She didn't ask why Zannanza had been killed. At least it saved me from having to decide how much to reveal.

"Our husband knows many merchants," she said. "I will ask if he knows of someone who is travelling to Babylon."

"We must be on the next ship going in that direction," I said. "Even if it cannot take us all the way."

"If you wait a few days, there will be someone who can take you. Merchant, trader, ambassador." She shrugged to suggest it didn't matter. "Better that you wait a few days and travel with someone our husband knows. It will be safer that way."

"We can look after ourselves." I tried to tamp down my offence at her suggestion but then remembered Intef's arm. He would need to learn to fight all over again. "But if your husband knows someone who will be travelling soon, we would appreciate the chance to go with them."

It took two days before Dakini's husband was able to locate someone who was about to sail to Babylon. She told us at the evening meal.

"He leaves tomorrow." Dakini gave me a sorrowful look. "Perhaps you would wait for the next ship?"

"We must go with him," I said.

"What is his business in Babylon?" Renni asked.

Once it would have been Intef who asked such questions, but he was staring down at his bowl and said nothing. I translated Renni's question into Akkadian for Dakini.

"He is a merchant," Dakini said. "He trades the most exquisite glass beads, as well as very fine cotton."

I relayed her words to Renni.

"I assume he will have soldiers on board to guard his cargo?" he asked.

"Of course. But he would not refuse an offer of additional men to aid them." She looked at Intef, including him in her reply to Renni, even though she knew neither could understand her.

"I am sure we can come to an agreement," Renni said. "I understand it is not much more than a week's journey from here."

"You would sail along the coast until you reach the mighty River Euphrates. Babylon is about halfway along it. But, of course, you have your own Great River. You might not think the Euphrates quite as mighty as we do."

Her tone was jesting and I offered a half-hearted smile to show I had understood the joke. Renni, however, countered her claim with details of why our river was the greatest in the world, and they sparred back and forth for a while, keeping me well occupied with translating their conversation.

"We are getting closer, Samun," Istnofret said, quietly, once Renni and Dakini finally fell silent. "I am sure of it. There is something that feels very right about this. The Eye will be found in Babylon."

"I am not so sure." But I, too, felt the rightness about going to Babylon, even if it was without Sadeh. "I expect the gods will tease us a while yet."

"But where else is there to go?" Her tone was despairing. "We have travelled over most of the known world. Are we to sail to the ends of the world to see what lies beyond the horizon? Are we to travel to the underworld itself?"

I suddenly remembered my dream from years ago, where I offered up a babe to a green-faced man. Of course, at the time I knew neither that Osiris was the god of the underworld or that he was typically depicted with a green face. Having grown up under Aten's rays, I knew no god but him at that point. Perhaps I would indeed travel to Osiris's domain. I placed a hand on my belly. There was no child inside of me. That was the only thing I was certain of, and that alone told me that my journey was nowhere near over.

THIRTY-THREE

Our new captain spoke neither Egyptian nor Akkadian. He issued a stream of instructions, waited only long enough for us to nod uncertainly, and walked away.

"Where do you suppose he wants us to go?" Istnofret asked.

"The hatch is that way." Renni pointed. "We will find an out-of-the way place for ourselves. I guess it doesn't matter whether we can understand him or not. We are familiar enough by now with what a captain expects, especially of the women. If you three keep below deck, I doubt that will make him unhappy."

The area below deck was crammed full of so many crates that we could scarcely slip between the rows of them, let alone find space enough to lie down. It seemed this captain's men must sleep above deck.

"Do we dare go back up?" I asked. "He might put us straight off the ship."

"There is really nowhere at all for you down here," Renni said. "Those boxes will shift as we sail and you may well be crushed if you sit in between them. I cannot think that this would be his intention. Come back up and we will find a place where you will be as out of sight as possible."

We found such a spot and settled ourselves there, although not without many a nervous glance towards the captain. He paid us no attention as the ship set sail. It was only once we were out in deeper water and the ship had caught the breeze that I started to relax. Surely if the captain objected to us being within sight, he would have said something by now. Being up here with the sun on my face and the breeze against my skin was infinitely more pleasant than being stuck below deck.

We kept the coast in sight as we sailed. With nobody else onboard who spoke either of the languages we knew, we had no way of telling where we were until the ship left the deeper waters and sailed into the mouth of a river. I could see why Dakini had called the Euphrates mighty although it was nothing compared to our Great River.

The landscape we sailed past was lusher than any I had seen before. Everywhere was tall trees, thick grass and lush crops. Surely the people who lived in this area didn't have to labour to feed themselves the way we Egyptians did. They must merely walk outside and harvest whatever food they desired.

The city the ship docked at a week later looked little like any I had seen before. It stretched further than we could see. Paved paths led between mud brick buildings, but that was the only familiar thing. There was greenery everywhere I looked. I recognised date, fig and pomegranate, but most of the other trees were unfamiliar. Flowers of types I had never before seen bloomed everywhere.

"It is amazing," Istnofret whispered to me.

"I can hardly believe it," I said. "I thought Memphis was large but this... this must be many times its size."

Ahead of us, a great stepped monument reached up into the sky. Its terraced layers were covered in trees, bushes and even flower gardens.

"Is that what the *mir* look like?" I asked. Istnofret was the only one of us to have seen the enormous monuments which were guarded by a giant Horus of the Horizon.

"Only in their scale," Istnofret said. "But the sides of the *mir* are smooth and there are no plants. I thought the *mir* were incredible, but this is something I could never have imagined."

The men and women who hurried past us wore something like a *shendyt* with a shawl around their shoulders. I no longer found it shocking to see women with their lower legs exposed. It was not until we stood on the dock that I was close enough to see the fringes and coloured beads that decorated their clothes. Wearing the brightly-coloured wraps Dakini had provided, we were clearly foreigners.

A young man, who I recognised as one of the crew, approached and said something in his own language. We looked at him blankly, but he smiled and waved his hands at us.

"I think he is telling us to stay here," Behenu said.

So we waited. I reached out to touch a fragrant white blossom and its yellow centre left a powdery residue on my fingers. Eventually a young woman who was dressed in the native garb approached us. She smiled and bowed repeatedly, and when she spoke it was almost a shock to hear a language I understood.

"I am Shala," she said in Akkadian. "Come, I will take you to my home."

She began walking away and we hurried to follow her.

"Shala?" I asked. "The same Shala who was corresponding with Bhumi?"

"The very same," she said. "I am much saddened to hear of her death."

"How did you know we were here?" I asked.

"Abha sent a message with the captain," Shala said. "He sent a boy to find me as soon as you docked."

"Can you help us?"

There didn't seem much point in going with her if she knew nothing.

Shala shot me a glance.

"Abha did not tell me what you wanted, only that you had questions about something I had told Bhumi. We can talk more in private."

Shala's home was modest, especially compared to some of those we had passed, but lush gardens around the house made it a cool and welcoming retreat. We eagerly followed her inside.

"Please," Shala said. "Remove your sandals. I will bring water for you to bathe your feet."

She left us in the entry and hurried away. I assumed she meant she would send servants, but a few minutes later it was Shala herself who returned bearing a large shallow basin and several towels. After we had washed our feet, Shala led us to a chamber which was comfortably appointed with cushions and low tables, and a large window to capture the breeze. Despite the foreignness outside, this chamber didn't look so different from what I was accustomed to and I settled onto a cushion with a sigh of relief.

Shala soon returned with a tray bearing a mug for each of us, a plate of bread, and a large bowl of purple berries. I sipped from my mug, pleased to find it was a barley beer. I hadn't realise how parched my throat was. I drained my mug and Shala refilled it quickly. Istnofret was eagerly eating a handful of the little berries. I took one before she could eat them all and found it to be sweet and juicy. With beer and food in my belly, I began to relax. Intef, Renni and Behenu busied themselves with the food and even Mau didn't look as dissatisfied as usual. Shala had left us again and from elsewhere in the house came the sounds of pots and utensils clattering.

"This is very pleasant, is it not?" Istnofret said. "It has been some time since I have felt so comfortable anywhere."

"I was thinking the same thing," I said. "This is not so different from home."

"And yet we are such a long way away," she said. "It seems strange, knowing that people so far away live so much like us."

"I don't know what I expected," I said. "I don't think I had ever thought about it before."

"And yet look out that window there," Istnofret said. "You cannot mistake this for anything other than a foreign country."

We stopped talking when Shala returned, for it felt rude to be discussing the foreignness of her home, even in our own language.

"Did Abha send any news with you?" Shala asked. "The boy relayed a brief message of Bhumi's passing but no details."

"She sent a letter for you," I said. "I will go get it."

"You can give it to me later." She waved at me to stay seated. "In the meantime, tell me, why are you here?"

I hesitated, unsure how to launch into my story. I hadn't quite expected to be telling her so soon.

"We are searching for an artefact that we believe originally came from Egypt. Abha thought you might know of it because your last letter to Bhumi mentioned it."

Shala frowned at me.

"I do not believe I have ever mentioned such a thing to Bhumi, not least in my last letter. I did, however, relay an old Egyptian tale to her. It was something my husband had come across in his work at the archives."

"It is exactly that tale we come in search of. We seek an artefact called the Eye of Horus. The tale you sent to Bhumi is the first confirmation we have found of its origin."

"I am afraid I can tell you nothing more," Shala said. "If Abha has read my letter to you, which I assume she has, then that is the entirety of my husband's knowledge on the matter."

"Could we ask him about it? There might be other details he did not think were significant enough to tell you about, but they might well help us to find the Eye."

"You believe the tale of the falcon god is about this eye you seek?"

"The falcon god is Horus," I said. "He is one of the most ancient of our gods and yes, I do believe that the story you sent Bhumi is about the Eye."

"And why do you seek such a thing?" She smiled a little. "What use could the shrivelled eye of a god have for you, even if such a thing still survived? Surely that tale was thousands of years old. It would not be possible for the god's eye to still be in existence. I know of no preservation method that would allow such a thing to last for so long. That is assuming there is any truth at all to the tale of a god meddling in human affairs."

I tried not to feel insulted. Shala's earnestness told me that she wasn't trying to offend. I knew nothing of what manner of gods the Babylonians believed in. Perhaps they had no gods at all. I could hardly fathom such a thing. Could barely imagine what it would be like to not know that Isis was merely a prayer away, to not have grown up knowing that whenever Aten's rays touched my skin, he saw me. It was a baffling concept and for some moments I couldn't reply.

"I have offended you." Shala's tone was more curious than contrite. "What exactly was it that caused such offence?"

I struggled with how to respond without offending her in return.

"It was because you suggested that Horus might not exist," I said, at length.

"I have no idea whether he exists or no. My interest is purely academic. I am, however, interested to know what you make of the tale. This is the sort of thing that Bhumi and I discussed, and I will miss her letters on such topics. I would welcome the chance to correspond with you on such things."

"I do not know where we are going, and thus I cannot leave any address for you to write me at."

"But you know where I am," she said. "And perhaps when you settle down again, you might write to me. I am sure that on your travels you will encounter all manner of new tales. I would love for you to share them with me."

"I will write to you. Later. Once we have found what we seek and have put things right again."

"Then tell me, and I will see if there is anything I can do to help. Where do you believe this eye to be located?"

"I have no idea. We went to Indou because we were told that someone there could tell us where to go next. But Bhumi had already died by the time we arrived. We were fortunate that Abha read your letter and realised it contained the clue we sought."

"And Abha sent you to me," Shala said.

"It is you who will tell us where we are going next."

"To find this eye?"

"Yes, to find the Eye."

"It sounds grotesque."

"I suppose it does." In truth, that hadn't occurred to me. "I am not sure it is actually Horus's eyeball we are seeking, though. Perhaps it is an amulet that has been modelled on his eye or something reminiscent of his eye."

"So you believe the tale to be allegory rather than literal truth?" Shala asked. "And yet you believe some version of the god's eye exists and can be found?"

"I…" I had no idea how to answer that. I hadn't even considered that Shala's story might not contain the exact truth of the Eye's origins.

"How will you find it if you do not know what it looks like? You have travelled a very long way to find something you are not even sure exists."

"I have to believe. There is no other option."

"But tell me, why exactly do you seek this thing?"

She noted my hesitation and eventually she waved away my lack of response.

"It is clear that you seek it for some great purpose and I understand that you may not wish to share this purpose with a stranger."

"There are many who would wish to stop me. I must be careful about how much I say and to whom I say it."

"Of course."

Shala tipped her head to the side as she studied me. She looked like an inquisitive bird. A tiny figure with her fringed shawl wrapped about her. Something told me I could trust her, yet I still said nothing further.

She turned to my companions and asked about our journey. Once again, I found myself in the position of translator.

We made pleasant conversation for a while until Shala excused herself to go check on something in the kitchen.

Sometime later her husband returned home. Belasi was a short, wiry man with a thick black beard. He smiled pleasantly at us and didn't seem at all perturbed to find his house full of strangers.

Shala brought out a large pot and my stomach growled when its fragrant scent reached me. She ladled the contents into bowls and we ate it piping hot with flat bread like we had in Indou. It was a stew of some sort, with vegetables and grains. I tasted leeks and onions but couldn't name any of the other ingredients. It was thick and hearty, and I ate with relish.

"Shala tells me you are here to learn more about the falcon god," Belasi said, when we had all eaten our fill. "You may come to the archives with me tomorrow and I will show you the scroll that records his story."

I wanted to ask him to take us there tonight, but Belasi worked long hours from what he said, and he looked tired. So I swallowed down my impatience and agreed that we would go with him in the morning.

THIRTY-FOUR

I barely slept that night for anticipation of our visit to the archives. I had never been to an archive before, although I understood it would contain stores of scrolls and other written records. We had archives in Egypt, of course. My father had always been particularly diligent about ensuring that copies of important documents were sent to multiple archives. I couldn't imagine, though, how an archive in faraway Babylon could have a scroll that told such an ancient tale of our people. How had I never heard this particular story before and yet the Babylonian archivists knew it? Shala's comment about allegories kept coming back to me. Perhaps we would find multiple versions of the tale? How would we know which to follow if that happened?

The air in the chamber I shared with Istnofret and Behenu was warm and somewhat stuffy due to the windows having been shuttered overnight. I was wide awake as birds began singing and dawn broke.

Belasi spoke little as he led me to the archives later that morning. It was hard to see him as a match for Shala, who was excessively talkative and friendly, but they seemed genuinely fond of each other.

Around us, Babylon was still wakening with hens clucking, goats bleating, dogs barking. A baby cried. Doors slammed. It was both familiar and exotic at the same time. These people didn't seem all that different from us. They lived in houses. They kept their livestock nearby. They kissed their families goodbye as they left. But the city was unmistakably foreign with its many lush gardens, fragrant flowers, and the enormous stepped monument which was, apparently, a temple.

This place, far more than any other we had seen, seemed foreign, and I was struck with home sickness. Not for my childhood home of Akhetaten. Too many years had passed since I had left, although I still remembered it well, with the marshy scent of the Great River, sand beneath my toes, and the ever-present sunlight bouncing off desert and white walls. But the memories had faded over time and Akhetaten no longer held the same pull for me as it once had. No, it was Egypt herself that I longed for. My beautiful country, with its Great River which rose up to spread its black wealth over the land every year. The people with their dark skin, their wigs and elaborate eye makeup. The clean-swept paths, dom palm trees, the endless horizon, the hot desert breeze. Belasi stopped walking, jarring me from my thoughts.

"This is the archive. I would ask that you speak quietly. It is a place of study and reflection. All who wish to learn are welcome so long as they do not interrupt anyone else's study."

The interior of the building was cool and dimly lit. Belasi led me through multiple chambers filled with shelves of baked clay tablets covered in a strange, triangular writing that I caught no more than a glimpse of. We reached a chamber which contained not clay tablets, but scrolls. I reached out to touch one, but Belasi stopped me with a raised hand.

"Please," he said. "Do not touch. Some of these scrolls are unfathomably old. The merest touch can cause them to crumble into dust."

"Then how do you study them? Surely you would need to unroll them to read them."

"We do it but once, and then very carefully. Scribes take several copies as quickly as they can. Then the original is stored away safely. There are some scrolls which we have never read because they begin to fall apart as soon as we touch them. Perhaps one day we will find a way to read them, but for now we keep them here so that they may be kept safe until that day."

"What do you do with the copies?"

"We keep one here and send others to archives elsewhere. That way if, Marduk forbid, this building is destroyed, we will not lose the knowledge we have accumulated here. We are preserving these documents for our descendants. Never will there come a day when people do not know everything we know today."

His words brought images of Akhetaten to my mind. When my father had been alive, I would have thought nothing could destroy his desert city. After his death, I had seen the city's fate in a dream: its mud brick buildings disintegrated, its people gone. Once we had thought the city to be eternal but nobody would ever live in Akhetaten again. I hoped Belasi's archive would not suffer a similar fate.

"This here is the scroll you wanted to see." Belasi tapped a wooden tray which contained a single scroll. "It is very old. Not, perhaps, the oldest scroll we have, but certainly many hundreds of years old."

"May I read it?"

My heart pounded. Finally I would learn the truth of the Eye. Surely, hidden somewhere within this scroll, was the knowledge I sought.

"Oh, no. It is far too old to be handled in such a way. This here is a copy." He pointed to the next tray. "You are welcome to look at that one. I doubt you will be able to read it, though."

"I can read," I said, somewhat indignantly. He clearly assumed I was illiterate just because I was a woman.

"It is written in a very old form of your language." Belasi continued as if I hadn't spoken. "We were fortunate to find someone who could translate it for us. It may be many years before we find another who can read it."

"Where do I find him?" I asked. "I will fetch him and have him read it to me."

Belasi shook his head. "He died shortly after he finished translating it. He was very, very old."

"But surely there is someone else who can read it. Show me the copy. Perhaps I can read it myself."

Belasi reached for the tray.

"Come, I will take you to where you may sit down and read. Or try to, at any rate."

I ignored his insinuation and followed him silently. He led me to a chamber which had two large windows and an excess of oil lamps. Their heat left the chamber overly warm, but at least they provided sufficient light to read easily. Belasi pointed to a table, beside which was a stool.

"You may sit here." He placed the tray on the table. "I have work to do. I will return later for you."

I sat down and took the scroll from its tray. It was nonsense to suggest I wouldn't be able to read it. But my first glimpse confirmed the truth. Its text was as foreign to me as if the scroll was in another language altogether. Still I made myself examine it line by line. Perhaps buried somewhere in its text was a passage I could understand. But I couldn't read even so much as a single symbol.

I was so absorbed in trying to understand the text, that it was only when I reached the end of the scroll that I noticed the drawing at the bottom. Half a dozen people were prostrated on their bellies before a man who towered over them. Behind them stood a woman, her gaze turned politely downwards. The man, who must of course be Horus, offered her something in the palm of his hand. I strained to make out the details but the ink was slightly smudged and all I could tell was that the thing he held was small. Surely this represented the moment when Horus gave his own eye to solve the dispute between tribes.

I worked my way through the scroll again, searching for anything that might be familiar. From time to time I found a hieroglyph that looked somewhat like one I knew but never in combination with any others that were intelligible to me. By the time Belasi returned, I had admitted defeat. I simply couldn't read any part of the ancient scroll.

"Have you seen enough?" Belasi asked. "I have a break now. I can take you back to the house. You will be more comfortable there and Shala would be glad of your company. She is always pleased to have someone to talk to."

"Are there other scrolls like this one? Anything else that seems to be written in the same language?"

"In the ancient form of Egyptian?" Belasi scratched his beard thoughtfully. "I do not know, but I know who would. Come with me."

I carried the scroll in its tray as Belasi led me to a small chamber which looked much like the others — long shelves filled with endless rows of scrolls.

"This is Naramsin." Belasi indicated a skinny little man who was hunched over a scroll. "His grandmother was Egyptian. He is responsible for seeking out Egyptian documents."

"Do you know where this scroll came from?"

I passed the tray to Naramsin. He peered shortsightedly at the label.

"Oh, this one. This is the one that tells of the falcon god."

"His name is Horus."

"Oh." Naramsin looked at me intently. "You know of him?"

"All Egyptians know of him."

"Oh." Naramsin's attention turned back to the scroll. He stared at it for long enough that I wondered whether he had forgotten I was there. "I remember now. We found it in a crate of old scrolls. Most of them have never been read."

"There are others?" My hope rose. "But where did they come from?"

"Oh, nobody knows." Naramsin was clearly disinterested. "The crate has been here for many years, but we have no scholars who read this language. If Yuny, who translated this one, had not died when he did, we would have asked him to look at the others too."

He breathed quickly now and I got the impression it had been a very long speech for the little man to make. He looked at me blankly, his speech concluded. It seemed he would offer nothing else unless I asked.

"Can I see the crate?"

"Oh." Naramsin seemed to consider my request for a very long time. "I suppose you can. I can think of no reason why you cannot. Belasi, would you agree?"

"Yes, yes, go ahead," Belasi said. "I need to return to my

work. Stay inside the building and I will find you at the end of the day."

He left quickly, leaving me wondering whether it was me or Naramsin he wanted to be rid of. I waited, but Naramsin was looking at me blankly.

"Will you show me to the crate?" I asked.

"The crate?"

I took a deep breath. Showing my exasperation was unlikely to hurry the man.

"The one this scroll came from."

"Oh." Naramsin looked down at the tray he still held. He considered it for a moment. "Yes, I will show you."

THIRTY-FIVE

Naramsin led me through a series of chambers, collecting an oil lamp on the way.

"We do not come to this chamber much," he said, when we reached our destination, which was all in darkness with not even a window. "I will leave the lamp with you. That crate there is the one you seek."

He deposited the lamp on a table and left without another word. At least I wouldn't have to suffer having him here with me. I dragged the crate over to the table. It was too heavy to lift so I had to leave it on the floor. I reached for a scroll, grabbing it a little too quickly in my eagerness. The papyrus cracked under my fingers. I placed it on the table, gentler now, but the scroll fell apart as I tried to unroll it. I inspected some of the larger fragments, but the script was faded and I couldn't make out even enough to determine whether it might have been legible.

I was more careful with the next scroll. It crackled a little as I unrolled it but didn't break. I scanned the text, but it was different to the language of the other one. I recognised the occasional symbol here and there. This scroll was not written in the language I knew, but it didn't seem as old as the other. I hunched over the table and moved the scroll closer to the lamp as I searched through it line by line. I could read no more than half a dozen words and none of them seemed to relate to the story I searched for. I found references to a feast, beer and bread, but nothing that spoke of Horus or eyes or power. I set the scroll aside and reached for the next.

Hours passed. My stomach began to grumble and my eyes blurred. I was not accustomed to reading for so long. I checked scroll after scroll, but none seemed as old as the first. None looked like they were written in the same ancient version of our language. And none had any words I recognised that might suggest it contained the information I sought. So absorbed was I in my task, that I didn't hear Belasi when he returned.

"Did you find what you were looking for?" he asked.

I placed a scroll in the growing pile of those I had checked and shook my head, not trusting my voice. I was ready to burst into tears. We had travelled so far and for so long, and yet it seemed Babylon was a dead end.

"You are welcome to return with me tomorrow." Belasi glanced down at the crate, which was still more than half full. "It looks like you have work to do yet."

"It is pointless. They are not old enough."

"Hmm. We have a storage chamber where scrolls that have not yet been reviewed by an archivist are stored. Scribes from all over the world send us documents. Far more than we have time to look at. Perhaps something there will aid you in your search."

"Can you show me?"

I stood up and my back burned after spending all day hunched over the table. Belasi led me to a large chamber.

"Here, these are all the ones we have not examined."

My heart sank. The chamber was filled with row after row of crates. They were piled on top of each other. The chamber was orderly enough, but there must be many hundreds, if not thousands, of scrolls in here.

"I will never be able to check all of these." Tears welled up and I dashed them away impatiently. "This is hopeless."

"Could your companions not assist? Surely they would be willing."

"They would gladly help, but they cannot read."

"I am sure Shala would be only too happy to help. Of course, you would have to tolerate her prattling all day, but she loves nothing more than trawling through musty old documents."

"A most fitting wife for an archivist."

I really should act more grateful. After all, it was not his fault that my task was so overwhelming.

"We shall go home now," Belasi said. "Things never seem quite so bad after a hot meal and some sleep. You and Shala can return with me tomorrow. Perhaps between you, you can come up with a system of some sort. Something that will make the job faster."

He pointed out various sights as we walked back to his house. The city was noisier at this time of day, with many people out and about. Children ran along the paved streets, shouting and waving tiny wooden daggers. Women carried jugs of water to their homes. The air smelled of cook fires and baking bread. Familiar things in an exotic city.

When we reached his home, the others took one look at my

glum expression and knew not to ask. Only Shala seemed oblivious.

"Did you find what you were seeking?" she asked, brightly, as she handed Belasi and I each a mug.

I sipped cautiously, but it was warm and a little sweet — a tea of some sort — not the sweet-sour drink that left a nasty taste in my mouth.

"There are too many scrolls," I said. "Thousands maybe. I could never check them all."

"I will help you," she said. "It will be an adventure. We will be seekers of truth, searching for a long-lost scroll."

"We can help, too." Istnofret's tone was more cautious. "You could show us the symbols you are looking for."

"If you wrote them down and gave us each a copy, we could have them beside us and check them against each scroll," Behenu suggested.

"I suppose." My heart lifted. Perhaps they could help after all. Surely between all of us we would find one that could tell us where the Eye could be found.

We passed a pleasant evening and Shala gladly entertained us until it was time for bed. Belasi appeared briefly to eat with us, then returned to wherever he had been hiding.

When we arrived at the archives the next morning, Belasi gave me some papyrus and a reed, and I painstakingly made several copies of the most common hieroglyphs from the copy of the original scroll. Then we set to work. Hours later, Istnofret pushed her crate back into its place beneath a shelf and stretched.

"My back cannot take this," she said. "I don't know how the archivists stand it."

"I suppose it is what they are used to." My back ached too,

but I was reluctant to stop. The harder we worked, the sooner we would find what we were looking for.

"I need some fresh air." Istnofret wandered out of the chamber.

Renni gave me a guilty look, which I pretended not to notice, and followed her. I went back to my work and noticed nothing other than the scrolls in front of me until Intef took one from my hands. I glanced up, startled. It still sometimes surprised me to look at him and see only one arm. He set the scroll aside on the table.

"Samun, it is time to stop."

Something inside of me twisted at the way my name sounded on his tongue. He so rarely called me that, even if the others had become more accustomed to using it.

"You can stop if you want," I said. "I will keep going."

"It is almost time for dinner. If we leave now, we can be back at Shala's in time to eat with everyone else."

I looked around the chamber. The two of us were the only ones there.

"I thought they were just going for a break. Did they not come back?"

"They did, and they worked for hours. They left a little while ago, as did Behenu and Shala. We should go, too."

I reached for the scroll he had taken from me, but he pushed it further away across the table.

"This will still be here in the morning," he said.

"Let me at least finish that one."

He shook his head.

"Then you will want to check another, and another, and we will be here all night. I am tired, Samun, and hungry and thirsty. I want to go back to Shala's."

"I will follow you in a little while."

I reached again for the scroll but he put his hand on mine to stop me.

"No more. You will be here all night if I leave you alone."

I looked down at our hands. It had been so long since he had touched me and the sudden longing for him almost took my breath away. He was so close that I could hear him breathing. When I finally dragged my gaze from our hands, he was looking at me with such tenderness. I remembered the day we had sat together on the couch in my little sitting chamber. I had rested my head on his shoulder and told him about my sisters. My eyes filled with tears and I yanked my hand away.

"Samun?" He gently placed his hand on my chin and tipped up my head, forcing me to look at him. "What is it?"

I shook my head, trying to pull away. For a moment he was unsteady on his feet — he was still adjusting to balancing without his arm — but then his hand was on my waist, trapping me there.

"Tell me."

His voice was tender and the shields I had put up around myself were cracking. I had to get away before I said something I would regret later.

"Nothing. You are right. It is time to go. I am hungry too."

My words sounded hollow even to my own ears.

"Not until you tell me why you are crying."

"I am not crying."

He laughed a little.

"Samun, I may have only one arm but I am not blind. I can see your tears."

I shook my head. It suddenly seemed important that I said nothing, although I wasn't quite sure what it was that threatened to burst from my mouth.

"Why do you keep pushing me away?" Sadness filled his

voice. "I have given up everything for you and still you keep me at a distance."

"I…" I had no idea what to say.

"Tell me truly. Do you really care nothing for me? If that is so, then tell me. I could put us behind me if I thought you didn't. But it is moments like this, when you look at me and your eyes are so full, that I wonder. Moments like this make me think that you do care, even if you will not let yourself say it."

I wanted to say it. Truly I did, but my throat was choked and I could say nothing. I avoided his eyes and tried to pull away, but he tightened his grip on my waist.

"No, Samun, I am not going to let you walk away this time. This is it. Either tell me you love me or tell me you don't."

I shook my head. Tears spilled down my face. Why wasn't I able to say what he wanted me to? Was it because after keeping my feelings bottled up inside me for so long, I had forgotten how to let them out? But still he held onto my waist.

"Let me go," I managed at last. "Please."

"If you care nothing for me, tell me. I will leave you at once and go home. I won't waste my life following you around the world if you don't care for me."

"You cannot leave me." I looked him in the eyes at last. "I cannot do this without you."

"You have other companions. Istnofret will not leave you and Renni will not leave her. They will stick with you until the end of your quest, wherever it takes you. But I will not. If you truly do not love me, I will go back to Egypt. Find somewhere to make a home for myself. A woman to marry. I want to settle down, Samun. Have my own house. A couple of children. Grow old with a woman who loves me. I cannot keep chasing a dream."

"Stay until I find the Eye," I whispered. "Please."

But he shook his head and there was a look in his eyes that I had never seen before.

"It is time," he said. "You need to make a decision. If you want me to stay, then tell me you love me."

"I cannot," I said, brokenly. "You do not know what you ask."

"No, I think it is you who do not know what you ask. How can you expect me to keep following you? You have said you can offer me nothing and yet you expect me to stay? You could at least give me your love, but if you will continue to withhold even that, then it is time I left."

He gave me a steady look, but when I still said nothing he shook his head and finally released me.

"I am sorry, Samun."

Then he walked away. I put my head down on the table and cried.

THIRTY-SIX

I waited for Intef to come back. He wouldn't leave me. Intef would never leave. My tears dried and still I waited. Eventually I convinced myself that he must have gone back to Shala's. I had thought I could remember the way, but I made a wrong turn somewhere and ended up in a part of the city I was not familiar with. I tried to ask a woman for directions but she looked at me as if I was mad. I traced my steps back and tried again.

The sky was fully dark before I found Shala's house. They were all in the dining chamber and looked like they were just finishing the evening meal. Everyone except Intef.

"Samun, what took you so long?" Istnofret asked.

She was lazing on a cushion with a mug of beer in her hand and looked perfectly content.

"Come, sit down." Shala jumped up and led me to a spare cushion, then began piling food on a plate. "You must be famished. Where is Intef?"

My throat choked up again. The chatter in the room died as

they all waited for me to speak. I could do no more than shake my head and burst into tears.

"He is gone," was all I could say.

They all spoke at once, but I was too busy crying to hear any of it. Renni crouched beside me and put his hand on my arm.

"Samun, where is Intef? Did something happen to him?"

I cried harder, big noisy sobs that some part of my mind was saying I would be horribly embarrassed about later. Then Istnofret was there, pushing Renni out of the way. She took me by the shoulders and shook me firmly.

"Samun, pull yourself together," she said in a tone she had never used with me before. "Stop crying and tell us where Intef is."

I tried to gulp down my sobs, but they kept coming out. Eventually I managed to get myself under control enough to speak.

"He has left me."

She waited for me to continue.

"He told me..." I hiccupped. "He told me that if I didn't say I loved him, he would go back to Egypt."

"And you still didn't tell him?" she asked.

The tears welled again and I shook my head.

"Oh, Samun," she said. "You are such a fool sometimes."

"I cannot," I said.

"So where is he now?" she asked.

"I assume he is looking for a ship to take him home."

Istnofret laughed. "You are indeed a fool. Intef is not going home."

"He said he would and then he left me."

"He would not leave you." Her voice held nothing but certainty. "He would not leave even if you ordered him away."

"I didn't say I loved him," I said, brokenly. "And he left."

"I will go look for him." Renni drained his mug and set it aside. "He has likely found somewhere to hole up for the night while he licks his wounds."

"I told you, he is gone."

"Even if he was planning to, no ships will leave port this late." Renni was already on his way to the door. "I will return when I find him."

Istnofret pushed a mug into my hand. "You may as well eat and drink while you wait." Her tone was all no nonsense now. "Renni will bring Intef back and then you will be sensible and tell him you love him."

The meal tasted like ash, but I forced myself to choke it down. When Renni finally returned, he was alone.

"I found him," he said. "But he will not come."

"I knew he wouldn't." I set my mug aside and buried my face in my hands. Why hadn't I said what he wanted to hear? Why couldn't I force the words out of my mouth? I did love him, didn't I?

"I think he will if you ask him yourself," Renni said.

"Of course he will," Istnofret said. "You should get some sleep now and go to him in the morning once you have both calmed down."

I shook my head, unable to summon any response. Couldn't they see I had ruined things between us forever?

"You will." Istnofret's tone was firm. "But first, some sleep. Nobody can make good decisions when they are so tired."

I didn't have the strength to argue but merely let her lead me to bed. Although I was sure I would lie awake all night, I must have fallen into a deep sleep almost as soon as I lay down. When I woke, the dawn light was already filtering into the chamber. Outside birds chirped and elsewhere in the house someone was talking quietly. My heart was heavy, but a quiet acceptance had come over me as I slept. This was Intef's decision. If I truly loved him, I had to let him be free to live his own life. The others were already breaking their fast when I reached the dining chamber.

"After breakfast, Renni will take you to Intef," Istnofret said, handing me a mug of beer. "Sit down and eat first."

I was thirsty after all my tears and drained half the mug before I spoke.

"Intef may return home if that is what he chooses." My voice was calm and gave no hint of the grief it gave me to say such a thing. "I will not force him to stay."

"Samun, he has never asked anything else of you." Istnofret shook her head at me. "Will you not give him this?"

"He wishes to be free to live his own life." My voice was a little less steady now. "He wants to marry. Have children. I cannot offer him a life like that."

"Why not?"

"Well, because…" I stammered, my mind suddenly blank. "Because he is a commoner. And I am the queen."

"You *were* the queen." Istnofret's tone was gentle. "And even if you still were, why would that stop you from marrying Intef? He is better than any of the men you considered when you were looking for a husband."

"He is a commoner." Could she not see the obvious? I could never marry a commoner.

"Horemheb is a commoner. Nobody argued against him when your brother named him as heir. You knew that for him to become pharaoh, you would have to marry him. It was not until after your brother went to the West, that you objected on that basis and that was only because you wanted to avoid the marriage."

Her words echoed through my mind. It was a good thing I was already sitting down or I might have fallen over. All that time I had spent searching for a lover. Someone — Sadeh? — had suggested Intef and I had dismissed him immediately, but none of the noble men I had considered were worthy of being pharaoh. What were the prerequisites I had set? Honest, strong, brave? There were surely others but I couldn't remember them. Whatever it was I had been looking for, Intef was the answer. There was none more loyal or trustworthy than he. Even with one arm, he was more than any of the foolish men I had considered back then.

"Now, are you ready to go find Intef?" Istnofret asked.

"I cannot." How could I expect him to come back to me?

"He will leave if you do not go to him."

"Will he really? Or is he testing me?"

I was ashamed of myself as soon as the words left my mouth and the look on Istnofret's face made me feel even worse.

"That is not the sort of man he is," she said. "And I think you know that."

Her rebuke was less than I deserved and when Renni offered his hand to help me up, I accepted without comment. He led me to the dock.

"Intef was planning to wait here until he could secure passage on a ship," he said.

"He was going to sleep here? On the dock?"

"He has no funds of his own so his options are limited. He can go nowhere until he finds a captain willing to exchange work for passage. Even with only one arm, any captain who turns him down is a fool."

We searched the area but found no sign of Intef. We tried asking passersby if they had seen a man with one arm, but nobody spoke either Egyptian or Akkadian. Renni seemed to have some success at miming his question but still everyone shook their heads.

"Surely someone has seen him," I said as we paused to rest beneath a shady tree. It must be mid *shemu* — the harvest season — by now at home. I had no idea what the Babylonians called their seasons, but the day was turning out to be warm with overcast skies. At least here by the water there was a refreshing, salty breeze.

"We might be too late," Renni said. "If he was still here, we would have found him by now. Or someone would have seen him."

"They are all speaking a foreign language. We have no idea whether they have seen him or not."

"I think we are managing to communicate enough for them to understand. We must face it, Samun. Intef is gone. There must have been a ship ready to leave first thing this morning and Intef has gone with it."

"That cannot be so. Even if a ship was leaving early, surely the chance of it heading to Egypt must be low."

"Then it means he has gone somewhere else. He has no ties to Egypt without his father. If he didn't want to be followed, he would go somewhere else."

"But where?"

"Anywhere in the world. We have no way of knowing."

"Can we get Belasi to come down here and ask some questions? We need someone who speaks the local language. He can find out if a ship left early this morning and where it was going."

"He doesn't want to be found, Samun."

I knew he didn't mean Belasi.

"He would have still been here if that was the case. He must have known you would come for him eventually."

"We will follow him," I said.

"Will you give up your search for the sake of one man? After all we have been through, does this search mean so little to you that you would walk away?"

"I am not walking away. I am going to find Intef and then we will find the Eye together."

But my words didn't sound convincing, even to my own ear.

"It has taken us so many months to get this far," Renni said. "We are getting closer to the Eye all the time. If we leave now, go in a different direction, we might never pick up its trail again."

"We still have no idea where it is."

But I was beginning to doubt myself. Was I wrong to search for Intef? After leading my companions halfway around the known world? If Intef had enough of a head start, we might follow him for months before we caught up with him. And if he didn't want to be found, he would know how to disappear.

"This is my one chance to save Egypt." The words came out slowly, unwillingly. "How can I walk away from that? No matter what it costs me, I have to continue."

"Intef would expect nothing less."

THIRTY-SEVEN

That night, I cried for a long time before I finally fell asleep. Istnofret and Behenu politely pretended not to notice. Memories of all the times Intef had asked me to tell him how I felt ran through my mind, and all the ways I had put him off. Now it was too late. Intef was gone and I had no way of following him. My grief was all the more bitter for knowing that it was my own fault.

But even in my sleep, I found no peace. I dreamed I walked along a paved street. The dress of the people I passed told me I was still here in Babylon. I reached an alleyway and paused. I had heard something there, although my dream didn't reveal what. I hesitated for some time, wondering whether to turn down the alley. At length, I walked on.

The dream changed and I found myself again standing at the alley. This time I entered it, but I had taken no more than a few steps before I realised somebody was following me. I darted a glance over my shoulder and saw a man who was a stranger to me. He licked his lips and reached for me. I tried to run, but he caught me by the arm. I woke just as I screamed.

I lay on my mat, panting. My heart pounded uncomfortably hard and my whole body trembled. It had been some time — months, at least — since I had had a true dream, but I could still recognise one. I had to make sure that when the time came, I did not turn down that alley.

THIRTY-EIGHT

We returned to the archives the next morning and within minutes of starting work, Shala brought me a scroll. She laid it out on the table and pointed to several symbols.

"See," she said. "Here, and here. These are what you are looking for, no?"

"Yes." I itched to run my fingers over the scroll, but it flaked apart even as I looked at it. It was old, possibly older even than the original scroll Belasi had showed me.

"What do we do now?" Istnofret asked.

Their hopeful expressions said they thought our task was over, that we could move onto the next stage of our journey.

"We keep going," I said. "If there are any other scrolls that mention the Eye, this is where they will be. We keep searching until we have checked every scroll. Then we find someone who can read them for us."

Somebody sighed — I wasn't sure who — and they all returned to their work.

I hadn't realised before how much space Intef took up. He was never one prone to chatter, but his silent presence seemed to fill a chamber. I felt very alone without him.

Shala's early discovery gave me hope, but that faded as the days passed. Every now and then someone would find a scroll that seemed similar to what we searched for, but when we compared the symbols more carefully, they were different. It took us three weeks to check the rest of the scrolls and in all that time, we found not a single other that seemed to be written in the same ancient language as the original one.

"Well, that is the last of them." Istnofret carefully placed her scroll back into a crate and wiped her dusty hands on her skirt. "Now what?"

"I suppose we find someone who can read these two," I said.

We had set the document Shala found and the copy of the first in a tray on a shelf well away from the other scrolls so they wouldn't get mixed up. I longed to open the new scroll and pore over its contents, but it was brittle. We couldn't afford to handle it any more than was necessary.

It seemed strange to leave that chamber, knowing it was the last time we would be there. Belasi had secured permission for us to take the two scrolls to his home for a little while and had repeatedly reminded us that we mustn't damage them or he would incur a heavy fine. So I carried them in the tray and didn't let myself touch them.

Dinner that night was subdued, although Shala worked hard to be an entertaining host. Having so many guests in her home must be wearying for her.

"It feels like we have reached a crossroads, does it not?" Istnofret asked as she reached for another of the juicy red-skinned fruit Shala often served.

They were sweet with yellow flesh and a large stone in the middle. My taste buds tingled at the thought and I reached for one too. I translated Istnofret's words into Akkadian for Shala's benefit, before I bit into the fruit. Juice ran down my chin.

"We need someone who can read the scrolls," I said around my mouthful.

"I will ask Belasi again," Shala said. "Perhaps he has finally found someone."

She collected an armful of dishes and left the room. Behenu jumped up to help her. I often wondered why Shala did such tasks herself rather than calling in her servants. She had two serving women whose duties seemed to include a variety of tasks about the house, but they never waited on us. I had been wanting to ask why but wasn't sure if Shala would be offended. Perhaps this was the Babylonian idea of hospitality. Maybe they thought the mistress of the house should wait on her guests herself. It was an interesting idea and I longed to know if I was right.

"Perhaps it is time to go home," Renni said. "Surely, if we are to find someone who can read those scrolls, it will be in Egypt."

"I don't think Belasi will let us take them away," I said. "He was very specific that we could only bring them to the house."

"Could we make copies?" Istnofret suggested. "If not you, then perhaps someone from the archives?"

"We need the original scrolls," I said. "A copyist who doesn't read the language couldn't accurately transcribe all those symbols without error. We don't know what any of them means. The smallest error may well change the meaning of an individual symbol, and anything we might otherwise learn from these scrolls could be lost."

"What about your dreams?" She dipped her fingers in a bowl of water to wash off the fruit juice. "Have you seen anything that might give us a clue? Perhaps something that suggests where we should go next?"

"They don't really work like that," I said. "But no, I haven't dreamed anything useful."

Except for the dream where I offered up a babe to a green-faced god. That, at least, gave me hope that we would return to Egypt eventually.

"Maybe we should find some lodgings of our own," Behenu suggested.

"I tried to pay Shala but she wouldn't accept anything." I had offered her one of my finger rings. She had laughed but looked more offended than amused. "Still, we cannot continue to impose on her hospitality. Maybe Behenu is right. We should find somewhere else to live for a while, and then figure out what to do next."

Shala didn't protest very hard when I told her we had decided to find a house of our own. I supposed five people — four without Intef — plus a cat must be an enormous burden on her household, but even though I offered another finger ring she still refused any payment, saying that her hospitality was in honour of Bhumi. She sent out a servant to make enquiries and the girl returned a couple of hours later to say she had located a house for us. The owners, an elderly couple, had both died and they had no children to inherit, so the house had passed to a friend who had no use for it and was happy to hire it out.

We moved that day and it was a relief to be surrounded by only my friends. We quickly settled into new routines. Renni secured some labouring work, saying that as long as we were going to settle here for a while, he may as well make an income. The fact that he spoke no language in common with his colleagues didn't seem to matter and he returned home each evening cheerful if filthy and exhausted.

Mau seemed content to spend her days lying outside in the sun. At first, I worried that she would wander off and become lost, but after travelling for so long, she seemed happy to be in one place and to have grass, rather than a ship's deck, beneath her paws.

Istnofret took in some sewing and quickly became known for her fine work. Behenu put herself in charge of preparing our meals, making bread each day and even tried her hand at brewing our beer. Soon it was only I who had no occupation. I tried helping Istnofret with her sewing once or twice, but quickly found she would unpick all of my work and do it again as soon as she thought I wasn't watching. I tried to help Behenu in the kitchen, but she sent me away, saying it took her twice as long to do anything with me underfoot.

I felt inadequate that it was only I who wasn't contributing to our household, but there seemed no task that I could do competently. So I resumed my visits to the archives, searching every day for more scrolls like the two we had found. At least I felt like I was doing something useful. After all, if we were ever to leave Babylon, it would be because I found the next clue.

After several weeks of searching the archives without success, I sent a carefully-worded message to Hemetre, along with copies of the two scrolls, asking if she knew someone discreet who might be able to translate them. I had painstakingly made the copies myself, spending several days on each. They undoubtedly contained errors, no matter how careful I had been, but I could think of no other way we might find someone who could read them. After all, the hymn to Isis that the priestesses sang every day was in an ancient version of our language. I even dared to hope that Hemetre herself might be able to read the scrolls. More weeks passed as I waited for her reply, and I began to wonder if we would be stranded in Babylon forever.

THIRTY-NINE

More than three months had passed since I sent the message to Hemetre. It was improbable that she had even received it yet, but the wait left me fidgety and restless. I had spent the day at the archives and decided to walk for a while before going home. Once again, I had found nothing useful and I was starting to lose my mind, spending all day poking through dusty old scrolls without finding even so much as a clue.

I walked for a long time, seeing little of the city around me. It felt good to stretch my legs. Clouds hid the sun and the afternoon air was still warm. It was mid *akhet*, by the way Egyptians measured the seasons, and the annual inundation at home would be at its peak. Here in Babylon the days were still long and hot, although the heat was not quite as oppressive as it had been a couple of months ago. I had visited Shala last week and she said the rainy season was approaching. Back at home, it rarely rained, but here the Euphrates didn't rise up over the land in the way the Great River did. Instead the rainfall was frequent enough to keep the crops watered and for a few weeks each year, the rain would come as often as every day.

We had taken to dressing as the local inhabitants did in bright fringed and beaded skirts and shawls. My hair had grown out almost to my chin and I enjoyed the freedom of going without a wig. Nobody paid me any attention as I walked. There were many people here whose appearance suggested they came from other countries and I supposed I stuck out no more than they did.

I walked all the way to the docks and stood there for a while, looking out at the ocean. Although I had no desire to ever step foot on a ship again, I itched to move on. Somewhere out there was the Eye. It had to be. Otherwise we had come this far for nothing. The sun was beginning to dip down towards the horizon and the crowds were thinning. I would have to hurry if I wanted to be home before dark.

I walked more briskly, a little uneasy now that there were so few people around. As I passed an alley, I heard a clatter from its depths, followed by the yowl of a cat.

"Mau?"

I peered down the alley but could see little in the fading light. I couldn't remember whether I had seen the cat today, but Behenu would surely have said something had she disappeared. Even if Mau had gone wandering, she couldn't have come this far. But the sound came again and now I was more certain. It was definitely Mau. I started down the alley.

The cat yowled again and something darted in front of me. I hesitated. It was orange, like Mau, but surely this creature was too big. I looked back, to the empty street behind me. I could go home, check whether Mau was there. If she wasn't, I could bring Renni back with me to search for her. But the cat might be long gone by the time I got back and I would never forgive myself if we lost Sadeh's cat. I put my hand to the spell bottle, which still hung on a cord around my neck, just as the woman who had sold it to me had said it must. It was as cold as ever. The warning from my dream of a few months ago had been clear: I must not go down the alley.

I straightened my shoulders and told myself to stop being a coward. I had long learned the futility of trying to choose which dream showed the best version of the future, and I couldn't risk losing Mau. I would find the cat and if it was Mau, I would grab her, and we would both go home. If my spell bottle warmed, I would turn back immediately.

I set off again, but before I had taken more than a couple of steps footsteps came from behind me. I glanced over my shoulder. A man approached down the alley. He breathed hard and when I caught his eye, he licked his lips and reached for me. I let out a surprised squawk and darted forward out of his reach.

"Easy, girl," he growled.

I screamed and ran.

But he was too close and grabbed me by the arm. He spun me around and pushed me against the wall. I thrashed, trying to kick him, but he just laughed at my efforts. My spell bottle remained cold. Perhaps the spell had worn off after all this time.

"Your husband know you are out wandering around on your own?" he asked. "Stop wriggling and let me get a good look at you."

I thrashed even harder, managing to land a kick on his leg but he didn't even flinch. He put his hand against my throat and pinned me against the wall. I froze. All I could think of was the time Ay had first come to me, when he had held me against the bed by my throat.

"Now, that is better," the man murmured. He brushed my hair away from my face. "Hmm, pretty enough. Plenty of strength. Well fed. Could make a good worker if you are inclined to obedience. Or perhaps you are a breeder? You breed yet?"

Distantly I wondered how this disheveled man could be educated enough to speak Egyptian.

"Answer me, woman," he growled. "I am short of both time and patience today, and I have a quota to fill. You a breeder?"

"N-no," I managed to stammer. I would not tell this beast of a man about my babe. Somehow I didn't think that was what he meant anyway.

"You know how to work? Skin's too pale to have spent much time outside." He grabbed my hand and turned it over to inspect the palm. "Hands look like a worker, though. What do you do? Brew beer? Make bread? Sew?"

I didn't know how to answer. He pressed harder against my throat, and I choked and gasped for air.

"I dinna like to ask questions twice, woman."

Then the pressure on my throat was gone and the man lay crumpled at my feet, a pool of blood spreading beneath his head. Behind him stood Intef.

He tossed a brick to the ground, gave me a dark look, then turned and walked away.

"Intef." I could barely breathe, let alone speak. "Wait."

"Leave me be," he said, without even turning back to me. He continued to walk away.

I stepped over the man and hurried after Intef. I grabbed his arm.

"Wait. Please."

He looked coldly down at my hand and shook his head.

"There is nothing to say."

"Where have you been? We thought you had left."

"As you can see, I didn't."

He shook off my arm and started walking again.

I should let him go. He clearly wanted nothing to do with me. But I had almost lost him once. Would I really let him walk away from me now? This might be my last chance.

"Intef, please. I... I need to say something. Will you stop and listen?"

His stride hitched, but he shook his head and kept walking. He walked differently now. It seemed he had found a new balance without his arm. Intef reached the end of the alley. I might have expected him to at least look back as he rounded the corner, but he didn't.

"Intef."

I raced after him, filled with sudden certainty. I wouldn't let him leave me again, no matter what I had to say.

"Intef, you wait right there."

I was sure he would be gone when I emerged from the alley, but he was still there. He slowly turned to look at me and my heart broke at the indecision in his face.

"I cannot keep doing this, Samun." The name he used for me told me he hadn't forgotten me, no matter how much he might try to pretend he had. "It is not good for any man to live like this."

"Please." I stopped an arm's length away from him. "Let me say what I must before I lose my courage."

He said nothing, but he also didn't walk away.

"Intef."

Where to start? My thoughts were jumbled, but as I tried to make sense of them, there was only one thing I was sure of — I knew what he wanted to hear.

"I—"

That was as far as I got before Intef grabbed my arms and pulled me to the side. Two small boys dashed past, immersed in a game of chase. They probably never even realised they had nearly knocked me over. He released my arms as quickly as if he had been burned.

"Is there somewhere quieter we can talk?" I asked.

He turned and walked away.

"Intef," I called after him.

"We can go to my lodgings."

He never even looked back to see whether I followed.

Intef led me to a house. There were other people inside, who took no notice of us as we entered. We went to a chamber and he closed the door behind us. It was empty other than for a reed mat, a blanket and an oil lamp. At least there was a window, covered with a threadbare curtain. He lit the lamp, then drew the curtain open to let in some air.

"Speak if you have something to say," he said.

Where had this coldness come from? I supposed it was no more than I deserved. He waited in silence while I gathered my thoughts.

"I have been a fool," I said, slowly. "No matter what I needed, you were there. I didn't really notice you for a long time. Like all good servants, you disappeared into the background. You were there when I needed you and you faded away when I didn't."

He inhaled a little shakily. My words hurt him. That wasn't my intent.

"But that changed the first time you came to my bed. I realised how kind you had always been to me. How safe I felt with you. I knew that as long as you were there, everything would be all right. And then…"

I paused, searching for the right words. I didn't want to open up old wounds, but I needed to say all of this.

"Then I thought you had betrayed me. When you went to Ay. That day in the audience hall, when you said you had been in my bed, that I had ordered you to entertain me. I was humiliated. I felt like a silly girl. For believing you, for trusting you. I thought I would never trust anyone again."

"After everything I have done for you. I followed you halfway around the world, with no promise of anything in return. All I asked was for you to tell me the truth of how you felt and you couldn't give me even that."

It was no more than he had said before, but his words cut me. I let them sink in. Let them hurt. I deserved it.

"I cannot explain why. I think… I think I was so used to believing that everyone would betray me if they had a chance. After Khay. And Tentopet. I assumed that Ay had offered you more than I ever could."

He looked me in the eye, only briefly, but long enough for me to see his hurt.

"I…" What was I trying to say? Why did I find it so hard to trust? "I was raised with the expectation that I would be used. That one day I would marry a man who would be useful to my father. That by allowing myself to be used I would serve my pharaoh. My body, my status, my actions — everything would be used to benefit Pharaoh.

"That was how it was for my mother. She was lucky that there was genuine affection between her and my father, but I had no expectation of that for myself. I saw how everything she did was for my father. For Aten's glory. Privately, she had some influence over my father, but in public she was always the perfect queen. It is… It is hard to forget that. To let someone in without expecting them to use me to their own advantage."

I waited, but he said nothing. Was I even telling him anything he hadn't already figured out for himself? He had been trailing after me since he was seven years old, after all. He had seen most of my life play out right in front of him. He knew what I had come from, how I had been raised. He knew who I was. He knew I could give him nothing, and yet he was still here.

"I am sorry."

He looked at me for a long moment.

"I accept your apology."

"Will you come home now?"

He looked away. At the wall, the floor. At length, he shook his head and my heart broke a little more.

"I cannot."

"Why? We miss you."

It wasn't what he wanted to hear, but I was getting closer.

"I cannot be near you anymore. Every time you don't see me, it is like a dagger to my heart. I was only watching over you until you left Babylon and then I intend to return home."

"You will not come back to us? Even now?"

Even after I had apologised.

He wouldn't look at me.

"Samun, you still don't understand or you would not ask this of me."

I inhaled shakily. My legs trembled and there was a buzzing in my ears. I knew what would bring him home again. I just wasn't sure I had the courage to say it. It would make me too vulnerable. Vulnerability made it easier for people to use you.

"Intef, please."

He looked resolutely at the wall.

"Intef. Will you not look at me?"

For a heartbeat, I thought he wouldn't, but then he dragged his gaze from the wall. I met his eyes and the rest of the world fell away.

"Intef, I am not good at letting people get close to me. Bad things happen to everyone who does."

"We all go to the West, sooner or later."

"But maybe I can protect the people I... the people I care about if I don't let them close."

I suddenly realised I was lying, and not only to Intef, but to myself. I had spent years pushing people away with the justification that I was trying to protect them, but that wasn't true. I was protecting myself. I didn't want the pain of losing yet another person who was dear to me. I didn't want the hurt of discovering that someone I thought cared about me had been using me to achieve their own ends. I had somehow believed that if I didn't let myself be vulnerable, nobody would be able to use me. I wouldn't be hurt.

"Maybe you are hurting them even more by pushing them away," Intef said.

I swallowed hard and suddenly found I couldn't look at him. Now it was me staring at the wall. He gently took my chin and turned my face back towards him.

"What are you trying to say, Samun?" he asked.

"I cannot do this without you." I had said this to him before and it made no difference. "I don't want to do this without you. I want you by my side. Now, while we search for the Eye, and later."

"Later?" His voice was a rasp.

"When this is all over. Istnofret wants to settle down in a seaside village. A little house for her and Renni. I thought..."

He waited, ever so patiently.

"I thought maybe we could do that, too."

Still he waited. I began to wonder if he would ever speak again.

"You and me, a little house somewhere. Maybe not by the sea, but not too far from Istnofret and Renni."

Dear Isis, he was not going to let me get away without saying it. I had already said so much.

"I love you," I said.

Still he just looked at me.

"Didn't you hear me? I said it, Intef. I said what you wanted me to."

"But you only said it so that I would go with you. You didn't say it because you mean it."

I found myself crying.

"You don't know how hard it was for me to say that. I thought it would mean something to you, but it doesn't."

He wiped the tears from my cheeks.

"It does, Samun. It means a lot to me. If you mean it."

"I do mean it," I said, between sobs.

He drew me into his chest and wrapped his arms around me, both the whole arm and the stub. I leaned against him and soaked his shirt with my tears. He didn't try to make me stop. At length, my tears dried up and I stepped back, suddenly embarrassed.

"Samun, will you stop pulling away from me?"

He drew me back to him.

"I am not—"

"I know. You are not used to letting anyone get too close. I know it well."

"There must be plenty of other women who would have you, if you offered."

"I don't want plenty of other women. I want you."

I dared to meet his eyes.

"Even after the way I have treated you?"

He smiled a little.

"I have seen the changes in you. It is slow, so slow, but you have gradually been letting people in. First Istnofret, then Behenu. Renni. Now maybe me. I know it is hard. Remember, I have known you since you were five years old. I knew you as a girl, and then as a woman. I knew you as a princess, and then as a queen. I have seen you at your highest, proudest moments and also at your lowest. The moments when you could barely find the strength to go on, and yet you always did. I have seen it all. I know you better than you could ever imagine."

My fingers wandered over his damp shirt, smoothing out the creases. It was easier to focus on his shirt than his eyes.

"I am not sure I can give you what you are looking for. I couldn't even..." My voice broke and it was a long while before I could speak again. "I couldn't even love my babe, and he came out of my own body. How can I think I could ever love someone else?"

"You don't think you loved him? Samun, I was barely aware of anything at that point, but even I felt your love for him. I saw the way you clung to him every moment until you had to hand him over. I saw the way you never took your eyes off him. If you didn't love him, it wouldn't have torn you apart like that."

I swallowed hard. All this time I had thought my son went to be embalmed without ever being loved.

"I named him," Intef said. "I know you said he wasn't mine, but whether he was or not, it didn't seem right that he had no name. I sent Behenu to find out where he had been taken and to tell them his name."

I waited, barely able to breathe.

"I named him Setau."

Now my tears came in earnest. He had named my babe for his father. Most sons were named for their father, or their father's father. We would never know whether Intef was truly his father, but he had named him as if he was. He let me cry until I ran out of tears.

"I am..." I could barely speak after crying for so long. I cleared my throat and tried again. "I am not the same woman who left Memphis, Intef. The things that were important to me back then are..."

"Samun." He interrupted me. "When are you going to stop talking and kiss me?"

I slowly raised my gaze to meet his. He looked at me steadily and waited.

"Why do I need to kiss you? Why don't you kiss me?"

"Because you already know how I feel about you. And you are the one trying to convince me."

His argument seemed fair enough, so I kissed him.

Intef finally agreed to come home with me. Istnofret and Behenu greeted him with enthusiastic hugs. Renni slapped him on the back and I was suddenly sure he had known Intef was still in Babylon.

I was relieved to find Mau curled up on Behenu's bed mat. Of course, she couldn't have wandered so far, but if I hadn't gone down that alley in search of her, I wouldn't have found Intef. But then, if I had taken heed of the warning in my dream, I wouldn't have gone down the alley at all. Perhaps I had never really understood how my dreams worked.

I had long given up trying to force one of the fates I saw in them. Every time I tried, it had gone badly wrong, and eventually I had concluded that my dreams were no more than the gods' way of forewarning me of what was to come. I no longer thought they intended for me to try to change the fates they showed. But the dream about the alley left me confused. If I had tried to choose the fate that seemed most desirable, I wouldn't have turned down the alley, no matter what I heard. And if I hadn't gone down that alley, Intef wouldn't have shown himself to me. Perhaps I understood even less about my dreams than I thought.

Dinner that night was raucous and I drank far too much of Behenu's newly-brewed beer. We joked about how Renni had at one time planned to introduce me as a beer brewer. Behenu had also turned out to be a surprisingly proficient cook. Shala had taught her how to make the flat bread and a type of barley stew the Babylonians particularly favoured. Between Renni's labouring and Istnofret's sewing, they brought in enough payment in barley for us to be reasonably comfortable without using any of the remaining jewels, even if we couldn't afford to be too extravagant.

When I stumbled off to the chamber Behenu and I had been sharing, I found her mat missing. Before I could go in search of her, Intef arrived with his mat and blanket.

"Istnofret sent me," he said, looking a little embarrassed.

"Behenu usually sleeps here."

"Apparently she is moving into the dining chamber with Mau. And Istnofret says she and Renni share the other chamber. So…"

His voice trailed away and we stared at each other for a moment. The air suddenly seemed far too warm.

"Of course." I broke our stare and leaned down to straighten my blanket. "You have to sleep somewhere."

"If I am not welcome here, I can trade with Behenu. I doubt she would mind."

"No, no. It is just…"

He reached for my chin and gently turned my face towards his.

"What is it? You do not want me?"

"I am just… It was…"

"Is it too fast?" he asked. "I can sleep elsewhere."

He waited patiently while I sorted through my thoughts. "It makes it feel so definite. You and me. Us. I am still getting used to the idea and already you are moving into my bedchamber."

"I will swap with Behenu."

He was already moving towards the door, but I grabbed his arm.

"No."

He turned back to give me a questioning look.

"Stay. Please."

FORTY

A week or so after Intef had come back to us, he mentioned the message I had sent to Hemetre.

"How long ago did you send it?" he asked.

"At least three months," I said.

"Closer to four," Renni said.

I shrugged, conceding that he was more likely than I to have kept accurate track of the days.

"It might take three or four months, or even longer, before it reaches her," Intef said. "She might not have received it yet."

"We thought at least seven months for a reply," I said. "Maybe longer."

"Undoubtedly longer," he said. "Your message has a long way to travel, and that assumes fine weather and that she is able to find a translator swiftly. She will have to be careful who she asks. It might take months before she finds someone suitable."

"We should have taken the message ourselves," I said.

"Should we go to Egypt?" The look on Istnofret's face said quite clearly that she didn't want to.

I was no keener than she to spend months on a ship but before I could say anything, Renni shook his head.

"We might miss Hemetre's reply if we leave. I don't think we can do anything now other than wait."

"But how long do we wait before we concede that no reply is coming?" I asked. "Messages go astray, boats sink. Hemetre might never receive it and we could spend the rest of our lives waiting."

"It is not so bad here, is it?" Renni wrapped an arm around Istnofret's shoulders. "We have a house, a garden, employment, friends. I wouldn't mind if we stayed here."

"But we need to find the Eye," I reminded him. "We cannot settle down in Babylon and never leave."

"Give it a year," Renni said. "If no reply comes in that time, we will think about what to do next."

"I cannot wait a year," I said.

Now that we had Intef back, I felt an increasing sense of urgency about resuming our search. Renni had heard yesterday that the Hittite and Egyptian forces had met in battle. Two of his co-workers had been discussing it, but each had heard a different outcome. One said the Egyptians had slaughtered the entire Hittite army and the other said the Hittites were victorious. Men were dying while we lazed around in Babylon.

"Wait a few more months, at least," Renni said. "It is not like we have any other leads. Where would you go if we left now?"

I sighed. "I don't know."

That was the most frustrating part. Although I grew impatient at the delay, I had no idea where else to search.

"I suppose we could go back to Egypt," I said. "To Behdet. We could try talking to the priests at the temple of Horus.

Since most boys follow in their father's profession, they are probably all descended from generations of priests. They might remember stories they heard as children. We could glean some clues from them."

"And we might not learn anything at all," Renni said, and although I didn't want to admit it, his words were perfectly reasonable.

"Someone must know something," I said. "I cannot believe we have travelled so far only to reach a dead end."

"Maia did say the gods would put obstacles in our path," Behenu said. "Perhaps this only seems like a dead end."

I took my frustration out on the garden, turning over the soil in an area we had not yet planted. Behenu came out to work alongside me and we toiled in companionable silence. As dusk approached, I leaned on my hoe and surveyed our efforts. I never would have thought I would dig a garden myself, but my blistered palms were evidence of my hard work.

"I have been thinking," Behenu said.

"I have been trying not to."

"The archives have a lot of scrolls we have not looked at."

"We checked all of the ones that came from Egypt."

"But what about all the others?" she asked.

"Surely you don't mean we should read every scroll? There are thousands of them. We could never read them all."

"It would give you something to do while we wait. I will leave you to your gardening now. It is time I began preparing dinner."

She left me alone in the falling darkness. I set down my hoe and went to sit on the front step of our house. Mau appeared from wherever she had spent the day and rubbed herself against my leg. She purred a little, but as soon as I reached for her she stalked away with her tail in the air. It was only then I noticed how skinny she was. She had had some periods of sickness over the years, where she would refuse to eat and would lose weight. Sadeh had always fussed terribly and would spend hours trying to convince Mau to eat. The cat always recovered, though, and regained the weight she had lost. I would have to ask Behenu if she had stopped eating again.

I sat there for a while, watching the sun as it sank below the buildings that surrounded us. It was in quiet moments like this that I particularly missed worshipping at the temple and I found myself humming the song we used to sing to Isis.

With dusk came swarms of tiny biting insects and I soon retreated inside. With the windows closed, the house was warm, but it was better than being nibbled at all night by the bugs. If anyone noticed that I didn't contribute to the conversation as we ate, they didn't comment. Later, as I lay beside Intef on my reed mat, I told him about Behenu's suggestion.

"What do you think?" I asked. "It would take years to look at all of those scrolls, even if the archivists would allow it."

"What other leads do we have?" He rolled onto his side to look at me. His ruined arm dangled over his chest and I tried not to stare at it. "I feel your frustration, but I agree with Renni that we cannot leave in case we miss Hemetre's reply. This would give you something to do in the meantime."

He leaned closer to kiss me and all thoughts of scrolls and archivists disappeared from my mind.

After breakfast the next morning, I went to the archives. I recognised most of the people there and a few even nodded at me. I found Belasi hunched over a clay tablet and explained what I wanted to do.

"You want to look at every scroll?" He frowned and

scratched his beard. "I would have to seek permission for that. How many people would be helping you?"

"It would just be me."

Intef had secured labouring work with Renni, proving that his one arm didn't slow him down much. He still had some difficulty balancing but was learning how to steady himself without his arm. He was learning to fight again too, sparring with Renni in the evenings. So once again it was only I who had no employment, being unskilled in anything other than sitting around while servants waited on me.

"Do you have any idea how many documents we have here?" Belasi waved his arm, encouraging me to look around the chamber. "Just this chamber alone has more than a hundred. We have thousands of documents in more languages than you have ever heard of."

"I cannot sit around all day. Even if it is a fruitless task, I want to try."

"What other languages do you read?"

"Only Egyptian and Akkadian. But if somebody could write down some key words for me, I can search for those. It doesn't matter whether I can read the language."

He gave me a stern look and I knew he would refuse me, but then he sighed.

"I suppose you could look at the Greek texts," he said. "There is a junior archivist working on them at the moment. He could give you some words to look for. But you must stay in that chamber and not wander elsewhere. I would need to request permission for you to do more than that."

"Thank you, Belasi. I am most appreciative."

He took me to a windowless chamber where a young man hunched over a table. He had the same distinctive features as Charis, who had been one of my ladies and whose family was

Greek. He had dark hair, a long nose, and skin that was several shades lighter than my own. Belasi introduced him as Dymas and explained what I needed. Dymas barely glanced at me as he reached for a reed.

"What words?" he asked.

"Eye," I said. "Power, magic, god, Horus, falcon, amulet." I listed off half a dozen others that might be useful.

Dymas wrote them down, along with the Akkadian word for each so that I would know which was which. He shoved the papyrus towards me and returned to his work.

"Thank you."

I waited but he didn't look at me again. I took a tray down from a shelf, fetched myself a stool and a lamp, and got to work. I quickly discovered that almost every one of the Greek scrolls contained at least one or two of the words I was looking for. God and power were particularly common. I reluctantly crossed them off my list. If Dymas had been more accommodating, I might have asked him to read me some of the scrolls, but he studiously ignored me.

When Dymas started to look like he might be preparing to leave for the day, I cleared my throat. He looked up, surprised, as if he had forgotten I was there. I pointed to two scrolls in which I had found references to an eye and an amulet.

"Would you read these to me?" I used my most conciliatory tone. "These have some of the words I am looking for."

"It would be quicker if you told me what you seek and then I can tell you whether these scrolls are relevant."

It seemed unwise to tell Dymas, of whom I knew nothing other than that he was Greek, what I was looking for. So I just smiled at him and held out the scrolls.

He took them with a grunt and read them out quickly, translating them into Akkadian as he went. The first was a story about two Greek gods. I didn't recognise either of their names but listened carefully in case perhaps one of them was really Horus. It described an argument between gods, which resulted in an earthquake, a flood and drought. The reference to an eye, which was what had caught my attention, turned out to be about one of the gods getting something in his eye and blaming the other.

The second scroll was a medical account of a boy who was poked in the eye with a wooden sword during a raucous game. The eye had festered and despite various medical treatments, had to be removed. The boy subsequently died. The scroll was mostly an accounting of the treatments tried and their effects, and concluded with the physician musing that perhaps the boy would have survived had his eye been removed sooner.

I returned every day for a month. Dymas didn't become any friendlier, but neither did he ask me to leave or refuse to read me the two or three scrolls I carefully selected each day. But none of them contained any references to the Eye of Horus. Like the first ones I had chosen, they were usually either medical accountings or stories about Greek gods who bore no resemblance to the falcon god. I had checked most of the Greek texts by now. Another three or four days and I would be finished. Then I would ask Belasi to show me another chamber, with texts from a different country, and I would start all over again.

"I only have one scroll today," I said to Dymas. "This one contains eye, magic and bird."

He took it without comment and began to read.

"This record is made by the priest Antinous, son of Antinous, son of Herodianus."

I tried to restrain my yawn. It had been a long day and my eyes were bleary after staring at dusty old scrolls for so long.

"I have in my possession a powerful amulet, which was given to me for safekeeping on the death of Djediufankh."

My fatigue disappeared. Although Dymas had pronounced the name awkwardly, it was undeniably Egyptian.

"Djediufankh was a priest of the Egyptian bird god, called Horus by the peoples native to that land. He was descended from a long line of priests of Horus, stretching many generations back into antiquity.

"Djediufankh possessed an amulet, which he believed to be the eye of his god. He said there were several versions of the story of how the god lost his eye, but this version was the one that he learned from his father.

"The Egyptian gods are just as jealous as our beloved Greek gods and the story Djediufankh told me was that Horus lost his eye in a fight with his brother Seth. He sought treatment from a priest, but the man was unable to restore his eye. In gratitude for the priest's attempt, Horus gifted him the eye, which he said would bestow great power on the one who possessed it."

"Does it say what sort of power?" I asked, as Dymas paused to take a breath.

He frowned at me.

"If you would allow me to read the rest of the scroll, we will find out. May I continue?"

I kept my mouth shut.

"Djediufankh said the eye was used a few times before the priesthood decided it was too dangerous and hid it away. It has been kept hidden ever since and memory of it has largely disappeared, except within the line of priests charged with its safekeeping. As Djediufankh had no sons, he gave me the amulet and asked that I take it somewhere it will be safe and where men will never again find it. He believed mankind was too irresponsible to wield such power as this amulet gave.

"I intend to take the amulet to the island of Crete. There is a place there where it may be secreted away and where I am confident that no man will ever locate it again. I make this record as evidence that I am discharging my vow to my friend, Djediufankh."

Dymas stopped reading.

"Is that it?" I asked. "Does it say where he took the Eye?"

"That is everything the scroll says. I take it, then, it was this which you were searching for."

"Can you make some copies for me? I need one in Greek and one in Akkadian."

Dymas frowned.

"It has been a long day. I will do it tomorrow."

"No, I need them now. Tonight."

"You have been looking for this for a month. Tomorrow will be soon enough."

"I can pay you."

I slipped a ring from my finger and offered it to him, albeit a little reluctantly. It was the one I had purchased myself at the bazaar in Akhetaten, a purple gem set into a gold band. It reminded me of a time when my life was so much simpler. My worries mostly concerned assassins and producing heirs, rather than searching the world for a magical amulet. We still had plenty of the jewels Istnofret had taken from my chambers, split between us for safekeeping. I never wore more than one at a time now that I understood how valuable they were.

Dymas looked down at the ring for a long time and I was beginning to think he would refuse when he finally reached for it. He held it closer to the lamp and turned it around to study it.

"This is a very fine item." He gave me a stern look. "How do you have such an item in your possession?"

"I purchased it."

"Indeed."

His tone suggested he didn't believe me and I pushed away a desire to convince him.

"Will you make the copies tonight?" I asked.

He looked at the ring for a moment longer and then tucked it away in his pocket.

"Fetch me some papyrus."

FORTY-ONE

I could hardly keep still while Dymas copied the Greek scroll. He studiously ignored me as I shuffled from foot to foot. His script was neat and even I could see that his copy was fairer than the original.

"Wait until they are dried properly before you roll them." He finally set his reed aside, then looked at me for the first time since he had tucked my ring away in his pocket. "I suppose we will not see you back here again?"

It must be clear to him that I would be leaving for Crete immediately. It was too late to cover my tracks. I should have thought of that before showing so much interest in the scroll.

"I hope that if anyone comes asking questions, you will remember that I paid you well for making these copies."

"You are a very determined woman." His tone was a little less cold now. "I hope you find what you are looking for."

"Thank you." I didn't want to give away any more than I already had.

"It has been a long day and I am going home," Dymas said.

"Leave the scrolls to dry for another few minutes and make sure you put out the lamp before you leave."

He left without another word. It was only after he had gone that I realised I hadn't even thanked him. I wouldn't have found Djediufankh's scroll without his help. I wrote a brief note and left it where he would find it in the morning, then rolled up the copies he had made and left.

Outside the sun was already setting, casting ribbons of orange and pink across the sky. Hopefully this would be my final Babylonian sunset.

I hurried home, clutching the precious scrolls to my chest. What if I crashed into somebody and the scrolls were damaged? I should have asked Dymas to make several copies. I burst into the house, slamming the door back against the wall in my haste.

"Samun?" Intef jumped up from where he had been sitting. "Has something happened?"

"Yes." I was suddenly laughing and crying at the same time. "And it is wonderful."

Istnofret and Behenu came running in.

"Where is Renni?" I asked. "You should all hear this at the same time."

"Here." Renni wiped water from his dripping hair as he entered. "I was just washing up."

"I found it." I held up the scrolls. "I found the Eye."

They crowded in, all speaking at once. I tried to tell them about Djediufankh, but nobody could hear me over the excited chatter.

"Will you all be quiet?" I shouted. "Let me read it to you and then I will answer your questions."

I read from the Akkadian scroll, translating into Egyptian as I went. There was silence for a few moments after I finished, then they all spoke at once. Eventually they stopped and we all laughed, although I wasn't sure why.

"I guess we are going to Crete," Istnofret said.

"We can discuss that after dinner," Behenu said. "Let's eat while the food is still hot."

She brought out the meal she had been preparing when I burst into the house and we all sat on cushions around the low table. Behenu poured the beer a little more liberally than usual and our meal felt like a celebration even if it was our regular fare of vegetable stew and flat bread.

"If only we had known," Renni said, when we all finally pushed away our bowls.

"Known what?" Istnofret asked.

"That the Eye was in Crete. We could have sailed straight there from Egypt instead of travelling halfway around the world."

"It might not still be there," she said. "We have no information about when the scroll was written."

"The papyrus didn't look very old," I said, slowly. "I have seen enough ancient scrolls to be able to identify them by now. That scroll was written not all that long ago. The Eye might still be in Crete."

"Maybe once we have found the Eye, we can settle down." Renni gave Istnofret a pointed look. "A little house by the sea, like we talked about."

"Soon." Istnofret placed her hand over his. "We need to find the Eye and get it back to Egypt first."

We sat up late into the night discussing the best path for our journey to Crete, which lay in the middle of the Mediterranean Sea. Once I would have let Intef and Renni's words wash over me, but now I listened intently, eager to understand our options.

We could retrace our original path, sailing back around the Persian Gulf and across the Red Sea, then make the trek back through the Valley of Many Baths to Thebes and follow the Great River all the way to where it met the Mediterranean. But that would take months, maybe as much as a year depending on the weather.

We discussed sailing along the Euphrates until we reached its end and trekking overland from there. Intef favoured riding horses along the length of a series of roads which ran all the way to the Mediterranean Sea.

"It is too far," Renni said. "Syria is to our east. We could ride across Syria and straight to the Mediterranean."

We all looked at Behenu.

"It is passable, although it will not be an easy journey," she said.

"How would you feel about going through Syria?" Istnofret asked, her tone gentle.

Behenu looked down at her hands. "I want to find the Eye. After all this time, I want to see this through to the end. But maybe after that, I will go home."

"The roads would be easier travelling," Intef said. "If we travel north-east from Babylon, we will cut across one of them. The journey may be longer, but we will only need enough supplies to get us from town to town, unlike crossing the wilds of Syria. We could follow the roads through Persia and Mesopotamia, all the way to Sardis."

"It will take a couple of months, though," Renni said. "Maybe three or four. We could cut through Syria much faster."

They looked to me for a decision. I sat up a little straighter.

"I want to take the fastest route, but maybe we should take

the safest. This is not the time to be hasty and run into trouble. Not when we are so close."

"Then we take the roads," Intef said. "Unless we come up with a better plan in the meantime."

He waited for further objections, but Renni merely shrugged.

"I will go see about purchasing some horses in the morning," Renni said.

"Are you sure?" I asked.

Renni gave me a quizzical look. "You do not want horses?"

"No, I meant are you all sure you want to come with me to Crete? You could stay here, or go where you choose. Take some of the jewels. You don't have to come with me."

"Why wouldn't we?" Istnofret asked. "Why would we abandon you now?"

"It wouldn't be abandoning me," I said. "It would be moving on with your own lives. I am not your queen anymore. I can offer you nothing other than a share of the jewels I have left. I have no right to expect you to stay with me."

"We are your friends," Istnofret said. "You do not think we would leave you to go by yourself?"

"You should," I said. "I think that the closer I get to the Eye, the more dangerous it will be. Maia said the gods would put obstacles in my path. I think the journey has barely begun."

"We will come with you," Behenu said.

"You are going nowhere without us," Intef said, covering my hand with his own. "Any of us."

They all nodded in agreement. Tears welled in my eyes.

"You are good friends to me."

It took less than a day to prepare to leave our Babylonian home. Behenu arranged for a neighbour to drop by and water our crops if they needed it. We packed up our personal items, purchased supplies, and farewelled Shala and Belasi.

I was a little sad to leave Shala, for she had turned out to be an interesting, if talkative, companion. I promised to write to her when we were settled in one place again and she agreed to send out word that if a message came for me, it should be delivered to her. I supposed it didn't really matter what Hemetre's reply said, if one ever came. We had found the information we needed. I prayed to Isis that the Eye was still in Crete.

On our final afternoon in Babylon, I worked on our garden, wanting to leave it in good shape for the next inhabitants. The onions and leeks were just starting to poke up above the soil. I pulled out a few weeds and picked the lettuces that were ready. I would be sorry to leave this little garden behind. It might not be as beautiful as my pleasure garden in Akhetaten, or even the one in Memphis, but I had created it with my own hands. Behenu had helped sometimes, and Renni broke a section of new ground for me, but I had done most of the work myself. I had never before known the satisfaction of a job well done and I would miss having my own little patch of garden.

Maybe once we had found the Eye and set things right in Egypt, I could have a garden again. Behenu would likely return to Syria, but as for the rest of us, I pictured two little houses, perhaps with a shared garden between them. Mau moving between the houses and lazing in the garden on sunny afternoons. The salty scent of the ocean in the air and perhaps the distant sound of waves crashing against the shore. Close enough that Istnofret could walk there whenever she wanted, but far enough that I wouldn't have to look at it.

For the first time, the future felt close enough to see. This was what was ahead of me. I just had to find the Eye and put Egypt to rights first.

FORTY-TWO

My Dear Sisters

I am not sure why I am writing this, given that I now know you have never received any of my letters. Did you think I had forgotten you from the moment I sent you away? Have you ever wondered if I still think of you every day? How I wish I could find a way to have this one letter delivered into your hands.

This is the final time I will write to you. Now that I know you do not receive my letters, there is no point. Before, I had hope. No, I had certainty that you were receiving my letters. The letters I sent have been burned, all but one that I have tucked away in my bag. I do not know which letter it is. Perhaps it relates something of momentous importance, something that in future years I might read and feel grateful that this letter was saved. Perhaps it contains nothing more than the ramblings of a lonely woman who thinks she is writing to her sisters. I do not know whether I will break the seal and find out which letter it is. I do not think I want to know.

We have left Egypt and are now in a faraway land. I never imagined that I would travel so far. After all, a queen's place is at home. But I am queen no longer and nobody but those with me care where I go. I do not dare document where we are or the reason we travel, in case this letter falls into the wrong hands before I can bring myself to destroy it, but I tell you this: we are searching for something. I can tell you no more.

We leave here tomorrow on what I hope might be the final leg of our journey. We have a long way to travel yet and it will take at least several more months. I hope it will be no longer than that, for I think I might have a babe growing inside of me. I have not told Intef yet, but he has been staring at my belly so I think he suspects.

I have no doubt that our journey will be long and dangerous yet. It will be even more dangerous if I must carry my babe in my arms rather than my belly. I fear the babe will be a target for those who wish to harm me. I dream night after night that those who pursue us have found me, that they are cutting the babe from my belly, and then I wake, sweating and trembling. There are not true dreams. There is no alternative future, only the babe being cut from my body.

I must finish here now, my dear sisters. I pray to Isis that you are well and safe and happy. I pray that you have found lives of your own, that you do not live in fear of me sending for you. I pray that even though you have never received my letters, you somehow know that I love you and I will never forget you.

Your sister
Ankhesenamun

Ankhesenamun's journey continues in
Book 4: *Gates of Anubis*

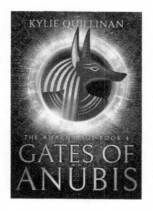

See kyliequillinan.com for more books, including exclusive collections, and newsletter sign up.

ABOUT THE AUTHOR

Kylie writes about women who defy society's expectations. Her novels are for readers who like fantasy with a basis in history or mythology. Her interests include Dr Who, jellyfish and cocktails. She needs to get fit before the zombies come.

Her other interests include canine nutrition, jellyfish and zombies. She blames the disheveled state of her house on her dogs, but she really just hates to clean.

Swan – the epilogue to the Tales of Silver Downs series – is available exclusively to her newsletter subscribers. Sign up at kyliequillinan.com.